Patriot of the Lowcountry

Eliza Wilkinson and the Fall of Charleston

A Ladies of the Revolution Novel by

TRACY LAWSON

Columbus OH • Dallas TX
graylionbooks.com

Distribution by Bublish
Published by Gray Lion Books

ISBN: 979-8-9876123-9-2 (ebook)
ISBN: 979-8-9943412-0-9 (hardcover)
ISBN: 979-8-9876123-8-5 (paperback)

Author photo by Owen Jones
Interior layout by Bublish
Cover model: Lola Kinsey
Cover photo by Brad Barton
Cover design by EbookLaunch.com

Manufactured in the United States of America

Contents

1779

1

In the pre-dawn of a late May morning, an unfamiliar sound brought me awake in an instant. I lay still, trying to separate what I'd heard from the mockingbirds' song and the swish of marsh grasses in the breeze off the water. Then I heard it again. The jingle of harness combined with a low rumble suggesting people and animals on the move.

"Quick, around back." The hoarse whisper below my open window spurred me to action. Had I locked the rear door? I put on my wrapper and ran downstairs on tiptoe. When I burst into the kitchen, I pulled up in surprise. A woman stood silhouetted in the faint glow of the embers on the hearth, clutching the fireplace poker. She turned, startled, and we both breathed a sigh of relief. Trust Jennie to be one step ahead of me.

Heavy footfalls crossed the back porch, and we shrank out of sight as the door swung open with a creak to reveal a tall, shadowy figure bearing a rifle.

The moment the interloper stepped inside, she leapt forward and hit him across the shoulders. The man cried out in surprise and his rifle clattered to the floor as he fell. I pulled the weapon out of his reach and raised it as Jennie slammed the door, turned the key in the lock, and readied the poker. Together we stood over the prostrate figure.

He groaned as he rolled over. "Consarnit, Eliza!"

"Will?" I lowered the rifle and frowned at the younger of my two brothers. "Why are you sneaking around in the dark?"

"Our unit's out on overnight patrol." He grunted as he got to his feet and reclaimed the gun. "If I knew you two were lying in wait I'd have let Frank come in first."

I unlocked the door, and as Jennie lit a candle and set it on the trestle, our older brother hurried a barefoot servant girl inside.

I asked, "Who is that?"

Will shrugged. The girl remained mute, but shot a desperate glance at Jennie.

"You Cora, from Mist' Ash's place, right?" When the girl nodded, Jennie put an arm around her shoulders. "You can tell my mistress what happened."

Cora gulped. "I went out visitin' last night and I was on my way home just now. I seen a squad of Redcoats at your gate and I hear them sayin' should they plunder the house. I tol' them it belong to a decrepit ol' gentleman who don't live here, and it ain't worth their trouble." She paused and gave me an apologetic glance. "It wasn't exactly a lie, ma'am, and they believed me, but I was scared to be around soldiers, so I run off."

Frank added, "We'd been tracking them all night, and took cover close enough to listen to everything they said—so close she almost fell over us in the dark."

"Please don't tell my mistress. I ain't supposed to be out."

"I won't. Wait here." I hurried to fetch a coin and handed it to her. "If the soldiers are gone, you'd best get on home."

"Yes'm." The girl curtseyed and slipped out the door.

Will took both rifles and stood them in the corner. "They were looking for Morton Wilkinson's place, but they couldn't find it."

Jennie laid slices of ham in the spider while I joined my brothers at the table. All of us had our mother's coloring, but they looked like wild men in their dirty, fringed hunting frocks. Their brown eyes glittered in their tanned faces, and their matted, dark hair was pulled back and tied with bits of leather.

In contrast, I was clean and well fed, even if my circumstances were more reduced than one would expect of a planter's widow. Doubtful anyone who saw the three of us would guess we had grown up in luxury.

Glad as I was to see them, their mention of my brother-in-law raised my ire. "If the Redcoats do find Morton's place and arrest him, I say it couldn't happen to a more deserving fellow."

Will spoke up. "You may not like the man, Eliza, but he's our company's ensign. Doesn't it frighten you that a squad of Redcoats out prowling in the night ended up at your gate? You'd be safer at Papa's."

Frank added, "You're only a few miles from where they're camped at the Ferry."

Jennie set plates of ham and buttered cornbread in front of us and my brothers dug in before she finished pouring the coffee.

"Papa's place is just as close to the Ferry." I stabbed at the ham with my fork. "I'm staying. The Redcoats have no reason to bother me. Even that servant Cora thinks this house is so shabby it looks abandoned."

Frank drained the rest of his coffee. "It's not only the Regulars you should be concerned about. Loyalists like Daniel McGirth and his banditti will use you harshly too. He's been spotted in the area."

Will nodded. "You should refugee while you can."

I laughed. "When did I ever take orders from my baby brother?"

"I'm only a year younger than you," he grumbled.

"I can't recall a time you listened to us." Frank gave me a knowing look. "I think you don't want to go to Papa's because you haven't made peace with Susannah."

"She hasn't made peace with me, either." Our stepmother was a mere ten years older than me, and more our contemporary than our father's. Rather than befriend us, she tried to rule over us—especially me, because I resisted her authority the most. "Papa is too feeble to

stand up to the Redcoats, so I daresay I'll be the one protecting them."
Besides, I had a reason for wanting to stay here at Plainsfield my brothers knew nothing about.

Frank pushed back his empty plate and got up to retrieve their rifles. "Our unit's been called to Willtown. No telling when we'll be able to stop by."

"Well, if our local militia isn't needed to protect us, the Redcoats must pose no threat. So much fuss over nothing–"

Will cut in. "No, it's the reverse. General Lincoln and the Continentals are on the march from Augusta and expected here any time."

"Why are they sending you away, then?"

Frank said, "Our primary job is to put down unrest and stop looting, but as soon as a battle's brewing they'll call us back. You're taking a pretty big gamble by staying here alone."

"You two risk running afoul of the Redcoats every day. I daresay you'd stay if you were in my shoes."

"Maybe. But you're our sister."

As Will got up to join him, they exchanged a worried glance. My relationship with my brothers had always been more roughhousing and pranks than expressions of affection, but this time I followed them outside and kissed each of them on the cheek in farewell.

Frank folded me in a warm embrace. "You look more like Mother all the time. Take care of yourself, Eliza."

They headed down the cart path with their rifles on their shoulders, and when Will looked back I smiled and waved. It was natural that we would not always agree. They believed Morton Wilkinson a great patriot, but I had no admiration for my brother-in-law or his supposed devotion to the Cause.

I was only seventeen when I wed Joseph Wilkinson, a dashing planter and physician twelve years my senior. We were married less than a year when he contracted smallpox and succumbed so quickly that his death left me stunned. Days later, I gave birth to our son, who did not survive. While I grieved the tremendous double loss, Morton schemed to make sure I received nothing from Joseph's estate. His treachery planted a simmering resentment in my soul I had been unable to reconcile for the past four years.

When my brothers were out of sight I went back into the kitchen, where Jennie cleared their plates.

"Sit with me."

She fixed food for herself and we took our usual places opposite one another.

I refilled my coffee. "Is it foolish to want to stay?"

She shrugged. "We've been hearin' for months that they soldiers be coming."

"I daresay Mr. Smilie over on Wadmalaw is the only man who still refugees every time soldiers are rumored to be in the district. If I'm going to do a man's work and run this place, I can't behave like a frightened girl."

"What about Mr. Joseph's plans?"

"After this harvest, I should have enough laid by." I leaned in. "We can't go refugeeing about the countryside if we mean to do right by his memory."

2

Over the next week I rode miles each day, searching roads and cart paths in the neighborhood for signs of the enemy. When I found nothing to raise concern, I felt confident enough to proceed with the indigo harvest.

Solomon, my foreman, was smiling when he came to the house to make his daily report on the plants' readiness. "I 'spect we start first harvest tomorrow, Miz Eliza. You'll see—them flowers about to bloom."

"Splendid. I'll come with you now." I fetched my sun hat, and as we started down the cart path toward the fields, I asked, "Do you have the vats ready?"

"Yes'm. The steepers all filled with water. I sent everyone to weed the rice fields today, since we gonna be busy pulling leaves and stems for a while."

Last year, my thirty acres of indigo plants yielded fifteen hundred pounds of dye cakes—around one hundred pounds of product per worker-and we were on pace to have a better crop this year. I was fortunate to have an experienced crew with knowledge of how best to coax the dye from the plants, a process half backbreaking labor, half miracle. I'd learned from them that pruning the plants just before they bloomed in early June allowed for enough regrowth for a second harvest in July.

When we arrived at the indigo fields, I paused at the nearest vat to put my hand below the water's surface. I discerned neither heat nor cold, just right for the dye extraction.

I imagined each stage as Solomon and I walked along the rows and inspected the plants. The harvested leaves and stems would soak for days to release the natural juices. Once the resulting liquid fermented, the workers would drain the liquor into the second vat.

The stench from the rotten plants would be so strong that the workers would take it in frequent turns as they stirred the liquid with paddles. When the water reached the desired shade of blue, a lime mixture made from burnt oyster shells and spring water would be added, and as it reacted with the liquor, a blue sludge would sink to the bottom. After the water drained and the sludge hardened, the workers would cut it into dye cakes.

"Everything looks favorable for a large yield." I brushed some dirt off my hands. "Solomon, I'm proud of all that you and the others have done and I thank you for being willing to teach me."

"Miz Eliza, yo' papa always been a fair man, but there ain't nothin' like working for you. Plainfield is our home too."

Unexpected tears welled in my eyes as I envisioned my workers' reaction to what I planned for them. I patted him on the arm. "That means a great deal to me. I'll see you tomorrow."

Buoyed by the prospect of a fine harvest, I hummed as I walked back to the house. The sun was overhead, and Jennie drove past me in the chaise on her way to deliver dinner to the workers.

I ate the meal she'd left in the kitchen for me and then went to the study, where I got out my account books and notes on the expected outputs of my salable crops. Pen scratching on parchment, I added the estimates to the amount of cash I kept hidden in the house and sat back in my chair, satisfied.

No one but Jennie was aware of the plan I'd held in my heart since the day my father asked me to manage Plainsfield. I meant to see it through, even if it branded me as a radical in South Carolina's planter society.

Every detail of that evening in March 1774 was as clear as if it happened yesterday. At Charles Town's winter social season, I'd met several men who possessed the qualities I favored in a beau, but as the months of revelry slipped by, Joseph Wilkinson stood out from the rest. Not only was he a pleasure to look at and an excellent dancer, he showed interest in my intellect and favored genuine conversation over meaningless compliments.

During an interlude in the dancing, we found a window seat in the hallway. Once we had exhausted the topic of the unrest simmering in Boston, he looked around to make sure we were not overheard. "I am plotting my own rebellion as we speak."

At first I thought he was joking. "Against whom?"

"My brother, for one. My parents died before I came of age, and Morton assumed the role of my guardian with uncommon zeal. Without asking me what life course I desired, he apprenticed me to an apothecary in Charles Town, and later sent me to the Medical College of Philadelphia."

I considered this. "No one has ever asked me what I wanted, but I did not know a white man could be denied his free will."

"What you want interests me a great deal." He took my hand. "Let me explain why. While I lived in Philadelphia I boarded at a Quaker home, and at first I found their wish to abolish slavery strange. But after I entered into discourse with them and my instructor Dr. Benjamin Rush, they opened my eyes to the sins we slaveholders commit against our fellow man. After I received my degree I considered not returning to South Carolina at all, but last autumn my friend John Laurens convinced me I should."

"I'm glad you came back, because otherwise we would not have met." I paused to make sure I chose the right words. "But what do you think you can do about people holding slaves? Slavery is everywhere, like the air we breathe, and it's protected by the law. I've never heard anyone question it before."

"Just because slavery is legal doesn't make it moral." He waited until another couple passed and then he went on. "I intend to put my own house in order first, and manumit the workers I inherited from my parents."

"You mean set them free?"

"Yes, free to leave, or to stay and work for wages. Free to marry and have children with no fear of being separated. Many people I spoke with in Philadelphia believe the tensions between us and the Crown will lead to war. Should the American colonies seek independency, slavery will be abolished, for how can it go any other way? We cannot cry tyranny while we force others to labor for our benefit."

"Why are you telling me of your seditious plans?"

"I want to know if you could come to believe as I do, so I might have an ally in my wife."

As I understood the full meaning of his words, a thrill swept through me. "I could, sir."

He knelt before me. "Eliza Yonge, you are not only the loveliest girl in all of Charles Town, but the one whose spirit and character I most admire. Will you consent to be my partner for life and help me change the world?"

I accepted without hesitation, for I understood a woman's personal liberty depended on the benevolence of first her father, and then her husband. I could make no better choice, for not only did he seek to challenge the conventions of society, he believed he could change them. His confidence in his convictions made me admire him all the more, until it was easy to adopt his abolitionist ideas as my own.

Satisfied with my figures, I closed the ledger. Joseph had not lived long enough to do more than manumit his workers. It fell to me to bring the whole experiment to fruition.

As I imagined developing my once-broken-down Plainsfield into a prosperous plantation with a thriving community of literate, skilled tradesmen, all of whom were freed former slaves, a distant rumble pulled me from my thoughts. The sultry Carolina heat often brought about an afternoon thunderstorm. I opened the kitchen door and scanned the fields, expecting to see everyone returning to their cabins under a cloudy, darkening sky. Instead, prisms of sunlight filtered through the branches of the live oaks that shaded the house. When I heard it again, I went to the front porch, where, a hundred yards distant, the road ran past my dock.

I leaned over the railing to check in each direction, and straightened with a gasp when I spied flashes of red through a thin part of the woods, realizing the rumbling noise came from the galloping steeds of a body of soldiers. I ran back inside and slammed the door. My breath came in panicked gasps as I prayed the soldiers would think the house unoccupied and pass me by. Instead, the sound grew louder, punctuated by their hoarse shouts.

"Where are the rebel bastards?"

"Surrender in the name of the King!"

I peeked through the sidelight curtain in horror as Redcoats charged up my avenue, urging their horses on as though they were in pursuit of a fleeing regiment of Continentals.

There was nowhere to escape. Heart pounding, I opened the door and stepped out into the coming storm.

A soldier at the fore leapt from his horse and took the porch stairs two at a time. I shrank back out of his way, but he was upon me in an instant and took my arm in a tight grip. "You must be one of their hussies. Any men in the house, missy?"

I wanted to retort that if my brothers were here, he would've been dead before he had time to ask, but the words died in my throat. I shook my head no.

He pushed me ahead of him and called to the others, "Search top to bottom! Likely she has some rebels hiding under her bed."

Inside, he backed me into a corner of the foyer, where the soldiers who streamed past me hurled insults and made threatening motions with their swords as if they would hew me to pieces.

Tears blurred my eyes as the men plunged their bayonets into upholstery, smashed tables and chairs, and destroyed anything too large to carry away. From upstairs came more crashes and the protesting screech of heavy furniture being moved.

As I squeezed my eyes shut and covered my ears to block out the scene, my guard grasped my wrist. Over the din, he said something I did not understand.

When I did not respond he leaned closer, his face twisted in anger. "I said, give me your ring, you little trull." He wrenched off my wedding band and then took hold of my chin and pushed back my hair. "What, no earbobs?"

The rum on his breath raised the bile in my throat. I jerked my chin away, and in response he yanked the linen cap off my head, along with a handful of hair. He turned it inside out, I presumed to make certain I'd hidden nothing in it. He pocketed it, and his eyes raked me from head to toe. "Where's the rest of your jewelry?"

"I have nothing else."

"I guess I'll take those buckles, then." When I did not remove my shoes to make it easier for him he knelt before me and pulled at the lappets so roughly I nearly fell. All the while a stream of soldiers carried out sacks of rice, cornmeal, and other provisions meant to last us for months. Squawks of the terrified chickens taken from their coop rose above the noise inside the house.

It was not until a trio of soldiers descended the stairs, their arms full of my clothing, that I pushed past my guard to protest. The first had stuffed one of my underpetticoats into his jacket front like a jabot. The second, who had my best summer gown in his pile of plunder, wore my split-rump bustle tied around his waist, and squealed falsetto protests as the third soldier swatted at the padding with the rug beater.

"Stop!" I moved to block them from leaving. "Sirs—if you please."

They halted, giggling like drunken schoolboys.

"Times are such that I cannot replace what you are taking. I beg of you, spare me a suit of clothes or two."

The one wearing the bustle replied with mock seriousness. "We're not heartless, madam—to prove it we'll swap you a gown for what you have on!"

His fellows burst into uproarious laughter, and the second one dangled a gown in front of me and then pulled it back.

My guard laughed along with them as he took me by the arm, drew his sword, and caught my petticoat on the tip. "Poor thing, worried about being without an extra suit of clothes. Here's how you deal with a modest maid, lads—put her skirts over her head!" He lifted his sword until he exposed my knees. My face flamed, and I tried to reclaim my skirts and my dignity as the other soldiers whistled and jeered.

"Here now, that's enough of that." The crowd at the door parted to make way for a soldier wearing epaulettes that marked him as an officer. He waved a careless hand toward me. "We've left her with plenty to remember us by. Form ranks!"

My guard waited until every man left the house. As soon as we were alone his hand closed around my throat and he backed me against the wall. "Consider this a lesson in submission. Rebel women are just another thing to be conquered."

Terror took hold of me and left me with no more agency than a rabbit caught in a trap, but when he laughed, something ignited deep within me. I raked my nails across his face, and he roared in pain, tightening his grip to cut off my airway. I thrashed and kicked, and just as my vision began to cloud someone wrenched him away. Gasping, I slid down the wall to the floor.

The ranking officer held my former guard by the scruff of the neck as he spoke through gritted teeth. "I gave an order, Corporal." He shoved him toward the door and left the house without an apology or a backward glance.

I remained where I was until the last hoofbeats faded, and even then I trembled so violently I had trouble getting to my feet. I stumbled across the foyer to close the door and hugged myself to quell my shaking. Why hadn't I taken my brothers' warning more seriously? My stubborn denial left me with no time to think, defend myself, or try to escape. I'd spent four years building an independent life for myself at Plainsfield, and it had taken the enemy less than an hour to destroy my home and my sense of security.

Upstairs, my clothespress was split in two. Its doors sagged on broken hinges, and the drawers were pulled out and emptied. I had no clothing but what I wore, not even a spare pair of stockings.

The escritoire was tipped on its side, and my books and writing paper smeared with ink and strewn around the room. Feathers from my torn mattress floated on the breeze and settled over the destruction like flakes of snow.

Then I saw the loose floorboard near the hearth was pulled up. I stumbled through the wreckage, fell to my knees, and plunged my hand into the space between the joists. My cache of money, everything I'd saved to buy my workers from my father, was gone.

The memory of the soldiers charging the drive flooded my senses, so intense that I imagined I could hear their shouts and the pounding of the horses' hooves. I shook my head to clear it, but the sound only grew louder. I hurried to my window and cried out in horror at the sight of more horsemen approaching.

From a distance, this group appeared to be a corps of natives, but as they drew near, I realized they were white men disguised with feathers and war paint. Were they friends, or more of the enemy?

I went downstairs on trembling legs and met them in the yard. "A party of British dragoons just left here."

The one who seemed to be in command of the squad motioned for the rest of the riders to dismount. "Not doubting your word, missy, but Colonel McGirth says we must search every house ourselves."

At the mention of their leader's name, I went cold. These men belonged to the Loyalist militia my brothers warned me about, and again, there was no escape. "I assure you I have nothing left for you to steal. Nothing."

"We'll be the judge of that, missy." He shifted in the saddle as his men swarmed past me into the house. "Would you be Missus Wilkinson?"

"Yes, I am."

"How far to Morton Wilkinson's?"

Despite what I'd said about Morton, I couldn't bring myself to aid these blackguards. I shook my head. "It's a great while since I've been there, and he's got a new road to his house."

He then said, "But you can guess."

"Indeed, sir, I can't."

"We've orders to burn that house."

"If you go, you won't find it in your heart to execute your orders. He has small children. You would not be so cruel as to turn them out of the house."

The officer considered what I'd said. "Well, if it's as you say, we won't burn it. Is this your place, madam?"

"Yes, it's mine. I'm a widow."

"We often bear the blame for these outrages, but I assure you we take nothing from ladies. The fellows who robbed you today can't have any feelings for the fair sex."

After he recalled his men, one came from the rear of the house and spoke quietly to him. He turned back to me. "What of the horses in your back pasture?"

"They belong to my father."

"Well, as they are not your property, we'll take them. That won't be injuring you, now, will it?"

How easily he'd tricked me! "Those beasts are past their prime and not suited for the army. I use them for farm work."

"So they are, but I'll take a rebel's horse any day."

"Would you take those poor, old creatures if they belonged to a Tory?"

"No, I would not."

Another of the soldiers laughed at him. "Faith, I believe you don't mind Whig or Tory, so long as there's something in it for you."

The officer motioned for some of his men to go fetch the horses. "Now, missy, what settlements are nearby?"

It would do no good to lie, for these men could find their way down the road just as easily as anyone. "None before you reach Willtown, but there are homes along the river to the southwest. When you come to my father's place, I beg you to treat him well."

"What's your father's name?"

"Francis Yonge."

"Yonge, you say?" He scratched his stubbled chin. "Why, he's a damned rebel. We'll tell him we left you as we found you, but if he's got anything left worth taking, we make no promises."

Tears welled in my eyes as McGirth's men tied ropes to my horses' halters and led them away. How I regretted my disregard for the danger and my belief that the British and their sympathizers meant civilians no harm.

As we are commanded to pray for our enemies, I prayed that none of those men would live long enough to attain my father's venerable age.

3

When Jennie returned, she found me huddled on the bottom step, clinging to the newel post. She knelt beside me and her dark eyes searched my tear-stained face. "What happened?"

I gulped. "Soldiers."

"Did they hurt you?" She seized me by the shoulders and shook me a little. "Eliza, did they hurt you?"

"One of them would have, but an officer stopped him. They stole horses, chickens, supplies, money, and all my clothes. We must go hide the horse you took to the fields in case there are more soldiers about."

Nightfall came too soon that evening, and with it every terror my overactive imagination could conjure. Despite the heat and humidity, I had Jennie build up the fire on the hearth in my chamber. I had no thoughts of sleep as I fed the flames and cowered near them like some primeval being.

The next morning, we both yawned and our bellies rumbled as we went about our work. As we cleaned up the shards, splinters, and horsehair stuffing that littered the house, I recalled the cobwebs, dust, and mouse nests we'd encountered when we first moved in. That evidence of years of neglect was far easier to put right than the destruction wrought in a single afternoon.

I sent Solomon and two other workers to Papa's with a handcart to beg for supplies. The men returned that afternoon with sacks of rice, cornmeal, salt, some vegetables, half a dozen bottles of wine, and news.

"Mist' Francis say the Redcoats busted up they furniture and broke some windows, but took pity on them because of the chil'ren and din' take much food. He say they got enough supplies to spare."

"Thank you, Solomon. Did you encounter any soldiers?"

"No'm. Look like they all gone off."

My joy and anticipation of the indigo harvest all but forgotten, I left that work to Solomon while Jennie and I repaired furniture, nurtured the kitchen garden, foraged for edible plants, and went to the marshy river's edge to fish and hunt oysters. Despite working harder than I ever had in my life, I could not let my guard down long enough to sleep. I spent restless nights feeding my fire as if the flames could drive away my fears, and greeted each day more tired and irritable than the one before.

This time, the ominous rumble came while I was in my chamber pinning up my hair. I ran to the window and as soon as I spied flashes of red through the trees, I dashed downstairs, shouting for Jennie. She came running, and I pointed a shaking finger toward the road.

At that moment the rear door burst open with a bang, and we both shrieked and clutched at each other. Solomon appeared in the dining room doorway, panting as he wiped his perspiring forehead. "Redcoats a-comin' down the road!"

"How many?"

"Look like the whole army, Miz Eliza."

Insides frozen with dread, I forced my feet to carry me onto the front porch. Everywhere in view were men in those hated red uniforms. I panted as I gripped the porch railing, fearing that without some anchor, I would give over to my terror and flee, screaming.

Jennie came to stand beside me, dignified and calm, and murmured, "Steady, Eliza. You ain't alone this time."

Only then was I able to take a deep, calming breath.

Two officers rode up to the porch. One was broad-shouldered, with a hawklike nose and graying hair pulled back in a queue. I guessed him for a contemporary of my father, and a good deal older than the men under his command.

The younger officer wore a powdered wig, and when he spoke, his accent revealed him as a foreigner. "Madam, please, I beg you not to distress yourself."

He was a Hessian. How could I not be distressed when I knew of their brutal reputation?

They both dismounted and climbed the porch steps, and the Hessian asked, "Will you join us?"

They paused to allow me to enter the house first. An aide-de-campe carrying a rolled map and some papers followed and spread the map on my scarred dining room table. When Jennie tapped me on the shoulder, I jumped out of my skin.

She motioned for me to follow her into the hall and whispered, "One of the soldiers gave me a silver coin and asked for milk. Why are they offering to pay?"

"I don't know," I whispered back.

"You sure they British?"

"Of course. Our men can't afford to pay for milk. Besides, they're wearing red uniforms, and they have a Hessian officer."

"But the ones who came here before busted up everything and stole from us. These men behavin' like gentlemen."

"They're still the enemy," I hissed. "I suspect they're planning to lay a trap for General Lincoln."

The Hessian came to the doorway motioned for me to come look at the map spread on the table. In his thick accent he asked, "How far is it to the river?"

"I can't rightly guess."

He tried again. "Can you guess the distance to Stono Ferry?"

I decided I would bite my tongue off before I gave away any information. "Indeed, no."

They regarded me in silence, and then the older one spoke. "Madam, if you have a sensible fellow about the place, I'd be glad if you could summon him here."

Before I had a chance to refuse, one of the soldiers brought Solomon in. "This one will tell you the way to the ferry."

They proceeded to ask the same questions they asked me, and tears of frustration welled in my eyes as he answered in detail. When I could stand it no more I cried, "Solomon, stop! I order you not to say another word."

My good and able foreman, who'd never heard anything but polite requests from me, fell silent.

All the soldiers looked puzzled, and the elder one asked, "Madam, what distresses you so?"

"I fear for my friends."

"Which friends?"

I stared at him in surprise. "Why, the Americans."

"But we are Americans. I am Major James Moore, and this is Colonel François Malmedy, of the North Carolina Light Dragoons."

"Truly?" He nodded and my face grew hot. "We have been plundered by the Redcoats of late, as you see from the state of my home. You are wearing scarlet and have a Hessian officer in your party. What else could I think?"

The major chuckled. "Is that what you deduced? Let me assure you that Colonel Malmedy is French, not a Hessian."

Malmedy added, "You were so upset we feared this was a Tory household. With your permission, we will camp here tonight."

Now that the misunderstanding was behind us, I was quick to agree. That evening, Major Moore and Colonel Malmedy and their subordinate officers dined as our guests. They added their rations to ours and even produced a bottle of sherry and some mismatched glasses. When the meal was over, Major Moore raised his. "To wanting liberty, for it is man's most natural state."

I responded, "Women have no less capacity for thoughts and opinions than men and we crave liberty, just as you do. We are capable of much more than minding the dairy, the poultry-house, and children."

Though I had thought about my own liberty many times, I had never spoken the words aloud. All the men burst forth with a hearty 'hear, hear!' and I flushed with pleasure as they raised their glasses to me.

Just then a young sergeant rushed into the room and snapped to attention. "Sirs, a party of the enemy is down the road, carrying off a family's provisions."

Colonel Malmedy nodded. "Tell the first troop to prepare to ride."

I followed our guests outside and after the riders departed, Major Moore said, "Madam, we have orders to take up posts to keep the Redcoats from crossing the Stono in the morning. General Lincoln intends to engage the British very near here. Is there somewhere you can refugee? If so, I will assign a detail to escort you."

"I could go to my father's."

"If you were my daughter, I would insist you leave straightaway. By now their scouts know we've camped here, and they'll come back and treat you worse than before."

That night I prepared for bed with a heavy heart, but I felt no compulsion to remain on guard. I crawled under the covers and lay back with a sigh. When next I opened my eyes, sunlight streamed in the window.

4

My plantation ledger and the letter book in which I transcribed copies of my correspondence, the evidence of my past four years' accomplishments, were all I carried away from Plainsfield. I had nothing else to pack.

I expected Solomon and the rest of the workers to accompany me to the island, but when he came to the house for our morning meeting, he refused to consider it.

"What we gon' do over at Mister Francis's? I already talk to the others and we want to stay here."

"If it's too dangerous for me, then it's too dangerous for you."

He shook his head. "Might as well finish the indigo harvest. I'll take care of everything until you come back."

It was not in me to compel my workers. "Very well. Jennie and I'll be back once the threat is over." I unwrapped my bundle, tore a page out of the back of my correspondence book, and retrieved a quill and the ink I'd made from blackberry juice. "I'll write you a pass so you can come to Island House if need be."

The dragoons were mounted and ready to ride when Jennie came back with my horse. While one of the dragoons saddled my mount, another helped her into the bed of their supply wagon.

Once I was settled in the saddle, Major Moore looked around. "Where are your field workers?"

"They chose to stay here."

He frowned. "Without supervision, they will run away. Who can say what may befall them if they are taken by the enemy?"

"I trust my people to take care of themselves." I changed the subject. "I would like to hear from you what's been happening. Out in the country, we get many conflicting rumors and have no way to determine what is true."

He obliged. "After the British captured Savannah they set their sights on taking Charles Town. But when word reached General Prevost of General Lincoln's approach, he abandoned his plans to attack the city in the face of our superior numbers. The Redcoats fled to James Island and built redoubts at Stono Ferry for the rear guard to cover the main army's evacuation. If Lincoln arrives in time, he will engage them."

"How can you predict what will happen?"

He chuckled. "From years of experience, good scouting, swift messengers, and intelligence gathered from civilians."

"If Lincoln engages and wins the battle, will that drive the Redcoats out?"

"No. Clinton wants Charles Town, and I daresay he'll not abandon his quarry, even if he must make a temporary retreat." He smiled. "Take heart. Every time an American surrender seems inevitable Washington finds a way to keep his army in the field. I daresay the men who defend the city are as worthy and as cunning as our commander in chief."

We were crossing a low-lying area known as The Sands when one of the soldiers in the ranks behind us shouted, "Halt! Show yourself!"

I turned in the saddle in time to see a dragoon leap from the saddle and dash into the woods. A moment later, a black man dressed in the rough clothing of a field worker ran into the road. Some of the mounted soldiers turned their horses to block his flight, and they soon had him surrounded.

The soldier on foot declared, "He was following us. He may be a spy for the Redcoats." He turned to the captive. "Have you a pass?"

I watched in distress as the man dodged the soldiers. One of them swung the butt of his gun and caught him across the face. Blood ran down his face and neck, and I cried, "Enough! I won't have you treat him so."

Major Moore intervened. "Tie his hands and have him walk alongside. We can't let him go if he could be a spy."

As soon as we were underway again, I watched the poor man stumble as he tried to keep up.

He looked at me imploringly. "Please, mistress–let me walk by you."

I prevailed upon Major Moore. "It would please me to see the poor man treated well. Please bring him up here."

"Madam, believe me when I tell you–your compassion would make you a bad soldier. Though if I was captured, I would prefer to fall into your hands." He turned his horse's head, circled back, and brought the captive forward. Whether friend or foe, he would suffer no more cruelty on the journey.

We rode along the causeway to Papa's island, and as soon as the house came into view, Major Moore handed the rope to one of the sergeants. "See that his wound is looked after and then lock him up so he cannot inform the enemy of our whereabouts."

As we neared the house, Papa hobbled out to meet us, leaning on his gold-headed cane. I saw the concern on his face at the sight of me surrounded by soldiers in red and hastened to introduce him to Colonel Malmedy and Major Moore so there would be no repeat of my comedy of errors.

The officers dismounted and as the three men conferred, I noted how Major Moore's broad-shouldered frame and military bearing stood in contrast to Papa's stooped shoulders and reliance on his walking stick.

Jennie took our things up to the little chamber that I had occupied before I took up residence at Plainsfield, and I went in search of my stepmother. Flora, the kitchen maid, directed me upstairs.

I found Susannah lying on the bed, one arm across her eyes. As I entered the room she raised herself up on her elbows. "Eliza? What are you doing here?"

"Some soldiers brought me here for safety. I hoped to borrow a suit of clothes."

She sank back and closed her eyes. "Take what you need from the second drawer in the clothespress and leave me be."

I put the clothes in my chamber, and when I went back downstairs, Major Moore asked, "Will you accompany me while I familiarize myself with the shoreline?" He offered me his arm and as we walked the property, he noted favorable places for troops and field guns. "You hesitated to leave your place, even though this seems the superior spot, and the house is commodious. May I ask why?"

"My father purchased this place when he married his second wife. After I was widowed, I found I preferred to be on my own."

"Where your liberty goes unchallenged." He patted my hand. "A courageous choice."

That night the men camped on the lawn and the officers slept in the downstairs hall. I offered to have pallets made for them, but they refused.

Major Moore took his overcoat and spread it on the floor. "There! That's how a soldier's bed is made. I assure you I sleep as well on that hard lodging as I ever slept on a feather bed."

Though I did not contradict him, I could not imagine experiencing restful sleep on a hard floor. When I went upstairs to retire for the night, I sank into the undamaged feather bed in my chamber and slept well for the second night in a row.

The next morning, I came downstairs to find the dining room turned into a military headquarters, with men sipping coffee as they conferred over maps and papers spread on the table. Moore and Malmedy introduced me to the officers from a detachment of Continentals that arrived just after dawn.

Flora served breakfast to Papa and me on the piazza. "Miz Susannah not feelin' well again today, sir. I'm takin' her up a tray."

He nodded and waved a hand to dismiss her. As we ate together, I recalled the last time I spent time with him without Susannah present.

After I lost Joseph and our son, the thought of continuing his experiment consoled me. My father, who had also lost a beloved spouse, understood that I needed something to occupy me. He drove me out past The Sands to Plainsfield, his plantation located at the confluence of the Wadmalaw and Stono rivers. There we walked the earthen bridge alongside the untended irrigation canals meant to feed the upland rice fields. Weeds choked the canals and protruded from a few inches of murky water.

Papa had purchased the property when I was four years old, and for a time he divided his attention between Plainsfield and our primary residence at Toogoodoo. A few years later when he wed Susannah, he sold Toogoodoo and purchased the island for their residence. Plainsfield, listed for sale at eight pounds the acre, had yet to find a buyer.

Papa pointed with his crop. "The greater part of the cleared land is well suited to growing indigo and corn. The stands of pine, oak, and hickory are good for construction and for use as fuel, plus there's money to be made in producing tar for the shipbuilding trade. Usually, the water supply is adequate to fill the tanks used to process indigo, but the rice fields languish for want of both water and workers to care for them." He paused. "This place wants a manager. If you don't mind that the overseer's house is a bit rundown, I'll lease you servants to work the land and cook for you."

I thought I'd misheard him. "Me manage Plainsfield? What about Frank?"

"Frank is older, but he'll inherit the Island one day and has no need for Plainsfield. I daresay your circumstances have matured you beyond your years. You may keep the profits. Does that suit?"

Managing Plainsfield more than suited. As Papa sipped his coffee, I felt a surge of affection for him and for his willingness to take a chance on me.

As soon as he was finished eating, he returned to the dining room with the officers, but I lingered on the piazza to watch the messengers on fast horses who galloped up to deliver dispatches. As the morning went on they arrived with greater frequency, and I began to wonder if I had refugeed away from safety and into the middle of the impending clash.

One dispatch reported that a flotilla of enemy vessels would soon pass our island. Soon after, a sentry posted on the mainland sent word that several schooners were following behind, and to prepare for attack. Then came a message from Major Pinkney, who was a few miles down the Stono Road with the First Regiment, asking for reinforcements.

By mid-afternoon I had seen enough of the comings and goings and went into the house, but when another rider announced the arrival of General Lincoln I rushed out to meet him.

He dismounted slowly, limped to the impromptu receiving line, and shook all our hands. Papa invited him into the house for refreshment, and I whispered to Major Moore, "What happened to him?"

He answered quietly. "He was wounded during the Siege of Savannah."

I nodded, veneration rising within me for his sacrifice to the Cause, and as I took in the scene and the soldiers standing ready to defend our shoreline, I wondered what sacrifice would be demanded of them before the war came to an end.

Though the presence of the friendly dragoons allowed me to sleep in complete security for two nights in a row, this night I lay awake listening to the officers as they prepared for battle. I fell into an exhausted sleep in the early morning hours, and by the time I came downstairs, Major Moore, Colonel Malmedy, and their men were gone from the island.

Susannah, who looked as tired as I felt, joined Papa and me in the dining room for breakfast. Letty had just set the final platter in place when we heard the first roar of the cannon and quit the table to hurry outdoors.

With the panorama of the island before me, I spied dozens of Continentals poised in defensive positions from the dock up to the causeway. In the distance, the cannon and small arms kept up a continual thunder.

Susannah staggered against me, and I turned in time to see her eyes roll up in her head. I made a grab for her and tried to keep her from falling. "Papa, help!" He caught her other arm and together we lowered her to the ground.

I ran back toward the house, shouting for Jennie. Within moments she came out and assessed the situation, and she and Flora supported Susannah back to her chamber with Papa following behind.

Too nervous to return to my abandoned meal, I stayed outside, listening to the battle sounds. How was our army faring? I both wanted and dreaded to know.

When the roar of the guns ceased, the quiet was more unnerving than the cannonades, and when the first messenger galloped up the causeway I ran to meet him. "How did the battle end?"

"General Lincoln and his army are cut to pieces."

The ground tilted beneath me and I sank to my knees as my imagination transported me to the field of battle. There I imagined the friendly dragoons, wounded and in agonizing pain, as the enemy brought them to their end with the thrust of a bloody bayonet. Still others were dragged away as prisoners and treated in the most insulting manner. The visions crowded so close I could not breathe.

The messenger dismounted and held his horse's reins as he helped me to my feet. As we made our way toward the house, two more horsemen galloped their mounts up the avenue. Startled, my escort's horse reared, and I dodged the metal-shod hooves as I pulled away and stumbled toward the new arrivals. I clutched the nearer one's stirrup and begged, "Please, tell me the truth of the battle."

He answered, "The shot fell thick as hail, and there were many killed on both sides. The troops on this island are ordered to retreat, for their number is too small for an adequate defense."

"If this detachment is called away and the Redcoats come ashore here, what will happen to us?"

The other messenger replied, "We shall stop them in their tracks before that becomes a worry, madam."

"But it seems you have not done so. Where is Major Moore? I want to speak with him."

"I cannot say, madam. There were many units on the field of battle."

Finding no comfort in anything they said, I went into the house. The hall clock struck ten and I realized it was not even midday.

Jennie and Papa were upstairs with Susannah and Flora was minding the little ones, leaving me on my own. I watched out the windows that faced the causeway for hours, and when Major Moore rode up, I reached his side before he dismounted. "No one will explain what happened during the battle. Pray tell me the truth, sir."

He patted my arm. "We suffered heavy losses and many of our men deserted. Though the British prevailed, General Prevost is removing his troops from the Ferry. Lincoln's presence prevented him from going on toward Charles Town. I daresay we'll return to Georgia and attempt to liberate Savannah before autumn. Does that satisfy your curiosity, my dear? If so, I will muster the men so we can move out."

"Oh, but I hoped you could stay longer. Now that it's over, will I ever see you again?" My tenuous hold on security would depart with this officer and his men.

"I hope the winds of fortune will guide us back together, Eliza. In the name of liberty, I bid you goodbye for now. It has been a pleasure to make you and your family's acquaintances."

He swung into the saddle, and as he rode toward the soldiers gathered near the causeway, he left me with the worry that our troubles with the Redcoats were far from over.

5

Colonel Malmedy's dragoons were the last unit to depart, and as soon as they were out of sight the island felt lonely and unprotected. I stood where I'd watched dozens of soldiers poised to defend the island that morning, and as I cast my eyes in the direction of Plainsfield, Papa came out of the house to join me.

"Is Susannah all right?"

"Yes, now that she's eaten something. It's particularly hot today. Come inside now." He leaned on his cane and I matched his labored pace. When we reached the shade of the piazza, he sank into a chair and untied his neckcloth.

"Stay here in the shade where it's cooler, Papa. I'll bring you something to drink."

I was on my way back to him, glass in hand, when through the window I saw two men emerge from the underbrush at the edge of the lawn. Crouching low, they made their stealthy way toward Papa, who was unaware of their approach.

They were not in uniform. Their clothes were smudged with dirt, their faces and hands blackened by powder and smoke. Were they more of McGirth's emissaries, fresh from the battle and back to their plundering ways? As I debated whether to call out, one of them spoke.

"Pa?"

My father turned, and my brothers hurried to him. When I came outside, smiles shone out of their tired, dirty faces and they wrapped me in a smelly embrace.

"Leave off, you rogues!" I held the glass of rum out of harm's way.

When Will released me, he swiped at a tear and left a trail on his smudged cheek. Frank took out his bandana and blew his nose.

"What ails you both? You're carrying on like a couple of old women."

In response, Will punched Frank on the arm. "I told you so!" With a whoop, he picked me up and swung me around, slopping the rum over us both.

"Have you gone mad?" Over his shoulder, I gave Frank a quizzical look.

He grinned. "We thought we must bring Papa tragic news. Turns out, it's not tragic. Just bad."

"We already knew the battle was lost."

"But you were not, Sister!" Will planted a sooty kiss on my cheek and I struggled out of his embrace.

"Of course not. I was here the whole time."

Papa shook his head at the three of us. "Can someone explain?"

Will looked at Frank. "You lost the toss."

"So I did." Frank sat in the chair beside Papa. "After the battle, we headed for Plainsfield to check on Eliza, knowing she was dead set against refugeeing."

"Well?" I set down the empty glass. "What did you find?"

"The Redcoats fired your place. The house and barns were burned to the ground. We searched all over the property and called for you—"

"What about my people? Didn't they tell you I refugeed here two days ago?"

Will shook his head. "There was no one in the fields or at the cabins."

I had underestimated the danger again, and this time I'd abandoned my workers to the Redcoats. "It's all my fault for leaving them behind."

Flora came out to announce supper, and pulled up in surprise at the sight of my brothers. In Susannah's absence it was my role to instruct house servants, so I pushed my distress for my missing workers aside. "Could you please set two more places for Mister Frank and Mister Will? After they wash up, I'm sure they'll want to eat."

She nodded and sped off. As I helped Papa to his feet, Susannah came to the open piazza door.

"Whatever is keeping you?" There was an irritable edge to her voice, and as soon as she laid eyes on my brothers she demanded, "Where did they come from?"

"Straight from battle, Stepmother." Will, with a devilish grin, pecked her on the cheek and left a smudge. "We'll go wash up."

Frank took off his hat and sniffed the aromas of the food as he followed. "I'm starving."

As soon as they were out of earshot, she rounded on Papa, hands on her hips, and hissed, "You promised–"

"Peace, Susannah. We'll give them a meal and they'll be on their way."

She harumphed. "See that a meal is all they get. The little ones and I will eat in the kitchen."

I rolled my eyes as she swept away.

When Frank and Will joined us at the table, Papa's gaze rested on each of us in turn. Despite Susannah's objections, he seemed pleased to have all three of his adult children together. "Well, son?" He turned to Frank. "Tell me about the battle."

Frank gulped down a mouthful of food. "Our unit marched out on Lincoln's right, with orders to attack the Hessians defending the post at the ferry." He refilled his glass from the decanter. "We carried the attack in and overwhelmed the garrison. We had a much better opening strike than the Continentals on the far side."

Will mopped up gravy with a slice of bread. "Those men from the Line got pinned down in a fire fight. There was a creek in the way that kept them from reaching the redoubts. We thought our unit would take the Hessians with no trouble, until their reinforcements arrived and stopped our advance."

"That, and the cavalry charge failed," said Frank. "By the time General Moultrie arrived from Black Swamp with reinforcements for our side, the battle was over and we were in retreat."

Will speared his last bit of meat on his fork. "I'll tell you this: too many of our comrades died today. Battles are the darndest things. All through it, I wondered if anyone—even the generals—really knew what to do. Eliza, are you going to finish that?"

Their unvarnished report of the confusion left me rattled, and I scraped most of my portion onto Will's plate automatically. "General Lincoln is a gentleman. What was it like to be under his command?"

Frank drained his glass. "I couldn't credit why he ordered us to attack the way we did. The British were already withdrawing from around Charles Town—word of Lincoln's arrival with superior numbers was enough to make them evacuate back to Georgia. We stirred up a hornet's nest. Yours wasn't the only place they burned."

"Anyway," Will wiped his mouth on his sleeve, "as soon as the excitement died down we got permission to go over and check on you at Plainsfield. You know the rest."

I sighed. "To be honest, I had nothing worth saving in the house. Likely the Redcoats meant to punish me for harboring a squad of rebel dragoons. I suppose I'll have to stay here until—"

"Mist' Francis!" Flora dashed into the dining room. "There's Redcoats at the dock, coming ashore!"

In a heartbeat Frank and Will were on their feet. I followed them to the window in the parlor that afforded the best view of the shoreline and let out an involuntary shriek at the sight of a dozen Redcoats advancing toward the house.

As one, my brothers wheeled around, ran into the hall, and grabbed up their rifles and haversacks. They burst into the kitchen, startling

Susannah and our little sisters. With Sarah and Harriet's shrieks ringing in my ears, I ran to the kitchen window. Will was at the back door when I cried, "Stop!" for I saw a trio of soldiers break away from the column and head for the rear of the house.

My brothers had no time to reach the safety of the woods, nor could they mount a successful defense against a dozen Redcoats.

Susannah rounded on them, her voice shrill with panic. "This will ruin us! They'll murder my babies and burn the house and—"

Jennie pushed past her, shoved a worktable aside and pulled up a trapdoor in the floor. "Here!"

They dropped their weapons into the hole before letting themselves down, and Jennie shut the trapdoor just as the kitchen door opened. Susannah moved to stand over the trapdoor's handle and took the wailing Harriet in her arms as the soldiers entered the room.

The one in the lead approached her. "Any rebels here, missus?"

Tears stood in her eyes, but she gave him a disdainful look. "Of course not."

"Loyal to the king then, are you?"

She did not answer, and the soldier scoffed.

"What's in your pocket?"

He reached out, but before he touched her she slapped his hand like he was a naughty child. "If you must see I'll show you myself." She brought out a sewing case, and the wretch took it from her.

I found my voice. "What use do you have for a lady's sewing kit?"

He replied as though it was obvious. "Why, my Nancy would want it."

Susannah gave him a scathing look. "So this is the noble service you do your king?"

His lip curled in a snarl as he took her by the arm and shoved her ahead of him toward the dining room. The other soldiers motioned for the rest of us to follow. I picked up Sarah before I obeyed. She hiccupped with sobs in my arms, and I stifled a cry as I entered the dining room, for two more soldiers had their pistols trained on Papa while an officer stood by.

Jennie and Flora backed against the far wall.

The soldier who held Susannah by the arm gave her a shake as he addressed Papa. "Your daughter is quite impudent, isn't she?"

Papa replied gravely, "She may well be, but that's my wife you have there. Take your hands off her."

One of the soldiers chuckled. "You look too feeble to service her— yet you have plenty of progeny. If you're not as helpless as you look, perhaps I should put a bullet in your head."

Susannah tried to free herself from the soldier's grip. "Leave him alone!"

The officer raised a lazy hand, and the soldier demurred. "See what's in his pockets."

The soldiers hauled Papa to his feet and he cast off his outer coat and spread his arms. "Search if you must, laddies."

The soldiers patted down his pockets and grunted with displeasure when they found nothing but a few coins, a tinder box, and a pipe.

One of them took Papa's cane. "This'll do, then, won't it?" He smashed the shaft beneath his boot heel and pocketed the gold head.

Their officer picked up one of the wine bottles that sat open on the table. His gaze flickered between the four place settings and Papa, Susannah, and myself, and came to rest on Frank's napkin, which was smeared with the powder dust that clung to his mustache.

He stared at the napkin in silence for a long, agonizing moment, slammed the bottle down with a crash that made us all jump, and barked at his men, "Search the house!"

They dispersed, and as I heard the familiar sounds of rending wood and breaking glass, the officer turned to Papa and demanded, "Where's your wine cellar, old man?"

The wine cellar was Papa's pride, part of the rabbit warren of chambers in the house's lowest level, accessed both by an exterior door and the trapdoor in the kitchen. The windows on all sides of the cellar were covered with narrow battens set close together to allow ventilation and keep out varmints. Its exterior door was kept padlocked and afforded my brothers no means of escape.

"It's below." Papa nodded to Susannah. "Open it."

Susannah blanched, but rose and handed Harriet to Flora. The officer followed her out. When I winced at a particularly loud crash, the soldier who stayed behind flashed an insolent grin.

We sat in silence for so long my nerves stretched to the breaking point. Then one of the men shouted, "Come out here! On the double!"

Soldiers vacated all parts of the house and stampeded outdoors. I hid my face in Sarah's sweaty hair as a great cheer went up, followed by laughter. The image of Frank and Will driven out of the cellar into a mob of jeering Redcoats rose in my mind, and I steeled myself for their executions.

Moments later two soldiers, their arms full of bottles, came into the dining room. One asked, "I say, give us a corkscrew!"

Flora, long trained to respond to orders, retrieved one from the sideboard.

"Here! Leave me one!" demanded our guard.

As the soldiers opened the bottles, Susannah returned and sank into a chair across the table from me. She would not meet my gaze.

The afternoon wore on and we remained under guard while soldiers rampaged through the house. When the children cried from hunger, Susannah fed them what was left on the plates at the table.

The sun was low in the sky when their officer joined us, shook Papa's hand, and complimented the wine and the rum. He motioned for our guard to come with him and called for his troops to return to the barge.

I waited until I believed they'd all left the house, and then handed Sarah to Flora. I checked each room for stragglers as I ran on tiptoe toward the open front door. From there I waited until the whole squad was aboard. When the barge pushed away from the shore, I returned to the dining room.

"They've gone."

Papa rose and picked up his coat off the floor, chuckling as he put it on. "Bless my stars, they may have smashed every window in the house, but they missed the three hundred pounds in my jacket pocket. At least I saved something from those marauding blackguards."

How could he laugh? "Papa, what about Frank and Will?"

"If they'd found your brothers, we would know. Light a taper and come with me."

I followed him down the front stairs and around to the cellar door. The path was littered with empty bottles, and as I followed Papa I stumbled over one and sent it skittering.

The single candle's flame threw tall shadows against the walls as we entered the wine cellar. Papa pushed on a section of the now-empty shelves, and it swung back to reveal steps that led to a subterranean room.

A sob escaped my lips as Will came out, brushing off cobwebs and dirt. "That was a close one!"

Frank emerged on his heels, and for the second time that day we three clung together.

Papa cleared his throat. "How fortuitous that I had this hidden room put in. I thought to use it to keep my most treasured bottles safe, but it came to a greater use today." He folded each of his sons in a lingering embrace.

Frank looked down at our father. "Good thing you told us about the secret room long ago. Otherwise, we'd have been cooked."

"We leaned against the door to hold it closed while they raided your stores, Papa." Will chuckled. "I was afraid they'd hear my stomach rumble, but they made too much noise. Can someone wrap up more food for us? We'll leave as soon as it's dark."

"Of course." Papa rummaged for a moment and then touched the wick of an unlit candle to mine.

I spoke up. "I counted the soldiers. They all got back on the barge."

Will ruffled my hair. "Good thing we have a scout."

"I hope I never have to scout for you again. Perhaps try to stay out of trouble?"

"Where's the fun in that?" Will's grin was so saucy I pinched his cheek before I followed Papa out of the cellar.

When we went back inside, Susannah, Flora and the children were nowhere in sight. Papa sat at the dining table and poured himself a glass of wine while I went to the kitchen to pack the food for my brothers. Jennie dried the last of the supper dishes and came to help me. Before we finished, Susannah stormed in to confront Papa.

"You must turn them away next time."

Papa sounded tired. "Dearest, remember yourself. I cannot turn away the Redcoats."

"I'm talking about your sons. If the Redcoats had found them here, they would have burned the house and murdered the lot of us."

"Poor lamb. You're overwrought from the strain."

Her voice broke. "I'm with child again! What if the Redcoats had murdered you and left me alone with three young ones?" She burst into tears.

Jennie and I both froze. I put a finger to my lips and we listened as Papa spoke in a grave tone. "I will not deny any of my children. They are every bit as much my family as the ones you have borne me."

She stood up so quickly her chair tipped over, and we stayed out of sight as she fled upstairs.

6

Though Papa and some of his workers went to work immediately to secure the house for the night, I slept in my clothes, and my dreams were full of lurking Redcoats and the distant thunder of battle.

The next morning, I awoke to a cacophony of excited voices outside. Jennie opened my chamber door and announced, "They's here, Miz Eliza!"

"Who?" I sat up.

"Solomon and all of them!"

This news brought me wide awake, and I hurried down to greet my workers. Every one of them was smudged with mud and dirt. Some wielded stout clubs, and others carried bundles of provisions and clothing.

Solomon hurried to clasped my hand. "You was right, Miz Eliza. We should've gone with you. When the battle come too close, we hid in the swamp. We seen the Redcoats burn the house and barn, and after we'd just got the finished dye cakes stored away, too. This morning we din' see no soldiers, so we came here."

"You did right. I'm so thankful you're all safe."

Cato, who was Papa's right hand about the place, came to see what the excitement was about. I asked, "Could you please help my people settle into quarters? After they've had a chance to rest and eat, Solomon can put them in work crews to assist you however you see fit."

He nodded. "That'll be fine, Miz Eliza. Mist' Francis and I goin' to the sawmill after breakfast to buy lumber for the repairs." He motioned to Solomon to follow him, and my people headed toward the row of cabins they'd inhabited before they came to Plainsfield with me.

Papa and Cato returned that afternoon with bad news. The Redcoats had rendered the mill inoperable, and every board in the miller's stockpile of lumber was already spoken for. Worse yet, his workers who ran the mill and fashioned doors and window frames had either run away or been taken by the enemy.

Papa directed his crew to tear down a storage shed and make the reclaimed boards into shutters to cover the broken windows, and then supervised the work, making me wonder if he was trying to prove he was not too feeble to take care of his young family.

I pretended I didn't know about Susannah's pregnancy, and even though I understood the fear of losing one's husband while one was with child, I could not forget she would have preferred to turn my brothers away rather than help them. I saw no reason to change my long-standing opinion of her, and, as always, we got along better from a distance. Most days I joined Jennie and some other women servants in carding, spinning, and weaving the yield from Papa's cotton fields.

Like most lowcountry residents, we made a practice of migrating to the city during the autumn months, but this year we remained at Island House when the marsh grasses faded to brown and the nights grew longer. Susannah's pregnancy was now evident, and she invoked it whenever she wanted to garner sympathy. Papa kept up a young man's pace, but as the weather cooled he began to complain of headaches and was often so tired he went to bed without eating supper.

Frank, Will, and their fellows in the militia stopped by when they were in the area, but we had no other visitors to the island until a few days before Christmas when a liveried messenger rode up the causeway. His arrival caused such a stir among the servants that Papa, Susannah, and I came out to the piazza to receive him. He carried a letter for me which bore my Plainsfield address, and apologized for the delay in its delivery.

I was mystified. Which of my correspondents had the time, paper, and ink with which to write to me? I broke the seal and unfolded the page, and as I read, I burst into incredulous laughter.

Papa asked, "What is it, Daughter?"

"An invitation to a Christmas house party." Did anyone in our area have nothing to do but eat, dance, and play games? I stuffed it in my pocket.

Susannah tossed her head in a feeble attempt at indifference and went back inside, but my father stayed with me. "Who is hosting?"

"Elizabeth and Philip Smith, of Airy Hall."

He nodded. "Ah yes. Old Doctor Skirving's daughter. They must not have seen much of the Redcoats over toward Pon Pon, if they plan to entertain. You should go."

I glanced down at my patched gown and rough hands. "How can I go without any party clothes?"

"It would be good for you." Though the day was not warm, he mopped his perspiring face on his sleeve, and it came away smudged with pink.

"Papa, you're bleeding."

His hand shook as he stared at his sleeve, and a rivulet of blood ran from his nose.

"You're not well. Let me help you inside." I put an arm around his waist to support him, but he took one step and collapsed. I staggered under his weight and was unable to hold him as he fell. My cries for help brought Susannah and Jennie running out of the house, and we knelt around him. He was breathing, but did not respond when I called to him and shook his shoulder. His forehead was burning hot. Susannah's swoons were mostly to garner sympathy, but Papa was unconscious.

I summoned four strong workers to carry him up to his chamber, and then Jennie took charge of the situation, and checked the pulse at his neck. "His heartbeat is too fast, and it ain't strong." She gently pinched the skin on his cheek. "Mist' Joseph used to say 'an imbalance of the humors' causes disease."

Susannah stared in surprise, so I explained, "My husband was training her to assist him."

She turned to Jennie, fear evident on her face. "How do you treat such an imbalance? Will you bleed him?"

"Not yet. I'll fetch him some wine and laudanum." She motioned for me to follow her.

On our way downstairs, I asked, "What do you think it is?"

"I jus' said that about imbalance of the humors so Miz Susannah wouldn't question me. Ain't no doubt. It's yellow fever." She went into the chamber off the kitchen she shared with Flora and brought out what had once been Joseph's medicine chest. I handed her a bottle of wine and then left her to her preparations, so overcome with dread I could not think what to do.

We should have found a way to leave the lowcountry during the sickly months. If Papa succumbed, I doubted Susannah could manage everything on the island, and responsibility for the whole family would fall to me.

Shouts and the sound of horses in the yard brought me out of my reverie. I wiped my eyes, and when I went to the front door I clapped my hand over my mouth to stifle a scream. A large party of Redcoats, both mounted and on foot, streamed up the causeway toward the house. There could not be a more inconvenient time for their arrival.

Susannah and I went out of the house together, and the officer at the fore stayed back a respectful distance. "Good day, ladies. Is this Yonge's Island?"

Susannah spoke. "It is."

"I beg you not to be under any apprehension. My officers require a meeting room and sleeping accommodations for the night. The enlisted men will bivouac on your grounds."

Neither of us responded, as any objection we might raise would be ignored.

He motioned to the officer who led the front company and said, "I leave you in the care of Captain Sandford, one of the best-bred officers in His Majesty's Army."

Sandford, a tall, imposing man who wore a powdered wig and was perhaps in his mid-thirties, puffed up at the praise. He dismounted as his commander rode away. "Which of you ladies is the mistress of the house?"

Susannah answered, "I am Missus Yonge."

He gave me a curious glance, but when I did not respond, he addressed Susannah again.

"Where is your husband, madam?"

"He is ill. Indisposed."

He turned to me. "And yours, madam?"

"I'm a widow."

This information seemed to interest him. "If you will lock up your poultry-house and anything of value, I will assign a sentry to stand guard over your larder."

He followed us from room to room as we gathered what we wished to secure. Susannah took a key off her chatelaine and whispered, "Go get the money pouch from your father's desk."

I slipped away the moment his back was turned, and ran on tiptoe to the study. I shut the door silently behind me, unlocked the desk drawer, and stuffed the money pouch into my pocket. As I left the room, I found the captain smarting himself up before the cracked looking glass in the foyer. He removed his wig and took a dainty little comb from his pocket to smooth its stray hairs. When he caught sight of me, I pretended I was headed for the parlor all along, and to my dismay, he replaced his wig and hastened to join me.

He gestured for me to sit and flipped out the tails of his coat as he took the seat next to me, but he did not seem to know how to begin a conversation. He cleared his throat and stroked down his ruffles as the silence between us stretched on. Under more favorable circumstances and with better company I would have had no trouble keeping the discourse going, but I decided to let him stew.

Soon some of his lieutenants came in, took seats, and stretched their legs toward the fire, heedless of their spurs digging into the carpet. When one of them smiled in my direction, Sandford made bold to speak.

"This is a very pleasant situation, madam."

"Yes, sir, it is agreeable."

"I admire it much, though it is rather sequestered. Do you spend all the year here?"

"We usually spend the sickly months in town, but this year we have resided wholly in the country."

"But why so? Are there not concerts, assemblies, and other polite amusements which ladies admire?"

"I would rather be where I am than in Charles Town just now." Could he not look around and understand that, in our current circumstances, taking part in polite amusements was the last thing on my mind?

This chit-chat might have continued forever, but Flora hurried in and interrupted. "Miz Eliza, some of the soldiers cut your homespun out the loom!"

I rounded on the captain and his smile faded in the face of my fury. "Do you command a gang of thieves, sir? Your countrymen won't let us buy yard goods in town for fear we'll supply our troops, so we are obliged to weave our own to clothe the family. You said you would not steal our possessions. Pray make them give me back the cloth."

My entreaty drove him to his feet and out the door. As Flora and I followed him to the lawn, a pig squealed in terror. In the sea of red I spotted Papa's largest sow, bleeding as she hobbled across the lawn on three legs. A group of soldiers had cut off the other and were laughing as they pursued the poor creature. Driven by rage, I picked up my skirts and ran toward them. The tortured pig limped past me, still squealing at the top of her voice, and I blocked the soldiers' path.

"Stop! I demand you stop at once!" I stepped up to the soldier in the lead, heedless of the bloody knife in his hand, and slapped him across the face. "Shame on you!"

A red mark in the shape of my palm blossomed on his cheek, and he raised the knife.

Captain Sandford, diverted from his original mission, panted as he arrived at my side. "Private! Stand down!"

He obeyed, but the manner in which he sheathed his knife was both an insult and a threat.

Sandford put a hand on my shoulder but I shrugged it off, never taking my eyes off the offending men. He waved them away and spoke to me as though to a child. "Madam, a lady of your station should not confront common soldiers. Neither should you have to wear clothing made from such rough, ugly cloth."

"What right have you to comment on my situation, sir? Your army has plundered us repeatedly. What we have left is supposed to be under your protection, yet you allow your men to create all manner of mischief!"

The pig's squeals ceased, and I whirled around to find the soldiers had slit her throat.

"David!" I beckoned to a servant boy of about ten, who was carrying a bucket and dipper among the soldiers. He slopped water over the bucket's sides as he hurried to me.

"Leave the water and go find Cain. The two of you bring all the pigs up to the house right away."

As he ran off, Sandford stared at me as if I had two heads, but I did not demur. "Since you cannot protect our stock from your men, I will see to it myself."

Soon the boys came across the lawn, herding the grunting pigs toward the house with willow switches.

David called, "Miz Eliza, them soldiers took and kilt three more."

"I see." I shot another angry glance at the captain. "Take the rest of them to my chamber, please."

I followed the boys to the house. The sentry laughed as the boys boosted the pigs over the threshold one by one, but I was far too angry to find the situation humorous. Those pigs were a food source necessary for our family's survival.

Sandford took exception to the sentry's mirth. He drew his sword and shouted, "If they kill another, why, I'll—" His voice trailed off as he charged back into the yard in search of the pig thieves.

Inside, the pigs squealed their objections and the boys muttered their frustrations as they coaxed them up the stairs. Cain was lifting the last one up to the second floor when the captain returned and gave me an ingratiating smile.

"Madam, when I first laid eyes on you, I couldn't help thinking, 'how I wish this little creature was mine.' But you scolded me—and for what? Some pigs."

"Despite your assurances, Captain, your men destroyed our property and stole from us. I shall scold as I see fit."

"Would you stop if you received half a dozen more tomorrow?"

"You mean if you stole them from one of our neighbors? No. I won't countenance plunder."

Disappointment and surprise were plain on his face. "Is your heart truly among the rebels?"

"After the way your army has treated us, how could it be anywhere else?" Hoping this exchange was enough to quell his clumsy overtures, I turned, marched upstairs, and locked myself in my chamber. The pigs were better company than the captain, though the combined odors of my four-legged companions and the fresh pork cooking outdoors left me feeling nauseated.

At early candle lighting, there was a quiet knock at my door. "Eliza?" Susannah's voice was a shrill whisper. "Stop this foolishness, come downstairs, and entertain Captain Sandford. He asked to be seated next to you at supper."

I answered through the door. "Tell him I am otherwise engaged."

She knocked again, louder. "Open up!" When I obeyed, she pushed past me into the room, gagged, and brought her apron to her nose.

I shut the door. "He enlisted you to plead for my affections, didn't he?"

When Susannah lowered the apron, she wore the same pained expression she'd had since I was eight years old and she realized the futility of trying to control me. "He favors you. If you don't come downstairs you'll humiliate him, and put all of us at risk. He could let his soldiers empty the larder and the wine cellar, murder your father in his bed, and claim one of us as spoils of war. There's no telling what his men will do, or how far they will go— "

"How far? How far would you have me go to entertain him? You guard your virtue, yet you have no concern for mine. I'm surprised you didn't invite him up here to rut with the pigs."

"How dare you speak to me that way." She gagged and pressed the apron to her nose again. "I have no idea what he sees in you, but come downstairs and be pleasant until they leave." She let herself out, but instead of following I went to Papa's room, where I gave Jennie a whispered account of the afternoon's events.

"Sandford frightens me. He knows we have no male protection. Oh, heaven. Papa will get well, won't he?"

She squeezed my hand as we looked down at my sleeping father. "Not soon enough to help you tonight. I can sleep in your chamber if you want me to."

"No. Stay with Papa. I'd rather you were here in case he grows worse. I have the pigs."

When I descended the stairs, Susannah was waiting, and inclined her head toward the candlelit parlor where the captain was waiting alone. When I entered he sprang to his feet, but when he drew close enough to take my hand, he wrinkled his nose. Pretending I smelled of orange blossoms instead of a pigsty, I swept across the room and resumed my place on the settee.

He followed and took a framed miniature from his jacket pocket, kissed it, and held it out to me with a flourish. "Won't you kiss our dear Queen Charlotte?"

"No, Captain. I do not worship idols."

He chuckled as though I'd said something amusing. "Your allies, the French, would make you worship the Virgin Mary."

"We may as well worship her as the queen's picture."

"How can you reject your queen, madam?"

"We have twice repulsed your army from Charles Town and have thrashed you up and down the Carolina coast all year. When will you realize that the United States rejects your monarchy?"

"How dare you say such things!"

I shrank from the anger in his voice and he leaned closer, speaking just above a whisper. "I am here to protect you from the rebels, and from yourself, if necessary."

Before I could reply, Flora came in to announce dinner. As Sandford escorted me to the dining room and held my chair, I glanced from Papa's empty place at the head of the table to the officers who outnumbered my family. Susannah gave me an encouraging smile, and I returned it with a stony glare.

I spoke little during the meal and intended to escape into the kitchen as soon as the wine was on the table, but when I began to clear the dishes, the captain put up a hand to check me. "You have servants to do the menial work. Pray, join me in the parlor." Reluctant to anger him again, I did as he bid.

This time I chose a chair near the fire, rather than the settee. He set another chair next to mine and scooted it closer by degrees. With no chaperone present, he mounted his next offensive, pressing his shoulder against mine and whispering close to my ear, "I vow there is no woman in all of the British Empire quite as bewitching as you."

I acted as though I had not heard. When his subordinates came in, I hoped he would desist, but he tried again. "The firelight makes your hair shine like ebony. A rare and most exotic wood indeed."

I tossed my head. "Elbow room, Captain Sandford—I beg of you, elbow room!"

No one dared to intervene, but he muttered under his breath and shifted his chair a few inches. While he sulked, the other officers entertained themselves by comparing the times they had been on duty in the presence of the king or been smiled upon by the queen.

After a few minutes Sandford gathered his courage and made another clumsy attempt to compliment me. "You seem different from when we met this afternoon."

"I assure you, sir, I have not changed at all."

"For God's sake, don't contradict and don't be so disdainful!" As the room fell silent, he continued in the same angry tone. "Don't you understand how much I love you? I may be a stranger, but I am a gentleman."

"Show me you are a gentleman and leave me be. I have no interest in you." I added, "Burgoyne for that!"

The other officers laughed and Sandford's knuckles whitened as he clutched the arms of the chair.

One of the lieutenants, seeking to break the tension, commented, "I say—we've been about this neighborhood for some time, and I'm surprised we've not been attacked by the rebels."

"Aye," said another. "No one has tried to prevent us from acquiring cattle and provisions."

"It may be," said Sandford, "that the rebels have sent word to Congress asking if they must fight us and are awaiting a response before they engage." He laughed at his own wittiness.

The lieutenant who first posed the question turned to me. "Pray, madam, which is it—a want of courage, or conduct?"

"Neither, sir. As they can take whole armies they don't think it worth their while to attack a detachment."

My reply was met by another uncomfortable silence. Finally Sandford addressed his fellow officers as though sharing a great confidence. "Did you know most of the royal family, including the king, are nearsighted?"

"Indeed he must be, or he would not have begun this war." The words escaped my lips of their own volition. "Now, if you will excuse me, I bid you good night." I rose and, without appearing to hurry, took up a candle. As soon as I was out of their sight, I ran up the stairs and unlocked my chamber with shaking hands. I'd forgotten about the pigs, and as I burst into the room, their startled squeals nearly made me drop the candle. I turned the key in the lock and leaned against the door, waiting for my pounding heart to quiet.

I held my skirts up to my knees as I waded through the pigs to my window and peeked through the shutters. Outside, the soldiers' campfires on the lawn dotted the darkness like dozens of fireflies. Shivering, I stirred up the coals on the hearth and crawled under the covers without undressing. It was late when the officers settled on their pallets in the downstairs hall, and even after all was silent, I dared not let my guard down.

7

The pigs snorted and grunted in their sleep, and woke before dawn to befoul my chamber with fresh droppings. Then, snuffling and squealing, they rooted around the room in a futile search for something to eat.

I nudged a few of them aside with my foot and stepped around the messes on my way to the window. In the gray light I watched soldiers strike tents, douse campfires, and form ranks to move out. Only when the creak of the supply-wagon's wheels and the horses' whinnies grew faint did I relax. I sank down on the edge of the bed, head in my hands, and uttered a silent prayer of thanks, but no sooner had I breathed my amen when I heard heavy footsteps in the hall and a knock at my door. On tiptoe, I ran to press my ear against it.

Sandford's voice resonated as if he wished the entire household to hear. "May God bless you with every happiness, Missus Wilkinson."

When I did not answer, he stealthily tried the door. He uttered his next words softly, for my ears alone. "Don't think you shall stay on this island long. I intend to return at the first opportunity and carry you off."

I trembled as I listened to his footsteps recede down the stairs. Suddenly Island House was more prison than sanctuary. As I wiped my clammy hands on my skirts I felt the lump of the money pouch in my pocket and brought it out along with the forgotten party invitation.

I need not cower in fear and await Captain Sandford's return to Island House. I would go to the party, and if he came back he would find me not at home.

I rang for a maid, but instead of Jennie, Flora answered the summons. She, like Susannah, did not hide her horror at the state of my chamber, and immediately brought her apron to her nose. "Oh, Miz Eliza! Miz Susannah ain't gonna like this mess one bit."

"What else was I to do? Those soldiers were brutes. They would have butchered all of the pigs and left us with nothing to eat. Please send for David and Cain to take them to their pen. Tell them to bring a bucket and shovel for the manure, and sand and water to scour the floor."

She dropped a curtsey, and as soon as she was gone I went down the hall to check on Papa. The door was open, and my heart lifted when he motioned for me to come in. I smiled my brightest smile. "How do you fare this morning?"

"Better." As if to prove his assertion, he set aside his untouched breakfast tray and waved away Jennie's assistance as he pushed himself up to sit.

I took the chair beside the bed. "Did Susannah tell you some Redcoats camped here overnight?"

"She did. Was I dreaming, or did she also say something about pigs in the house?"

"Yes, I daresay there were two types of pigs under this roof last night. The human sort have moved on, thank goodness, and the others will soon be going back to their pen." I decided not to burden him with my fears. "Papa, after more consideration, I believe I shall go to the party."

"I hoped you would change your mind." He gestured toward a small trunk against the wall. "I had Cato bring this down from the attic for you this morning. "

I knelt in front of it and as soon as I raised the lid I recognized the contents and tears welled in my eyes. "You saved some of Mother's gowns."

"It was difficult to part with things that reminded me of her. I had her maid pack these away, and now they are a boon, for you can wear them, can you not?"

I lifted out a coral-colored damask and shook out the folds to inspect it. "It's as beautiful as I remember, Papa, and looks as though it will fit. I'll be proud to wear it." I held the gown up to my front.

He caught the hem between his fingers. "You're as lovely as she was. You'll turn every head in the room."

When he did not let go, I asked, "What is it?"

"Four years and more have passed since you were made a widow. It's time you began to socialize again. Promise me you won't forget to live."

"I promise, Papa."

When he closed his eyes, he looked so waxy and pale he might have been laid out in his coffin. I brushed a kiss on his forehead before I left the room.

Flora, David, and Cain scrubbed and scoured my chamber until no trace of the pigs remained. After dinner Jennie helped me try on the coral damask, a robe *a la francais* of turquoise flowered silk, and a red floral polonaise with a lace-trimmed stomacher and petticoat. At the bottom of the trunk was underthings, stockings, a pair of embroidered dancing slippers, and a pocket containing a cameo brooch, a necklace and earbobs of rose-cut garnets, and a topaz in a gold filigree setting on a turquoise velvet ribbon. When Jennie clasped the garnets around my neck, I surveyed my reflection in the looking glass and felt wickedly glad that Papa never offered any of the jewels to Susannah.

My stomach fluttered at the thought of attending a party. Since Joseph's death, I'd told myself I was busy and content at Plainsfield. Now I wondered if I'd ever truly confronted my grief over losing him.

Cato drove Jennie and me to Airy Hall on the morning of Christmas Eve. The weather was sunny and fair, and I enjoyed watching the changing landscape as we traveled northwest toward Willtown. Once we crossed the Edisto River, the tidal marshes that sparkled in the sun gave way to the upland country's fallow fields and forests. Mistletoe hanging with the bearded moss on the live oaks brought back memories of other holiday seasons, but the sight of so many homes damaged by the Redcoats quelled my happy thoughts.

It was mid-afternoon when we turned into the avenue of oaks that led to a sprawling brick house pleasantly situated overlooking the Ashepoo River. The instant Cato stopped the chaise, liveried servants hurried to attend to us. One offered a gloved hand to help me down, and another took my trunk.

As we went inside, I handed the wool blanket I was using as a shawl to Jennie. She followed the footman upstairs, leaving me in a world I'd almost forgotten existed.

None of the looking glasses at Airy Hall were broken. There were no bullet holes in the walls, no rips in the upholstered furniture. Garlands of evergreen boughs brought a fresh, piney scent indoors, and from beyond closed French doors came the muted clink of silver and china as the servants laid the dining table.

Alerted by her butler, Elizabeth Smith met me in the great hall with a warm smile and clasped both my hands. "Eliza, how good it is to see you! Would you like refreshment, perhaps a glass of wine?"

"That would be lovely." In response to her subtle gesture, a servant brought me a crystal glass of Madeira on a tray. I murmured my thanks and took a sip.

"We hear the Redcoats caused a great deal of trouble along the Stono. I trust all is well with your family?"

I forced a smile. "We have dealt with all manner of pests in the past, but I daresay there's nothing worse than the Redcoats."

Her laugh was gentle and ladylike. "Everyone has gone outdoors to enjoy the gardens. I would walk out with you, but I must oversee the preparations for tonight. Shall I call someone to escort you?"

"No thank you. I'll find my way."

Her silks rustled as she hurried away. Instead of going directly outside, I wandered from room to room, admiring the walnut paneling, silk portieres, and imported furnishings. I caught sight of myself in a full-length pier glass and paused to straighten my skirts and smooth my hair.

My family lived well, but not nearly so well as the Smiths and the Skirvings. Though I had been content at Toogoodoo with Joseph and on my own at Plainsfield, when I spied the library, I felt both envy and loss. Joseph's collection of medical, philosophy, history, and religious books had been sold at the estate sale.

On the far side of the room I spied a dark-haired man on the settee by the window, engrossed in the book open before him. After the unwanted attention I'd received of late, someone who was unaware of my presence seemed like the perfect companion. I set my glass of wine aside, selected a book, and took a seat. At first I stole glances at him, but when I realized I could look at him as long as I cared to, I took the opportunity to compare him to the image of Joseph I held in my mind's eye.

I remembered My husband as tall and well-formed, with a cheerful countenance and hair the color of dark amber honey. He was fond of bright waistcoats and well-tailored clothes, and he wore them well.

A few strands of the silent stranger's black hair framed his forehead, and the rest was pulled back in an indifferent tail and tied with a knotted ribbon. He'd tossed his walnut-brown coat across the back of the settee. His linen was rumpled, his stock crooked, and he had a dirt smudge on his stocking where he rested his ankle on his other knee. He did not look dressed for a party. I glanced down at the everyday gown I wore. Perhaps I didn't either.

Taken with the sudden urge to remain where I was rather than seek the rest of the guests, I decided to create my own fun. I opened my book to a random page and began to read aloud. *"I know not whether some deceitful spirits haunt this spot, or whether it be the warm, celestial fancy in my own heart which makes everything around me like paradise."* I paused and gave him a sidelong glance. He shifted in his seat but did not respond.

I stifled a giggle. *"In front of the house is a fountain—a fountain to which I am bound by a charm..."*

He turned a page and began to read aloud from his book. *"After the fall of the Roman empire, on the contrary, the proprietors of land seem generally to have lived in fortified castles on their own estates, and in the midst..."*

I raised my voice a little, and a smile quirked at the corner of his mouth as he matched my volume.

"...a pleasant but sublime impression. Not a day passes in which I do not spend an hour there..."

"...chiefly inhabited by tradesmen and mechanics, who seem, in those days..."

He looked over his shoulder at me and when our eyes met, he gave a tiny nod, like a challenge. We both read faster.

"...they formed their friendships and contracted alliances at the fountain-side..."

"...ancient charters to the inhabitants of some of the principal towns..."

"...guarded by beneficent spirits."

"...what they were before those grants."

We finished our sentences at the same moment. He laughed and turned in his seat to face me, but before he spoke, a third voice broke in.

"Women, play, and wine divided my hours..."

I turned to recognize the blond young man who stood behind my chair. "Why, Hext McCall!"

He shut the book he held with a clap and tossed it on a table. "Dearest Eliza! Oh, to have a fresh face to gaze upon!"

The dark-haired man cleared his throat and turned his attention back to his book.

Hext's family owned a place near one of my father's properties, and when we were children he was a favorite playmate of my brother Will. I remembered him as prone to silly pranks and teasing. When he extended a hand to help me rise, I took it half expecting him to have a frog ready to slip down my back.

Instead, he bowed and touched his lips to my hand. "The weather is too pleasant to stay indoors. Come, my dear, and take a stroll in the gardens."

Before I let him lead me away, I turned back and dropped an unacknowledged curtsey. As soon as we were outside, I asked, "Who is that man?"

"One of the Porchers." He shrugged. "Who can keep track of them all?"

It appeared I would learn nothing about the dark-haired stranger from Hext, so I changed the subject. "My brother will be sorry he missed seeing you. You never write, and it's been years since you made a visit to your friends in the country."

"My law studies consume my every waking moment."

"Truly?" I could not imagine him applying himself to such a serious pursuit.

"No." He laughed. "I daresay there's too much going on in the 'Ton."

"You study law when time permits?"

"It satisfies Papa's ambitions for me. He insists I have a profession. Tell me, how do you stand it in the country? It's so terribly dull."

He would not say so if he had been present for any of my recent adventures. "I've had plenty of callers lately. Most of them were Redcoats. With my brothers serving in the militia—"

He broke in. "I did a stint in the militia in seventy-six and have no desire to return to military life. No thank'ee! "

As we approached the guests gathered in the garden, some of the young ladies gave me appraising glances, and others looked longingly at Hext. On his arm, I was the object of their envy, but I would have preferred the company of the boy who loved to fish, hunt oysters, and play pranks with my brothers and me.

I nodded to everyone as we promenaded past. "I believe I'll always relish country life. Remember when we were children? You used to love our humble amusements."

He led me away from the other guests and paused in a secluded spot. "No matter what you claim, Eliza, only those of decrepit old age enjoy the country. You would be quite a success at the Season. Your charms are so devastating, no man should face you unarmed." Without warning, he grasped my shoulders and kissed me on the mouth.

I pushed him away. "What the devil, Hext? Must you fall on me like a hawk on a dove?" I looked around to make sure no one had seen.

"Come, Eliza, don't deny me. I might be the first to claim a kiss this weekend, but I shan't be the last."

When I started to retort he kissed me again, and I slapped him. He touched his fingertips to the red mark on his cheek. "I wish to be hanged if you do not return my affections."

"I trust you can find your own way to the gallows." I pushed past him, and as I headed for the house, I wished I had remained in the company of the indifferent Mr. Porcher.

8

The walk back to the house gave me a chance to regain my composure. When I arrived I sought directions to my chamber. The upstairs hall seemed to go on forever, and I counted the doors until I arrived at the one I believed was mine. Jennie answered my knock, and if I still looked flustered she made no comment as she helped me change into the pink damask.

When the bell summoned us to supper, guests streamed downstairs. Hext entered the dining room with a young lady on each arm. One of them tossed her head and gave a high-pitched giggle as he held her chair. I hoped they would hold his interest until the party was over, and headed for an empty seat at the other end of the table.

Mr. Porcher, who had also changed for dinner, took the place across from me and acknowledged me with the same slight inclination of his head. I returned his bow, and as the last of the guests took seats, I cast glances at the men present. Some of the older men, including Colonel William Skirving, my hostess's brother, wore their dress uniforms, while the bachelors favored embroidered suits of blue, green, or mustard. As I scanned the faces of the youthful, smiling men and listened to their conversations, I recognized names and characteristics that hinted at their aristocratic French and English bloodlines. I wondered if any of them were, like me, wearing borrowed clothes and concealing a sudden descent into financial difficulties.

Startled from my thoughts by movement all around, I rose and lifted my glass as Colonel Skirving spoke from his place near the head of the table. "Savannah—may she throw off the yoke of British oppression in the new year."

Mr. Porcher murmured, "Savannah," before he drank.

The man at my left offered the next toast. "The memory of General Pulaski."

Two men spoke in rapid succession from the far end of the table. "Our absent friends on land and sea."

"Charles Town, the most beautiful and prosperous city in the United States."

Hext raised his voice above the others. "The season which engages the whole world in a conspiracy of love."

The dark-haired young woman seated next to Mr. Porcher gave a shy little giggle at Hext's words. I rolled my eyes, and the corner of Mr. Porcher's mouth twitched in almost imperceptible commiseration. Hext's was the last toast, and I set down my glass and smoothed my napkin on my lap as the servants brought out the first course.

The soups and roast oysters alone made the most satisfying meal I'd eaten since June, but soon the servants cleared away the used plates and bowls and served the second course of turkey, ham, pigeon pie, creamed vegetables, and rice. I ate some of everything as I listened to the men discuss the failed attempt to liberate Savannah the previous October. Captain Skirving decried the French commander's decision to bombard the city rather than attack the British defenses. The man on my right declared hardly a house in town had not been shot through.

Hext, bored with any conversation that was not about him, reiterated the sentiments he'd shared with me earlier. "No thank'ee! I'll leave the soldiering to my brothers."

"A wise decision, no doubt." Mr. Porcher delivered his dry observation and took a sip of wine. Several of the men chuckled, and the talk continued as if Hext had not interrupted.

The orchestra began tuning their instruments just as we finished the dessert course. When Elizabeth Smith rose from the table, the guests followed her to the hall and the butler shut the French doors behind us so the army of maids could clear the table and reset it for the late supper that would be served at midnight.

Dancing at parties commenced with individual couples stepping the minuet, and when I spied Hext shouldering his way through the crowd toward me, I wheeled around and retreated. The young woman who sat next to Mr. Porcher at dinner motioned for me to join her on a settee, and within moments, Hext was at my elbow, hand outstretched. "Eliza, will you be my partner?"

"No thank you. I believe I will sit out for now."

He didn't spare a glance for the girl next to me, and as he turned to go, another young lady sidled up and took his arm. After a quick word, they joined the waiting couples.

My companion sighed. "He's so dashing, isn't he?"

"I suppose." The young woman's round chin, full cheeks, and the modest cut of her pink gown made her appear too young to attend a house party, and too innocent to recognize Hext for the rake he was. I extended my hand. "I'm Eliza Wilkinson."

After a moment of hesitation, she clasped mine. "I'm Mary Porcher."

"Oh! So are you and Mister Porcher—"

"Peter is my brother." He took the chair nearest her, and she beamed at him as she introduced us.

I asked, "Why were you inside by yourself on such a lovely day, sir?"

He chuckled and responded as if the answer was obvious. "I soon lost interest in the company of men who lead a supine and easy life, and elected to spend my free time on self-improvement."

"What were you reading?"

"The newest work by Adam Smith. I can't believe our hosts have a copy."

"My late husband had a copy of Smith's *Theory of Moral Sentiments*. Perhaps I will enjoy his new book as well."

He nodded and then lapsed into silence as couples danced their minuets. When the dancing master called for a reel, I wondered if he might ask me, but before he took any action a red-haired young man approached me and bowed. "Do you remember me, Eliza? I'm James Kennan."

"Why yes! You're my brother Frank's friend."

"Will you favor me?"

"I'd be delighted."

James proved to be an excellent dancer, and when the song was over, he introduced me to his brother Henry and Edward Hall and Samuel Ash, their comrades from the Second South Carolina Regiment. I took it in turns to dance with all of them and had no problem avoiding Hext.

At the midnight supper, we toasted the arrival of Christmas, and then the dancing resumed until the clock struck three. After the musicians played *Hark! The Herald Angels Sing,* our host addressed his guests. "To honor those of us with Huguenot roots, let us keep to the French tradition and leave our shoes by the parlor hearth so Père Noël may fill them with gifts. A joyous Christmas to you all!"

We laughed like children as we removed our shoes. I looked around for Mary and Peter, but they were not among the guests.

The next morning the shoes were lined with colored paper and filled with beribboned packets of cookies and sugar candy. I put the treats in my pocket to save for my little sisters.

I sat with Mary and Peter at the church services and the elaborate Christmas dinner, and when the meal was over, our hosts announced games of ninepins, quoits, and shuttlecock were set up and waiting in the garden.

Mary shrank close to me as we headed outdoors. "What should we do?"

I looked around, intending to ask Peter his preference, but again he was nowhere in sight. "Shall we join the games?"

"I've never played any of them. Would you care to walk instead?"

"Of course."

Once we were away from the group, Mary grew more talkative, and we found we both enjoyed classical literature and religious study and had read some of the same philosophers. All of her pursuits seemed quite serious, so I asked, "Which novels do you enjoy? I recently read *Evalina*, which I found most diverting."

She glanced around as if we would be overheard. "My mother doesn't approve of girls reading novels."

"Oh, I see." It was odd to think of anyone questioning what I read for pleasure. I changed the subject. "How do you know our hosts?"

"I don't. Colonel Skirving stayed at Peter's home before the battle to liberate Savannah. It was he who invited him." She lowered her voice. "I'm doing the Season in Charles Town again this year, and I sometimes suffer from attacks of nerves. Maman thought it would be good for me to meet people at a smaller gathering first."

"Who have you met thus far?"

"Just you." She paused before taking me into her confidence. "My mother is determined I should make a match this year. She's holding back my younger sister Jane's debut until I am wed." She took my arm and steered me closer to where Hext was playing shuttlecock with three other men. Completely without the artifice of Hext's other lady friends, she planted herself directly in his line of sight.

Attention diverted, he waved, and his opponent scored a point.

She wore a wistful expression. "Mister McCall favors you."

"He probably still thinks of me as a childhood playmate. Let's go walk by the lake."

Hext shouted, "Eliza, come and play! We have another racquet!"

"No, thank you." As I turned away, the cork stuck full of feathers they'd been batting across the net struck me on the shoulder.

Hext waved again. "Bring it back!"

I left the shuttlecock on the ground, and as we walked toward the river, I spoke loud enough for him to hear me. "It's no wonder Mister McCall disdains rural pursuits. He seems to have lost all his skill at games."

Peter ate supper with us, but as soon as it was over he excused himself. This evening the married ladies assembled in the salon for cards, backgammon, and mancala, the gentlemen in the fumoir with their brandy, cigars, and talk of war, and the unmarried belles and beaus gathered for the fun and flirtation of parlor games.

Without her brother present, Mary's courage faltered, and she hung back until I insisted she sit by me and participate. Though sometimes she didn't understand what was funny, she laughed when I and the others did. The young men's roughhousing during Blind Man's Bluff frightened her, but she beat everyone in a skip counting game.

Late in the evening, Hext called for attention. "Everyone must put a personal item into this box, and we shall have forfeits to reclaim what is yours."

I dropped one of my garnet earbobs into the box as it passed, and when everyone had paid in, Hext grabbed the box. This brought shouts of protest, but he brushed off the complaints as he held up a cuff link and a tie pin. "Where are the gentlemen who wish to retrieve these?" When James and Edward came forward, Hext set their task. "You must have a drink and shake hands—while blindfolded!"

One of the young ladies helped Hext blindfold the two men and spin them around until they were quite dizzy. They put glasses of wine in their hands and pointed them toward each other. Neither could walk a straight line, and everyone laughed as they spilled canary down their shirts and staggered about with hands extended, trying to find one another.

Hext had a store of humbling tasks in mind, and each guest redeemed their forfeit amid good-natured jibes from the onlookers. Mary was given Contrary, in which she must perform the opposite of whatever she was commanded. Gamely she spun to the left when bid to turn right and sat down when told to stand, completing a dozen such tasks with no errors. She blushed crimson when Hext returned her ribbon.

Most of the forfeits had been redeemed when he held up my earbob. One of the young ladies who had been at his side all evening smirked and whispered something to him, and a devilish grin spread over his face. "If the owner of this wants it back, she must kiss the one she loves best."

Several of the young ladies gasped as I rose, face flaming. Until yesterday, I had not kissed any man other than my husband. Hext meant to pay me back for snubbing him.

What would put him in his place and still satisfy the forfeit? As I crossed the room, it came to me. I gave Hext a quick peck on the cheek, and proceeded to bestow lingering kisses on Edward and Samuel. The rest of the men stirred in anticipation. I would kiss all of them, revealing nothing of my true feelings—except I favored Hext least.

I made my way around the room until only James remained, and he grinned as I drew near. Just then Peter walked in, unaware of the game in progress. He was in my path, and without hesitation I put my arms around his neck and stood on tiptoe.

His eyes widened in shock, but when our lips met, it was as though the Fates had chosen us for each other. His hands gripped my waist and the heat of desire surged within me, along with the notion I'd found something precious I'd lost long ago. I wanted to prolong the moment until I made sense of my feelings, but everyone was watching. I pulled away and bestowed the final kiss on James, claimed my earbob from the sputtering Hext, and returned to my place on the settee where I stared down at my shaking hands.

I recalled nothing of the last forfeits. When our hosts summoned us to the great hall where the married couples were waiting to begin the mistletoe, Peter was gone.

Old Dr. Skirving took the first turn. He plucked one of the white berries from the bunch suspended over the doorway and gave Charlotte, who was his fourth wife and young enough to be his granddaughter, a chaste kiss on the cheek. He bowed, she curtseyed in return, and as they recessed he leaned on his cane, working to keep pace with her.

Our hosts Elizabeth and Philip Smith and Colonel Skirving and his wife Ann kissed in the same formal manner, but the young married men displayed no such decorum. They pinched and tickled until their wives squealed and giggled, and one gave his blushing wife a swat on her backside. That kind of grown-up play, usually private, left me wistful and lonely, but it fired the passions of the unmarried beaus.

They pushed and shoved as they culled the remaining berries, and gave up trying to take turns as they claimed kisses from the blushing belles. Though Hext made a show of avoiding me, all the others were eager to kiss me again. I played along, laughing and making appropriate protestations against the occasional groping hand, but none of the attention roused me like the brief kiss I'd shared with Peter.

When the berries were gone, the party came to an end. Couples and unmarried women took lit candles from the hall table and started up the staircase. Hext, clamoring for brandy and cigars, led the other young men toward the fumoir.

As everyone drifted away, I imagined Joseph was here, engaged in conversation with the men, paying compliments to my friends, excelling at the outdoor games, and holding me close under the mistletoe. Scenes from a life that would never be mine left me even more heavy-hearted. As I started upstairs, a man spoke behind me.

"Missus Wilkinson?"

Peter emerged from the shadows. "A moment, if you please." He met me where I was, one step above him, and we stood eye to eye. "Why did you—"

"I had to kiss all the men to get my earbob back. I'm sorry if it embarrassed you."

"I wasn't embarrassed. From the moment you joined me in the library, you have had me at a disadvantage." His gaze darted toward the picked-over mistletoe. "I'm not good at silly games."

"The berries are gone, so the game is done."

"Not all." He opened his palm to reveal a sprig of green and a single, white berry.

"Indeed, you are not good at games." I tried to jest but I felt my cheeks grow hot as I watched his chest rise and fall in the flickering candlelight. "Why didn't you claim a kiss from someone?"

"I didn't want to kiss you in front of everyone a second time. We're alone now. May I?" When I nodded, he set my candle aside and laid a gentle hand on my cheek.

The touch of his lips was soft at first. As his kiss grew bolder, his arms went around me and our shared excitement swept me away on a fast-moving current. I well knew where this kind of passion led, and after years without a man's touch, my desire surged shamelessly. When I envisioned us rolling together in the featherbed in my chamber, it shocked me into pulling away.

"What you must think of me," I whispered, knowing it was not I who held him at a disadvantage, but the other way round.

His smile was self-deprecating. "I confess I wasn't thinking at all. It's not my usual way, though I would be quite content to continue. Not thinking, that is." He added, "Unless you wish me to escort you to your chamber?"

"No!" My response came out more forcefully than I intended, for I had already pictured him there. "I mean to say, I can find it on my own, thank you." I took the candle and climbed the stairs, feeling the heat of his gaze long after I was gone from his presence.

Jennie was waiting up to help me undress. Though I had never kept a secret from her, she was part of my life with Joseph, and even more dedicated to his memory than I. It was too soon to say anything about Peter Porcher.

My thoughts roiled as I burrowed under the thick counterpane. When I was a bride I expected to lead a merry life, for Joseph seemed to have no worries at all.

The years of grief and loss changed me.

Peter's reserve and his habit of seeking quiet solitude appealed to me in a way they never would have when I was younger. It was his face that came easily to memory now, and I longed to peel back the layers until I learned what was on his mind and in his heart.

The next morning, the departing guests gathered for breakfast in the dining room. Mary motioned me to a vacant chair next to her, and as I sat, I noted that again, Peter was nowhere in sight.

"Eliza, you *must* come to Charles Town and do the Season so I'll be brave enough to bear it."

"Parties and balls are supposed to be fun." I spread butter and jam on a biscuit. "You shouldn't dread going to them."

She shuddered. "I haven't had any fun at all the past two Seasons, but I did have fun last night. Say you'll come with me."

"I don't know if I can be ready in time. I need to have gowns made." Even as I demurred, Captain Sandford rose in my thoughts. He was unlikely to seek me in Charles Town while it was garrisoned by the Continental Army. I turned my attention back to what Mary was saying.

"Maman's dressmaker has finished sewing for me, and I'm certain she will dress you. You can get anything else you need in the shops once you arrive."

"Will your brother accompany you?" I tried to keep my tone casual.

"No, Maman is coming with me." She looked up and waved. "There he is."

Peter addressed his sister as he drew near. "The carriage is out front and our trunks are loaded. Are you ready to leave?" Then his eyes came to rest upon me, and he fell silent for a long moment before he said, "Good morning, Missus Wilkinson."

"Good morning, Mister Porcher." I held his gaze and willed him to read my thoughts until Mary interrupted the moment.

"Eliza, you must! Say you will."

"Very well. I'd be delighted to join you in town for the Season." If he was interested in me beyond a few kisses, he would know where to find me.

Mary threw her arms around my neck. "Come to our house in Ansonborough right after the new year. We'll have such a good time, Eliza. It's all going on in the 'Ton!"

9

The warm, sunny weather of Christmas Day was gone. The temperature had dropped overnight, and an icy drizzle fell from the steel-gray sky as we departed Airy Hall that morning. As soon as we turned out of the avenue of live oaks onto the road, Jennie and I abandoned propriety and scooted closer together, rearranging the blankets to better share each other's warmth.

I spent the first part of the journey picking apart my interactions with Peter, from our first encounter in the library to his greeting this morning. Next I pondered whether it was a mistake to do the Season with Mary, for I lacked the money to buy gowns and all the things I would need, and I refused to ask Papa to help when he had so many repairs to make at Island House. We were about halfway home when I concluded I must write to her with my regrets. Shivering, I pulled the blanket closer around my shoulders.

"You awfully quiet." Jennie cast a sideways glance at me.

"I'm just tired. I forgot how much effort goes into having a good time."

After my visit to Airy Hall, the damage to Island House seemed worse by comparison. The makeshift shutters that covered the house's broken windows did nothing to keep out the cold, and it was as chilly inside as out. Susannah and my father huddled before the parlor fire, and I kept my blanket around my shoulders as I joined them.

Though Papa brightened when I took the chair opposite him, it was clear from the yellowish tinge to his skin and in the whites of his eyes that he was no better.

At his behest, I described the food and the entertainments, but he pressed for more. "What about suitors?"

"There are none, Papa, but Mary Porcher invited me to stay in town with her for the Season." I brought the the wrapped treats from Père Noël from my pocket and handed them to Susannah. "I saved these for the children."

As she accepted them with a curt nod, Papa rose shakily to his feet. "Come, Daughter. We must have a word in private." Leaning on the tree branch he now used as a cane, he led the way to his study, took the chair behind the desk, and gestured for me to close the door.

"What you have done to rejuvenate Plainsfield these past four years has not gone unnoticed. I expect your brothers would have done no better."

His praise refocused my thoughts on my heart's true desire and my words spilled forth. "Perhaps after the spring planting is done, we can hire a carpenter to supervise rebuilding the house. Jennie and I can stay in one of the cabins so I will be on hand—"

He coughed into his handkerchief. "I wager the Redcoats are not finished with us. When I die, I must leave bequests for you and your brothers and provide for Susannah, our little ones, and the babe she carries. With my poor health, the Redcoats making free to destroy our property, and Frank and Will committed to the militia, I don't see the point of holding onto both places."

"Papa, I don't understand. What are you saying?"

"While you were away, I received a fair offer for Plainsfield."

"You decided to sell it without consulting me? But why? Plainsfield is—" I stopped short of saying the plantation was mine. "I thought you knew I intended to go back once the Redcoats moved on." My throat constricted and tears welled in my eyes. "Plenty of widows run plantations."

"Though you are a widow, you're young enough to make an advantageous match. You don't need Plainsfield."

"You just said I managed it well."

He gave me a shrewd look. "You'll never be serious about finding a husband as long as you have Plainsfield to retreat to. The buyer signed a promissory note to make annual payments, plus interest, for the next three years. The note will be part of your dowry, and the cash from his initial payment is a bird in the hand." He opened a drawer and laid a sizable stack of Carolina dollars on the desk.

I ignored the money. "May I read the contract?"

He handed me a folded sheet of parchment. "If the British take control of South Carolina and seize patriot property, we will lose Plainsfield and the Island. It's wise to sell off what we can."

My vision blurred, and I delayed looking at the contract until I could read it without crying. "The buyer knows the house was burned?"

"I daresay he cares more about the loss of the barns. He plans to use the place to raise crops and livestock to sell to the army."

"And what about my people?"

"Your servants are not part of the purchase agreement."

I unfolded the contract, and my anger flared when I read the buyer's name. It was my brother-in-law, the man I distrusted above all others! "Papa, why did you sell to Morton, of all people? He owns thousands of acres, and as executor of his brothers' estates, he controls all the family holdings until his nieces and nephews come of age. When he takes Plainsfield, he'll own everything in this district but Yonge's Island. If we don't keep a sharp eye, he'll have that, too! Why not name him your executor and make it easier for him to steal it from you?"

Papa waved his hand to dismiss my concerns. "Frank is my executor and will inherit the Island." He looked at me over his spectacles. "Don't worry about Morton getting his hands on your bequest. I've also willed you fifty pounds sterling and gifted you the servants from Plainsfield, which you may take to your next household."

Vowing to draw up manumission papers for my people before they became the property of my hypothetical next husband, I stuffed the money into my pocket. "How long before he takes possession?"

"The first of the year. Daughter, it will ease my mind if you marry well and find the kind of security you cannot have on your own."

Though he was only trying to do his best for me, his betrayal cut me to the bone.

After I left Papa, I sought Jennie and asked her to bring my supper up on a tray. When she joined me in my chilly chamber, she built up the fire and unpacked my trunk while I relayed my conversation with Papa between bites.

"So we ain't got Plainsfield to go home to." She fixed me with a penetrating stare. "You never said you was wantin' a new husband."

"No, I didn't."

"Then why you goin' to do the Season? How can you tell what some other man gon' be like?"

She looked away, and I believed I understood her worry. "I'll always need you, Jennie. Your status as a free woman won't change if I remarry." I added, "Perhaps you'll want to leave me and marry someday."

She looked startled. "No'm, I won't." She gestured toward the tray. "You finished?"

"Yes, you can take it away."

She paused at the door. "Miz Eliza, where you go, I go. Mist' Joseph 'spect me to watch out for you."

Her disapproval stung. From our first meeting she'd been both forthright and protective of me, and she was bound up in both the good and bad memories from my brief marriage.

I recall I was overjoyed when I learned I would be returning to my childhood home as its mistress, but when Joseph and I came to Toogoodoo for the first time as a married couple, I was surprised to find the house's interior looked nothing like I remembered. The chandeliers, wallpaper, draperies, and furniture were all new and of the brighter hues that befitted my husband's taste.

A young woman in a crisp gray uniform and starched turban was waiting in the foyer. Joseph put an arm around my shoulders. "Jennie, this is Missus Wilkinson. Eliza, meet Jennie, your wedding gift."

Confused, I murmured, "You bought me a maid?"

"I hired you a maid. Jennie works for wages. She will help you settle in." He gave me a lingering kiss. "I'll be along shortly."

"This way, Miz Wilkinson." Jennie started up the stairs.

In what had been my parents' chamber, a fire snapped cheerily on the hearth, but the inevitability of whatever happened on a wedding night loomed before me and I hugged myself to stop my trembling.

"You cold, ma'am?"

"No."

"I'll help you undress." She gave me an encouraging smile. "Since Mist' Joseph hired me, he ain' talked of nothin' but you."

"Jennie, how old are you?"

"Eighteen, ma'am."

"A year older than me." I gulped. "Do you know about marital relations between men and women?"

"No'm."

"Nor do I. My mother is dead, and my stepmother's advice was no help at all. I thought I had come to love Joseph even before he proposed. I hold him in high regard, and my heart flutters when he touches my hand and kisses me. Is that what I should feel? I read in a novel that true love comes after the wedding. Undoubtedly there are unhappy marriages, so love does not come without fail. How will I know if I love him the way a wife is supposed to?"

Jennie laughed. "You all twisted up in knots. Stop worrying and let me help you." She unfastened the front of my gown. I untied the waist tapes on my petticoats, letting them pool around my feet, but when she started to undo the laces on my stays, I felt shy and pulled away.

"Miz Wilkinson—"

The name sounded like it should belong to someone older. "Please, call me Eliza."

"Yes'm, Miz Eliza." She set the gown aside, brought my silk wrapper from the clothespress, and helped me into it. "If you ring for me later, I'll come back. Otherwise, I'll leave you be."

"Thank you Jennie. I'm glad you're here."

She flashed a quick smile, picked up a taper, and shut the door behind her.

Alone, I cast my eyes toward the bed. It did look inviting, with a thick feather mattress and plumped pillows. What would it be like to share it with my husband?

A heartbeat later, a gentle tap sounded at the door and I squeaked, "Come in."

Joseph had shed his coat and stock, and his shirt was open at the collar. He showed no sign of shyness as he approached me. "Candlelight becomes you." He took my hand, and a look of concern crossed his face as he raised it to his lips. "Why, you're trembling." He folded me gently into his embrace and as he held me close I felt his quickened heartbeat and breathed in the fragrance of citrus and herbs that clung to his clothing and mingled with his scent.

"Just think of this as a dance, my dear. A most intimate, pleasing dance."

"I don't know the figures."

"I shall lead. You have only to follow."

A gentle kiss was enough to thrill me when our engagement was new, but now his mouth opened against mine and his hands roamed freely over my body, evoking feelings that set me trembling from anticipation, not fear. He trailed his lips down my neck and along my collarbone, and as he pushed my wrapper off my shoulders, I felt the weight of it fall away.

I never rang for Jennie.

Sunlight was streaming into our chamber when I opened my eyes. Joseph did not stir, so I propped myself on one elbow and watched the rise and fall of his bare chest, studying him with a mixture of curiosity and possessiveness. I was a wife now, several times over. I suppressed a giggle as I reflected on the loss of my innocence and concluded that I was well rid of it.

During our brief time together, Joseph was a loving and devoted spouse, and under his hand I came to know myself and understand my desires. What I'd learned about relationships from him would guide me when I must consider a new partner. Though I was becoming amenable to the prospect of marriage, I feared Jennie's devotion to Joseph was so fierce she would not accept any new husband I might choose.

1780

10

On New Year's Day, everyone on Papa's island ate Hoppin' John and cornbread for luck. It was a work holiday, and when evening came, the servants lit bonfires and gathered for music, dancing, and storytelling. I had been welcome at the bonfires at Plainsfield, but this year Jennie and I went straight to bed after supper. We would leave for Charles Town in the night to take advantage of the outgoing tide.

I drifted off to the music, and when the clock struck one, Jennie rose and stirred up the fire on the hearth. I gave the room time to warm before getting out of bed, but still I shivered as I layered on two pairs of stockings and every petticoat I owned before donning my mother's red floral polonaise. No matter how many layers I wore, the hours spent on the water would leave me chilled to the bone.

We ate a hasty, warmed-over breakfast and ventured out into the windy night. Two of Papa's oarsmen were to deliver us to Charles Town and return with an order of lumber. Jack carried a lantern to light the path to the dock and Grafton brought my trunk in a small barrow. Once aboard, Jennie and I huddled under blankets and an oilcloth with the pewter foot warmer and a lunch basket at our feet.

Jack and Grafton pushed the boat away from the dock and rowed into the Sound until the current carried us toward the winding Wadmalaw River. Jennie dozed off, but as we neared where the Wadmalaw flowed into the Stono, I strained to catch a glimpse of the dock at Plainsfield. My heart reached out to the beloved acres, and I was glad it was too dark to see the destruction wrought by the Redcoats. Plainsfield belonged to Morton now, and like my marital home at Toogoodoo, it had never really been mine.

On a windy day in March 1775, the last guests left after my son's funeral. I was numb with grief and wanted nothing more than to retreat to my chamber, but Morton summoned me to Joseph's study. Without preamble, he asked, "When do you intend to vacate?"

My sole comfort was the thought of remaining at Toogoodoo. "I don't plan to leave. Do I not inherit?" I knew widows could hold real property, for my paternal grandmother had first inherited the plantation many years ago.

Morton scoffed. "There is nothing to inherit. Joseph only rented this property. It belongs to our late brother Edward's estate, held in trust until his eldest son comes of age." My disbelief must have shown on my face, for he added, "Surely you did not expect to run the place on your own."

"I wish to see the account books."

"There is no need. The lion's share of the crop yield goes to Edward's estate. Joseph's share, along with the sale of his household effects and livestock will not be sufficient to settle his debts, but I am willing to return your dowry. " He picked up a stack of papers on the desk. "Proceeds from the sale of his slaves would have left something to provide for you, but instead we have manumission papers, signed and witnessed, freeing the lot of them. They will be transported to another colony."

"But they don't have to leave South Carolina. I'm certain the law requiring that has changed."

"Nonetheless, they will have a fresh start elsewhere." He flipped through the pages. "It appears only one can be sold. Jennie."

I never questioned Joseph's spending and knew nothing of his debts, but I was certain about Jennie's status. "She came to us as a free woman. Joseph paid her wages."

"She has no papers, so she shall be sold."

Within the week, I found myself back on my father's doorstep with empty arms and a shattered heart, and minus the portion of my dowry I used to purchase Jennie from Joseph's estate. I could not imagine life without her then, nor could I now.

The Stono River, a quarter mile wide with a half-mile of marsh on either side, looked like an endless expanse of black in the pre-dawn. When the first rays of sunlight broke in the east, the layers of pink and orange on the horizon melted into yellow, and the water changed from black to a misty gray. A strong wind gust rocked the boat and sent spray over the side, and I shivered as I pulled the blankets closer.

We ate while we waited for the tide to turn at New Cut, and later, when we emerged from Wappoo Creek to cross the Ashley River, the men pulled hard against the current to bring us alongside the pier at Gibbes' Wharf. The bustling commercial concern had piers that extended more than one hundred yards in either direction. As soon as the boat was tied up I stood to stretch. Jennie and I were both cold, stiff, and clumsy as the harbormaster's assistants helped us disembark, but I looked around with interest. I had never visited the wharf on business. Papa's agents had always managed the sale of my crop yields.

It was a noisy place, and the way the dock workers moved about their tasks put me in mind of an anthill. I delivered Papa's bank draft to the lumber dealer and while they loaded his order into the boat I watched transactions at the scale-house, where rice was weighed and sold. I could imagine the fruit of our labors at Plainsfield going to market thus in times past.

The activity was not confined to the quay. Upriver, dozens of soldiers and crews of enslaved men worked repairing and reinforcing the batteries and defense works.

With my errand for Papa completed, Jack carried my trunk to the carriage stand, and soon Jennie and I were on our way up East Bay Street toward the fashionable Ansonborough neighborhood. The genteel and prosperous Charles Town I had known all my life was now rowdy, raucous, and noisy. Jennie shrank from the window as we passed a slave auction in progress on a street corner.

Soldiers were everywhere, and it was my turn to draw back in alarm as a squad rushed past us with weapons drawn and burst into a nearby house. I rapped on the carriage wall. "Driver, what's happening?"

He called down from his high seat. "Likely they're searching for a reluctant soldier. Punishment for shirking duty is twenty lashes."

On Society Street, we came to a stop in front of a white stucco-over-stone with black shutters. Twin staircases with delicate wrought iron railings curved up from the street level to meet at the front door. As I alighted from the carriage, I wondered what Mary and Peter's mother was like. If she was as shy, intellectual, and unmindful of the nuances of social intercourse as her children, perhaps that was why she had trouble guiding Mary into a favorable match.

The clock was striking five when the butler answered my knock, and Mary flew to greet me with cries of delight. A middle-aged servant woman accepted the blankets serving Jennie and me as wraps while the butler went out to fetch my trunk.

"Mary, this is Jennie, my maid." Jennie and I had agreed in advance not to mention her free status until we assessed the Porchers' feelings about abolitionism, but I hurt for her as she kept her eyes cast down and dropped a small curtsey.

Mary barely glanced her way. "Letty will acquaint her with the house." She squeezed my arm. "You're just in time. We have supper early on the nights we stay in."

She led me past well-appointed double parlors with creamy walls, mahogany furniture upholstered in a berry red damask, and thick Turkish carpets on one side of the hall. Cheery fires snapped on all the hearths, and the cold and tension ebbed out of my shoulders as we went into the dining room. Whatever the cook had prepared smelled like the perfect thing to warm me.

Mrs. Porcher was already seated, and in her presence, Mary's tone turned formal. "Maman, may I present Eliza Wilkinson?"

I bowed. "Pleased to make your acquaintance, ma'am."

Mary and I took seats, and as Letty brought out the first course, my hostess gave me a long, appraising look.

"Mary tells me you are a widow. What is your family name? Which of the Wilkinsons did you marry?"

"I was born Eliza Yonge. My husband Joseph was a physician. We were married less than a year before he died."

"How tragic. So, you last went through the Season—"

"Oh, some time ago. Six years, I suppose."

"My! Why didn't you aspire to a new match before now?"

"I was content managing one of my father's properties after I was widowed."

"Most irregular." She gave me another, sharper glance, tilting her head in a manner that put me in mind of a pigeon. "Mary did not consult me before she invited you here."

"Please don't feel responsible for me. I already know some Charles Town folks. After living alone in the country, I look forward to seeking daytime amusements outside the house, so I won't crowd you. I hope I won't be a bother at all."

"When Mary described you as a widow, I assumed you would be less–" she let the sentence trail off as she searched for the right word.

I chose to believe she was commenting on my independence. "You are so generous to provide me lodgings. I'm sure Mary and I will have a lovely time attending events together."

After eating my fill of stew, fresh bread, and pudding, I wanted nothing more than to go up to my chamber and retire, but Mary took my arm and led me into the parlor. I took a seat in one of the wing chairs near the fire and reveled in the warm comfort for only a moment before Mrs. Porcher bustled in, carrying a newspaper and three white envelopes.

She opened the first one and drew out an engraved card. "Expected." She set it aside and opened the other two, tutting as she read. She dropped the invitations on the side table and gave a dramatic sigh.

Mary's distress was genuine. "What's the matter, Maman?"

Mrs. Porcher opened the newspaper and read aloud. "'The managers of the city's subscription concert and dancing societies announce that fortnightly balls and entertainments will commence in early January.' Hmm. It's a pity the Saint Cecilia concerts are suspended due to the war." She paused, and fixed Mary with the same critical consideration she'd given me. "You have been invited to a concert at the Assembly Room in the Exchange, one at Society Hall, and an evening of country dancing at McCrady's Tavern. There are many more choice parties mentioned in the *Gazette*, and it appears you will not be attending them this year."

"What? But why?" Mary wrung her hands, instantly on the verge of tears.

"Who can say?" Mrs. Porcher's shrill tone conveyed her frustration. "We should have already received the invitations. Unless you attend the best of the Season's events, you have no hope of finding a match. Whatever are we to do?"

Mary turned to me. "What if we prevail upon Mister McCall? Surely he can secure invitations to any party in Charles Town. Will you ask him, Eliza? Please?"

Mrs. Porcher chimed in. "Oh, yes, dear Eliza! For Mary's sake?"

I couldn't avoid seeing Hext while in Charles Town, but neither had I intended to seek him out. I sighed. "I can send a note to his father's house."

"Oh, splendid!" Mrs. Porcher beamed at me. "I'll ring for pen and ink right now."

I wrote the brief request, convinced with every scratch of the pen I would live to regret begging the favor.

As soon as one of the servants departed with my note I rose. "I left home before dawn and am weary from the journey. I shall take my leave and bid you goodnight."

"Oh but you cannot!" Mrs. Porcher exclaimed. "The mantua maker will be here for your consultation any minute. I took the liberty of engaging Elizabeth Thompson for you. I'm sure you'll be pleased with her work."

I scarcely had time to smooth my hair before Mrs. Thompson and her assistant, both dressed in gowns suitable for tea with the governor's wife, arrived. After the usual polite greetings, I asked, "Shall I bring down the gowns I have?"

Mrs. Thompson bowed. "If you please, miss."

I rang for Jennie, and when she brought the coral damask and turquoise silk downstairs for inspection, Mrs. Thompson clucked over them. "These are not suitable for Season events, miss. The robe *a la francais* is woefully out of date."

Mary spoke up. "I think Eliza looks lovely in whatever she wears." Her mother shot her a warning look, and the girl bit her lip and fell silent.

Mrs. Thompson waved a hand and her assistant brought forth samples of silks. Mary laid them out on the card table. "I can't say which is my favorite. Eliza, don't you love this one?" She held up a swatch of jade green with a pattern of flowers and vines.

Over the next hour, Mrs. Thompson's assistant took my measurements while I stood, sat, bent at the waist, and froze in the different positions of the minuet and quadrille. Mrs. Porcher and Mrs. Thompson debated styles, colors, and trims, leaving me out of the conversation altogether until I asserted myself and chose the swatch Mary favored, a creamy moire embroidered with sprigs of flowers, and an indigo damask that reminded me of Plainsfield.

Mrs. Thompson made some notes. "Now we must discuss your day gowns."

When I started to protest, Mrs. Porcher wagged a finger at me. "Three is the bare minimum you can get by with." When Mary chimed in agreement, I chose fabric swatches just to be done with it all.

My impatience turned to shock when Mrs. Thompson presented me with a bill totaling a quarter of the funds Papa had given me, with the evening gowns costing close to three pounds apiece. Loath to embarrass myself or my hostess by canceling the order, I paid the deposit.

Jennie collected my mother's gowns while Mrs. Porcher saw the seamstresses out. I bid goodnight to Mary and followed Jennie upstairs to my chamber.

The walls were painted a soft shade of blue, with blue-and-white chintz draperies and counterpane. A cot in the alcove meant Jennie would be close by. It was a comfortable private space, and I began to relax as soon as I shut the door. I sank down in the overstuffed chair while Jennie put my mother's gowns away. "I must have new clothes, but I did not enjoy that consultation in the least."

She shut the clothespress door. "You sure you wanna do this?" When I did not answer, she scooped glowing coals into the copper bed warmer and shoved it under the counterpane.

I undressed and crawled into bed, but sleep did not come, and I pondered Jennie's question. Did I want to do the Season? Was I prepared for the months of parties and whatever they might yield?

The twelve-year age gap between Joseph and me had not seemed too great when we married, but I was older now, and I had to consider the possibility of a second marriage like my father's. He was thirty-eight and Susannah twenty-four when they wed. From the beginning, my stepmother scolded and pecked and rarely seemed happy. It was hard to imagine her having romantic feelings for my white-haired father, yet he always seemed to have a child on her. I shuddered as I pushed the image from my mind.

A wealthy man could seek a young, attractive wife at any age. A woman had to take what she was offered or bear the consequences of stigma and poverty. If it came down to it, was I willing to enter a loveless marriage in exchange for security?

No. I touched my fingers to my lips, and as I recalled the thrill of Peter's arms around me and the crush of his mouth on mine, I vowed I would marry for love or not at all.

11

The next morning there was no answer from Hext, and Mrs. Porcher's anxiety spiraled. I tried to concentrate on writing a letter to Papa while my hostess paced, wringing her hands and sighing in a dramatic fashion. Mary, her embroidery tambour abandoned on her lap, was again on the verge of tears.

I sprinkled pounce on the letter to dry the ink, folded it, and rose. "I must post this and then go to the shops. Mary, will you accompany me?"

Mrs. Porcher seemed annoyed to lose her audience, but I acted as if I hadn't noticed and shepherded the girl out of the parlor. Out on the street, the breeze off the bay exhilarated me and lifted my mood. Mary, slower to recover her good spirits, shivered in her woolen cloak.

"Can you tell me if there are any new shops on King Street? I prefer to do my trade with patriots, of course."

"Père set up accounts for Maman and me at some of the newer patriot-owned shops. We'll go to them." She took a deep breath. "I hope Mister McCall doesn't answer your note. I was glad when I received so few invitations. Maman worries so, and she makes me nervous."

"She's concerned for you."

"She has to have a hand in everything."

It soon became clear that Mary had never made a purchase without supervision. She did not know what she liked without being told. To give her the opportunity to grow, I sought her counsel and encouraged her to voice her opinion.

Her confidence grew as she helped me choose, and finally my parcels, containing an embroidered reticule, four pairs of stockings, an embroidered shawl, a sturdy pair of shoes for city walking, a pair of dancing slippers, and the blanket I had been using as a shawl were on their way to the Porcher residence, along with yard goods to make two new suits of clothes for Jennie. As we stepped out into the windy street, I luxuriated in the warmth of my new rose-colored wool cloak.

I counted more than a dozen batteries along the bay, and as we passed each one, soldiers called greetings from the ramparts. I replied with words of encouragement, and could have traded compliments with the smiling soldiers for the better part of the day, but Mary was shivering, so I suggested we stop for refreshment.

Mary pointed out the Carolina Coffee House. "That place is quite popular with Charles Town's ladies."

"Do you go there often?"

"No, I've never been."

Inside was warm and fragrant, but the service was slow. We found seats in a quiet corner and as soon as we received our drinks I wrapped my cold fingers around my steaming coffee can. "You mustn't let your mother worry you so much that it ruins your fun."

"How can I have fun when all I do is disappoint her?" Mary's shoulders slumped. "I wish I had your confidence. Perhaps men would like me if I was more like you."

I laughed. "I'm sure there are plenty of people who do not enjoy my company. Once you learn to relax and let people see your true self, you will have more friends—and beaux. If they don't appreciate your personality, you are not well matched."

She considered this for a long moment. "Did you love your husband?"

"Yes, very much. I believe we would have had a happy life together."

"Why haven't you married again? You certainly could."

"Just because I could doesn't mean I should. I am determined not to settle."

She sighed. "Right now, I would accept any proposal that would make Maman happy."

"That could be a terrible mistake. You, not your mother, could live out your life in the bonds of an unhappy marriage." I reached across the table and took her hand. "I know how it feels to be loved by another, and to love myself. I would only resign my liberty to a generous companion and an equal partner, so we might rule over one another with love."

"Does such a man exist?" Mary's smile was sad. "If he does, he will choose someone like you." She fell silent and sipped her hot chocolate.

I took out the receipts from my morning's shopping and looked through them. Wartime inflation had driven up the prices of both staples and luxury goods, and what I considered trifling purchases totaled almost as much as my new gowns. It was only my second day in Charles Town, and the cash from the sale of Plainsfield was half gone.

The winter sun was slipping toward the horizon when we left the coffee house. We returned home, rosy-cheeked and windblown, to find Mrs. Porcher more agitated than when we left. The moment we stepped inside she demanded, "Where have you been? All these packages arrived from the shops, but you were nowhere to be found!"

Mary, cowed by her mother's scolding, quavered, "What's happened, Maman?"

"After you went out, an invitation arrived for a concert at the Assembly Room this evening. Mister McCall intervened on your behalf, Mary, and you will be sure to thank him. Now make haste! You haven't a moment to lose. Letty has prepared your bath."

With a terror-stricken expression on her face, Mary picked up her skirts and dashed upstairs. I started after her at an unhurried pace.

"Eliza?"

I turned. "Yes, ma'am?"

"None of your new gowns are ready. Perhaps you should stay home this evening."

"Nonsense. I'll wear one I brought with me."

"Mrs. Thompson gave her assessment." She pursed her lips as she picked up the sheaf of invitations.

I kept my voice cool. "Last summer, the Redcoats plundered my home and stole all my clothes, save the ones I was wearing at the time. The gowns I brought with me once belonged to my mother. When I wore them to the Christmas party, no one was rude enough to comment on their unsuitability."

She sniffed. "I warrant your attire was less noteworthy than your conduct."

Was she referring to the game of forfeits? I could not imagine Peter telling his mother about it, but perhaps Mary had. Retreat was in order. "Excuse me, my maid will be waiting."

With her usual efficiency, Jennie arranged my hair, helped me dress in the turquoise silk, and tied the ribbon on the topaz necklace. I surveyed my reflection in the pier glass. Though I had seen no other gowns of this style in the shops, I didn't care. I loved how the back draping ended in a short train that swished and whispered when I moved. New stockings, slippers, and gloves were enough to update my ensemble.

I closed the door behind me and started downstairs, determined to put Mrs. Porcher's remark out of my mind. Mary looked up and clapped her hands in delight as I joined her in the hall. "Oh, Eliza, how lovely you look!"

"As do you, my dear!" I returned the compliment, though the yellow gown she wore did not flatter her figure or her complexion. It was cut much lower than the pink one she'd worn to the Christmas party, and was decked with enough bows, lace, and pleated trim to overwhelm her slender frame.

In the carriage on the way to the Exchange, Mary wrung her gloved hands and chewed her bottom lip until Mrs. Porcher ordered her to stop. We had yet to arrive and already the poor girl looked ready to crack under the pressure.

In the Assembly Hall on the second floor of the Exchange, I scanned the room, taking the measure of our competition. To my eye, most of the other girls looked too young to be seeking a husband. It was hard to believe I was the same age when I met Joseph in this very room.

"Come, Eliza." Mary pulled on my arm, bringing me out of my reverie. I followed her and Mrs. Porcher to seats. During the concert, I spotted Hext on the far side of the room but avoided meeting his gaze. When the musical program ended and the liveried servants moved the chairs and prepared the space for dancing, he hurried over to present his compliments. Resplendent in a burgundy velvet ensemble with dozens of brass buttons, embroidered flowers and vines, and lace cuffs that covered his hands, he was so powdered and perfumed I wondered if it took him longer to dress than the women present.

"My dear Missus Wilkinson!" He gave me a rogueish wink before he bent over my hand.

I pulled free of his grasp but matched his formal tone. "Thank you for the invitations, Mister McCall. I'm sure we will enjoy every event."

"It is my pleasure to please you. Oh yes, and Miss Porcher." As he bent over Mary's hand, she giggled and dropped a half curtsey.

Mrs. Porcher nudged her and muttered, "Stand up straight!"

Hext turned his attention back to me. "May I presume you will honor me and step a minuet?"

I hesitated. I had not thought to make my re-entry into Charles Town society with so conspicuous a partner. "Oh, I don't know, it's been years since I—"

"Nonsense! I have already secured our position with the dancing master." He placed my hand in the crook of his elbow and led me away.

While we waited our turn, I took the opportunity to observe my hosts. Mrs. Porcher, seeming ever more like a pigeon, bobbed her head and uttered clucks of displeasure as she scanned the room. Mary's face reddened as one young man after another bypassed her in favor of other partners. If only Mrs. Porcher would realize that her hovering presence put her daughter at a disadvantage.

I came back to myself with a start when Hext put his hand on my waist and said, "Come along, my dear." He led me to my place and faced me from across the room with a flourish. The musicians began to play, and we stepped off the pattern, passing each other, turning, and returning in perfect rhythm until we met and clasped hands in the center of the room. With all eyes on us, we step-hopped through the second movement and finished without missing a beat.

Hext escorted me back to Mary and Mrs. Porcher and excused himself before either of them could speak. Before long James Kennan asked to be my partner for an upcoming reel. As we danced, I caught myself scanning the room, half expecting to see Joseph. A glimpse of a man with the same color hair or in the midst of a familiar gesture caused my hopes to soar and plummet so fast it made me feel ill. I excused myself when the song ended and retreated to the chairs along the wall. Before I had a moment to collect myself, Mrs. Porcher bustled over, her mouth pursed in disapproval.

She sank heavily into the chair next to me. "You must prevail upon young Mister McCall to ask Mary to dance." She had worked herself into such a state that she was trembling. "He invited her here, and he has not said three words to her."

I decided not to remind her Hext issued the invitations at my request, and rose to do her bidding. Two songs later I found him in a secluded corner, where he was attempting to charm a girl who could not have been more than fifteen. My skin crawled as I heard him croon,

"Your laughter dances like the sweetest melody upon a gentle breeze." When she giggled and blushed, he added, "and your eyes sparkle like the morning dew."

When I cleared my throat to get his attention he hurried to my side without bothering to excuse himself. Behind him, the girl's giggles turned into a pout.

"What is it, my dear?" He spoke in the same, crooning tone.

"I didn't mean to interrupt. By all means continue showering compliments on Miss—"

He scoffed. "Now that you are with me, I can't recall her name." His breath smelled of rum as he leaned closer and tried to nuzzle my ear. "Fie on the custom of wives obeying their husbands. If you were mine, I would give myself entirely to your will."

I took a hasty step back. "Hext, please."

He advanced. "Your least indication would be my command. I'm sure you know what you like."

"Ah, there you are!" Mrs. Porcher, Mary in tow, joined us.

Hext regarded the stout, panting woman with surprise as she spoke breathily. "Mister McCall, Miss Mary Porcher wishes for a moment of your time so she can thank you for your invitation this evening."

He looked puzzled. "Who is the lady, madam?"

She took Mary by the arm and pulled her forward to present her.

"Oh, yes. Of course." Hext bowed. "It would give me great pleasure." He escorted Mary to the dance floor, and from the way she blushed, I was sure he was plying her with a stream of meaningless compliments.

"I will be in the card room." Mrs. Porcher turned her attention away from Mary, though the girl had never needed a chaperone more in her life, so I stayed where I could see them. They danced a reel, and Hext was not quick enough to hide his displeasure when the dancing master shifted them farther down the line for the next one.

Mary was so rattled by the demotion she made several mistakes, and demurred when a trickier dance was announced. His obligation satisfied, Hext escorted her to the chairs along the wall. I assumed that was the end of the matter, but after the supper interlude, Mrs. Porcher delivered Mary back to Hext, and whatever she said spurred him to engage her in the dancing again.

The party ended at dawn, and I stifled a yawn as Hext walked us out of the Assembly Hall. The Porchers' footman, who was waiting outside the carriage, helped Mary and her mother inside. I tried to follow, but Hext blocked my path.

I tried to sidestep him. "Goodnight, Hext. Thank you again—"

The smile left his face and he said in a furious whisper, "By all the saints, Eliza! How dare you saddle me with that–that dolt?" Then, as though nothing was amiss, he took my hand and helped me in.

On the drive home, Mary sighed blissfully, and Mrs. Porcher made no criticism. I feared both their heads were already full of wedding plans. Could I protect Mary from Hext McCall, her mother's schemes, and her own naive, romantic notions?

12

Over the next several days, both Mary and Mrs. Porcher mentioned Hext in every conversation. They asked me about his favorite foods and his family tree, and assigned unwarranted significance to the amount of time he'd danced with Mary.

If I let on he'd called Mary a dolt and told them how he'd begged favors from me, I feared Mrs. Porcher would presume I encouraged him.

Then there was the matter of Jennie. Used to being my co-manager, she was now relegated to the role of lady's maid, and as I required less attention than another young woman might, she was bored.

In truth, neither of us was used to being this idle. During our years at Plainsfield we managed the plantation together. I had always counted on her thoughtful advice, but, knowing she disapproved of my decision to do the Season, I hesitated to voice my concerns about Hext and Mary to her.

The day before the next event on our social calendar, Mrs. Thompson sent over the finished jade green gown. Jennie brought the box up to my chamber and together we removed the lid.

When I held up the gown, words failed me. Though it was made in the style we discussed, Mrs. Thompson had added yards of lace, pleated trims, and bows. Jennie smothered a laugh, but I sighed. "It's far too fussy. I paid three pounds for it, so I suppose I may as well try it on."

When Jennie finished fastening the stomacher, she stood back and shook her head. "You look like a fancy dessert."

"It's awful."

"If I take off mos' of the trim it'll be fine."

The simplified version of the gown better suited me, but when I appeared in it Mrs. Porcher rushed at me with a cry of alarm and inspected me from all angles. "It's so plain! I've never seen this level of disinterest from Mrs. Thompson before."

"It's just what I wanted." I hooked the clasp on my cloak and headed out to the coach.

By the time we reached the Assembly Hall, Mrs. Porcher had tired of tsking and tutting about my lack of good taste. She scanned the room for Hext the moment we entered the Hall, and an eager smile spread over her face when she spotted him. While she helped Mary with her cloak and fussed over the flounces on her gown, I hurried over to speak to him alone.

"That color becomes you." As he bent over my hand, his eyes lingered on my bosom. "I knew you couldn't stay away."

I went straight to the point. "I beg you to be kind to Miss Porcher. If you cannot engage with her sincerely, then leave her be."

His smile twisted into something ugly. "Very well. As you say, my dear." He made an exaggerated bow and stalked away. Mary, midway across the room to join us, fled back to her mother.

No one was dancing yet, and I overheard two women engaged in conversation. The younger one said, "I tell you, Kitty, I've never heard so many excuses. There are twenty-four hours in a day, yet these young girls refuse to commit one or two of them to relieving the sufferings of those in need."

"I fear you have let your passion ruin your diplomacy, my dear."

"They have no sympathy for the plight of the indigent and the sick. Why, just one of their gowns likely cost enough to feed and clothe—"

I broke in. "I'll help."

They both turned in surprise.

"I'm sorry to eavesdrop. I'm Eliza Wilkinson." I held out my hand, and the younger woman clasped it.

"A pleasure to meet you. I am Lucretia Sarrazin, and this is my sister, Kitty."

I bowed. "Last summer when the Redcoats terrorized our neighborhood near Stono Ferry and destroyed my home, I was fortunate to have family to turn to. I feel a particular sympathy for the women who have no one."

Kitty Sarrazin gave a sympathetic cluck. "You poor dear. We serve food to the displaced at Saint Philips Church, and we can use your help. Will you join us, Miss Wilkinson?"

"Yes, of course. And it's missus. I'm a widow."

Lucretia added, "One of our committee members is also a young widow. We will be pleased to introduce you."

When I took leave of the sisters, Hext was nearby, surrounded by a group of young men. I heard one of them ask, "And what did you do with your partner from last week?"

"Nothing!" Hext replied in such an exasperated tone the men all burst out laughing. "I quite fatigued myself with efforts to engage her in conversation."

Another protested. "She seems quite agreeable."

"If you think you'll have better luck I invite you to try."

The first one said, "Her father is a Justice of the Peace, isn't he?"

Hext scoffed. "I would have thought him a country priest. Rustics like her are a waste of time." With a laugh and a shrug, he took leave of his audience.

I followed him into the ballroom and grasped him by the arm. Though I was furious, I modulated my voice. "Fie on you! Miss

Porcher does not deserve your ridicule. Had you entertained her with pleasing and instructive conversation, she would have endeavored to excel in what was praised. You did not even try to get to know her before you used her for jest. How would she feel if she knew what you said about her?"

"You ordered me to leave her alone tonight, and I did as you asked. The debts do mount up on your side of the ledger, my dear." He gave an exaggerated sigh. "I shall say nothing more about Miss Porcher if you favor me with a dance."

For Mary's sake, I let him lead me out to the floor. When the song ended I tried to excuse myself, but he checked my flight. "What does it feel like to hold another's fate in your charming hands, Eliza? I daresay you don't want poor Miss Porcher to fail for a third Season, do you? Stay."

As we danced on and on, Mary sat off to the side, eyes downcast, while her mother fixed me with a malevolent glare. To make matters worse, I saw James Kennan watching me, a hurt expression on his face. He looked away when I tried to catch his eye.

Though I left Hext before I met the Porchers at their carriage, the damage was done. We rode home in a smoldering silence, and in the privacy of my chamber, I lamented Hext's treachery as Jennie helped me undress.

"I can't tell the Porchers I'm only trying to stop him from ruining Mary's reputation. Missus Porcher is so angry she's not speaking to me."

Jennie offered, "Don't play his games. Let them tend to they own business. Miss Mary can find out for herself he ain't no good."

"If Missus Porcher would stop interfering, I know I could make Mary see Hext for the cad he is."

"Ain't nobody in this house who stands up to her."

"No, there isn't. I'll set things right with Mary in the morning."

Despite my assertion I doubted if anything I said could overcome Mrs. Porcher's influence over Mary, and I wondered if she held as much sway over her husband and son.

After evening social events, breakfast in the Porcher residence was served late. Even without the aromas of cooking and brewing coffee that signaled it was time to rise, I was up with the sun and eager to be on my way to the church.

I dressed in the gown I'd been wearing the day Plainsfield was plundered, which had been mended too many times to be worn for anything but work, and I was pinning up my hair when Mrs. Porcher's irritated voice pierced the quiet.

"Faugh! What do you mean by coming in here so early, girl? How dare you wake me at such an hour?"

I hurried to Mrs. Porcher's chamber and found her squinting in the sunlight that streamed in through the open portieres while Jennie stood by, an unreadable expression on her face. "What's the matter?"

The lady rounded on me. "I ask you, what kind of servant is simple enough to wait upon a town lady at seven o'clock in the morning? She ought to be whipped for opening my drapes!"

"I will not allow anything of the kind! Jennie didn't realize–" I cast about for some excuse "–that the nights are much longer in town than in the country. In the future, she will conform to Town customs and fashions."

"I should hope so. Have her bring me my breakfast on a tray. In an hour." She pulled the pillow over her head to indicate the discussion was over.

We left the room without delay, and as Jennie started downstairs she whispered, "Now go talk to Miss Mary alone."

"Did you wake her on purpose?" When she gave a noncommittal shrug, I demanded, "Why would you do such a thing?"

She looked at me as though the answer was obvious. "Now she's speaking to you again. I'll make breakfast so we won't be late to the church."

As I tiptoed down the hall, I tried to think of a logical explanation to shield Mary from the truth of Hext's treachery. I let myself in her chamber and gave her shoulder a gentle shake. "Mary? Wake up."

She opened her eyes, but as soon as she realized it was me she sat up, crossed her arms, and regarded me with a sullen expression.

I perched on the edge of the bed. "Let me explain about last night."

She pouted. "Maman counted how many times you danced with him."

"I assure you I was not keeping count. He begged for those dances so we could talk uninterrupted."

"Why would he do that?"

"Hext has always liked to be the center of attention, and I fear I wounded his vanity at the Christmas party. I did not mean to make you unhappy. Can you forgive me?"

She hesitated only a moment before she nodded. "Thank you for telling me, Eliza. I understand him better now."

As she settled back against the pillow, her blissful expression filled me with dread.

13

The chilly wind whipped at my cloak as I hurried down Meeting Street. Jennie carried my basket and walked two paces behind me, like the other ladies and their maids who filed inside the church gate past the crowd of shivering, poorly dressed women and children.

In the courtyard, Lucretia and some other women were setting baskets of food on a long table, and as soon as she saw me she hurried over. "Missus Wilkinson! We are delighted to have your help today. Your maid can help unload the crates from the wagon in the alley. Did you think to bring an apron?" Jennie gave me one backward glance before she headed off.

Lucretia went on. "Saint Philips and Saint Michaels churches have long been responsible for the care and upkeep of the city's poor. The parishes rely on donations to carry on these good works." She lowered her voice. "Since the Redcoats plundered the plantations outside the city, we have seen increasing numbers of respectable folks who are dispossessed of their homes and have nowhere else to turn."

I nodded as I watched two of the women on the committee hand out slices of bread to the children. My eyes lingered on one little girl of about six who ate rapturously, butter smeared on her face. I walked over to the child's mother. "Good day. I am Eliza Wilkinson."

"I'm Priscilla Jenkins. This is our first time here." She laid a hand on each of her little one's heads as she introduced them. "This is Robert, and George–"

The little girl broke in. "I'm Rebecca."

I bent down to her eye level. "I'm very glad to meet you. I also have two brothers, Frank and Will. They're soldiers."

"Our papa is a soldier. He bought me a pianoforte." Her face fell. "I just started learning to play. Now it's broken."

"I'm sure you'll have another one someday."

Priscilla said, "Our house was burned and our servants taken by the Redcoats. It's been a terrible burden, trying to provide for the children on my own. When we arrived here, there was no place to live except the refugee camp. We have no friends in the city, and my husband's army rations barely sustain him."

""I'll do everything I can to help you." I spoke to the children. "Let's make sure you get some food to take with you, shall we?"

Their mother gave me a grateful look. "Do you have children?"

"No. Perhaps one day."

Priscilla drew another woman with a baby on her hip into our group. "This is Lucy Crosse, and little Edward. We were close neighbors. We've been talking and perhaps it's silly, but we thought if we worked and earned something it would ease our minds. The army hasn't paid our husbands, and we don't have any possessions to sell. Lucy's an expert with a needle, both plain and fancy work."

Lucy added, "When Priscilla was a girl, her family's cook was trained in the French style, and Priscilla learned to bake from her."

I nodded as a plan began to form. "Please don't leave until I return. I must speak to someone." When I found Lucretia, I asked, "What else can we do to help these women and children?"

"What do you have in mind?"

"Could we help find work for those who are able? The last time I visited a coffee house they were short staffed."

"That's a wonderful idea. Would you make some inquiries?"

"Of course. Why don't I speak to the women in the line about their skills and abilities?"

By the time I left the church at noon, I had a list of women who were eager to work, and on the way home I visited a number of shops and coffee houses to tout the willing workers who were seeking employment. Encouraged by the responses, I sailed home on the chilly breeze.

I hung up my cloak, hastened to wash my face and hands, and took my place at the table, where Mrs. Porcher and Mary were finishing the first course. Letty brought me a plate and cutlery, and my stomach rumbled as I thanked her.

Mrs. Porcher regarded me with curiosity. "Pray, where have you been, Eliza?"

I picked up my fork. "I was doing charity work at Saint Philips, helping distribute food to some of the displaced people in the city. Perhaps you and Mary would care to come with me next time."

"Oh." She made a face like she'd smelled something unpleasant. "I think not! I wouldn't dream of exposing Mary to the diseases carried by the likes of them." She waved a hand to dismiss the topic. "You may do as you like, but Mary must be well-rested for the events in her social diary. Mister McCall's interest in her has led to more invitations."

When Jennie and I made our first visit to the soldiers' hospital a few days later, she looked around eagerly. We found Kitty Sarrazin, who was swathed in a large apron, and she led us to where the supplies were kept. "Thank you for giving your time. If we conscripted every woman in Charles Town to serve in the hospital, we would still need more pairs of hands."

"I'm happy to help. You mentioned another widow when we spoke at the Assembly Room."

"Yes, Missus Brewton is here somewhere." Kitty helped me into an apron that covered my whole front and introduced me to a bespectacled, sandy-haired gentleman who wore a blood-stained apron under his coat. "Doctor Mosse, may I present Missus Wilkinson? Eliza, if you accompany the doctor he will acquaint you with your duties. Your maid can go to the scullery."

Jennie's face fell, and I wouldn't let her be discounted. "A moment, please. My maid was trained by my husband, who was a physician. She is a competent healer, and is more than capable of assisting a doctor."

Kitty looked at Jennie with curiosity. "I see. I suppose we can try her with Doctor Chapman. Come along, girl."

"Are you ready, mum?" Dr. Mosse motioned for me to follow him to a supply room where he placed towels, bandages, and a basin on a tray. I liked him right away, for he had a kind smile and a pleasant lilt to his voice. "Many of the men contracted the grippe while working outside in the freezing rain. How fortunate elderberries grow in abundance here, just like in my native Ireland. We treat the mild cases with elderberry syrup, tea, and broth to build back their strength, but the seriously ill benefit from clearing out the weakened blood. Tell me, lass, do you faint at the sight of a bloodletting?"

"No, sir. I do not faint."

"You say your husband was a physician. Where did he study?"

"The Philadelphia Medical College."

"Och, aye. Many of their faculty came from the renowned medical college in Edinburgh." He peered at me through his spectacles. "Am I correct to assume you have not had smallpox?"

"Yes."

"Then you must stay out of the ward over there." He indicated a doorway on the far side of the room. "We only allow people who have had the disease to tend to those patients."

I nodded in response and followed the doctor up and down the rows of cots, dispensing doses of elderberry syrup. Many of the men tried to flirt with me, and though none breached proprieties in front of the doctor, I did not encourage them.

Dr. Mosse saw my reluctance. "Our labors are not just about healing bodies, but also nurturing the spirit." He smiled. "Chatting with a bonny lass like you makes any man feel better."

"Yes, sir." At the next cot, the soldier was too weakened by his illness to be interested in me. Dr. Mosse brought a leather case from his pocket and withdrew an ivory-handled knife and a brass lancet. I held the basin steady while he opened a vein in the soldier's arm. Watching so much blood flow into the basin did make me feel queasy, but I did not swoon.

Finally the doctor wiped the knife and lancet on a towel and put them back in the leather pouch. "That will be all for today. If you'll take the tray to the scullery, please."

On the way I noticed a tall, broad-shouldered officer pull up a chair next to a soldier's cot and recognized Major Moore, the fatherly commander of the North Carolina dragoons.

Eager to see him, I hurried down the aisle, a greeting on my lips. I was just feet away when someone bumped into me from behind and a wave of blood slopped out of the basin, soaking me and a soldier who lay on his cot.

"Oh, bother!"

A dark-haired woman brushed past me. It was she who caused the spill, yet she left me to move the soldier to a chair, strip the bed, and fetch fresh linens from the laundry. When at last I had him settled, I found the same woman engaged in what looked like an intimate conversation with Major Moore.

Too proud to interrupt them, I returned my tray to the scullery and left the bloody apron to soak. I retrieved my cloak and as I looked around for Jennie, Major Moore called, "Why, it's Missus Wilkinson, isn't it?"

I feigned surprise. "Major Moore! How good to see a familiar face."

He hurried over and took both my hands in his. "What a surprise to see you here, madam. I trust you are well?"

"Yes, quite well. I came to town for the Season. This is my first day doing charity work here."

"I'm visiting one of my men." He gestured toward the woman. "Are you acquainted with Missus Brewton?"

So this was who the Sarrazin sisters meant to introduce me to. I tried not to sound icy. "I have not had the pleasure."

"I say, you two look enough alike to be sisters!" Major Moore looked from one of us to the other.

She looked me up and down. "I see no resemblance."

"Nor I." I had no desire to foster an acquaintance with this woman. "It was a pleasure to see you, Major. I must find my maid, for we are expected at home." I made an about face and hurried away, and when I found Jennie I caught her by the arm and fled without explanation.

"Missus Wilkinson! Eliza!" Major Moore caught up with us outside. "You say you came to Charles Town for pleasure, but I am glad to see you helping at the hospital. They need every pair of hands."

"Kitty Sarrazin said the same thing."

"She is quite right. If I recall, you once chided my men for underestimating women's ardor for the Cause. Your own commitment remains firm?"

"Of course it does."

"There are many women in Charles Town who are as passionate about liberty as you. Like Polly Brewton, for instance."

"I can't imagine having anything in common with her."

"You two are more alike than you think. You should get to know one another."

"Perhaps. It was nice to see you, sir."

"And you. I hope we meet again soon. Please give my regards to your father."

He turned to go, and I called after him. "Do you know if the post from the island parishes has been interrupted?"

"If it has, I am not aware. Do you need a new pen friend? I'm sure any of my men would be pleased to start a correspondence."

"No, nothing like that. My papa has been unwell. I write home each week, but I've had no word from the family." I smiled to downplay my concern. "Perhaps I shall receive a letter in time for my birthday next week."

"I will inquire about any letters that may have gone astray. Allow me to be the first to wish you all the felicitations."

As soon as he was gone I remembered Jennie. "How did you fare? Did they let you do anything worthwhile?"

She looked happier than I'd seen her since we left Plainsfield. "The doctor seemed pleased that I can work on the smallpox ward."

"Doctor Mosse told me to stay away from that ward."

"That's because you ain't never had it."

I looked at her smooth, caramel-colored skin. "You haven't either, have you?"

"No'm. But I been inoculated. I can't get it."

"Joseph died of smallpox. Did you not think I might want to be inoculated?"

"It wasn't safe to give you the treatment while you were carrying a child. Since then, we ain't been around nobody who had it." She gave me an appraising look. "I can do it whenever you got two or three weeks between parties. Inoculation still make you sick."

I did not reply.

On the way back to Society Street, Jennie and I assumed our city roles, with her walking behind and carrying my basket. We could not have a conversation in public, and so my thoughts turned to Major

Moore and Mrs. Brewton, an odd pairing if there ever was one. He was fatherly and kind, and she brusque, even rude. Why in the world did he think she and I would be friends?

14

My efforts to assist the displaced families at St. Philips bore fruit, and soon dozens of women who had relied on charity to feed their families were hired into domestic and service positions around the city.

Though I was buoyed by that success, I worried about Mary and her continued infatuation with Hext. At the last party, he focused his attention on her, and I saw him whispering to her in a conspiratorial way. It would do no good to voice my concerns, for Mrs. Porcher was blinded by the desire to see her daughter wed, and Mary by the naive belief that Hext cared for her. When his true nature revealed itself, I feared it would break her heart.

Six years ago I began the Season with romantic notions, but this time it felt more like a business transaction. The arrival of my birthday served as a reminder my youth was slipping away. Why did twenty-three sound so much older than twenty-two?

St. Valentine's Day was a week away. The Season's belles and beaus would exchange tokens, sweets, and letters, while the lovelorn and hopeful turned to ritual and superstition to divine who their future spouse would be.

Though I was no closer to satisfying Papa's ambitions for me, I was not desperate enough to sleep with bay leaves pinned to my pillow or eat a salted, hardboiled egg before bed to help me dream of my true love.

When I awoke on my birthday morning I went straight to the looking glass to inspect my face for wrinkles. No one here but Jennie knew it was my birthday, and though I had sworn her to secrecy, Mary was waiting in the dining room, a broad smile on her face. "Happy birthday, dear Eliza!"

I returned the smile so I would not disappoint her. "How did you know?"

"Mister McCall said you love having a fuss made over you on your birthday. I chose the supper menu and asked Letty for two desserts because I couldn't decide which you would prefer."

"Mary, that's sweet of you, but there's no need to do anything out of the ordinary."

"Nonsense!" She stood to embrace me. "We are your family while you're in Charles Town, and we shall celebrate. Let's go to the shops."

"I'm expected at Saint Philips today. Come with me."

She hesitated. "Maman says I mustn't associate with anyone from the refugee camp."

"Nonsense! These are women from homes like ours, you'll see."

She glanced around to make sure we were not overheard. "All right, but we must let Maman think we've been out shopping all day."

Jennie was not disappointed when I told her she need not accompany me today. She teased, "Now I have time to bake your cake."

When we arrived at the church, I greeted the women and children who waited in the food line, but Mary hung back until I took her by the arm and drew her toward them. "No one is going to bite you, Mary. It could have been us who lost everything. Wouldn't you want help if you were in need?" At the main table I retrieved the basket filled with sliced and buttered bread and handed it to her. "Why don't you give one to each of the children?"

"All right." The children clustered around her, and soon she was smiling and giving words of encouragement to each of them. I felt a mix of affection and sorrow for her. Despite her mother's influence, her heart turned with little trouble. I wondered if her anxieties could also be overcome in time.

That afternoon we browsed in the shops, and Mary gifted me a new pair of gloves. I treated her to hot chocolate at the Carolina Coffee House, where the woman who was waiting tables came over to us, beaming. "God bless you, MissusWilkinson! Thanks to you, my sister found work in a print shop, and with both our incomes, we could afford to move out of the tent and into proper lodgings. We work different shifts and take turns minding the children. We never could have improved our circumstances without your help."

I clasped her hand. "No news in the world could make me happier."

Mary watched her as she cleared a nearby table. "What a gift you gave to those women." Tears welled in her eyes. "I apologize for Maman and for myself."

"You're a grown woman, and you must decide for yourself what is important and how to do good in the world."

She dashed away a tear. "I wish you were my sister. It's too bad you and Peter didn't get on. I daresay he's lonely too." She stopped, as though she'd said too much. "From now on I shall think about the example I set for my own little sisters."

We returned home in time to warm by the parlor fire before we were called to supper. Mary insisted I take the place of honor at the foot of the table while she took the host's chair. The roast chicken with rice, creamed vegetables, and a selection of cheeses with benne wafers more than satisfied. When the dishes were cleared, Letty brought in a Floating Island of meringue on crème anglaise, and Mary clapped her hands like a child. "This is to represent your home on your father's island, Eliza."

Jennie followed, bearing a chocolate cake ablaze with candles. Mary was as excited as if it was her own birthday. "Don't forget to make a wish so the smoke can carry it to heaven."

I closed my eyes and blew out the candles. As Jennie cut slices of cake, drizzled them with raspberry coulis, and set them before us, Mrs. Porcher asked, "What did you wish for?"

I fibbed. "A visit from General Lincoln."

Mary giggled. "The general was too busy to accept our invitation to dinner tonight, but I composed this for you." She unfolded a sheet of parchment and read,

> In February, month of love and mirth
> We celebrate Eliza's birth.
> Tho the urchin Cupid, that busy one
> Shoots his arrows in the 'Ton
> Eliza, thou alone doth wish
> To stay in the country to ramble and
> fish.
> So may you catch upon your line
> One whose heart you'd trade for thine.

Someone began to clap behind me. Mary cried out in delight, and I turned in my chair as she rushed around the table to greet her brother. "I was thinking of you this afternoon!"

Peter put his arm around her and kissed the top of her head. "Hello, Maman, Mary, and Missus Wilkinson. Maman, I received your letter begging me to hasten to Charles Town without delay." He turned to me. "I see I arrived in time to celebrate your birthday. I wish you many happy returns." He bowed, and I silently thanked Cupid for the speed with which he made my wish come true.

Peter turned his attention back to his mother. "What is the great emergency that requires my presence?"

Mrs. Porcher cleared her throat and took a sip of wine. "I have not been feeling well, and need you to escort Mary and Eliza to the remaining events of the Season."

Mary and I exchanged surprised glances, but Peter looked stunned. "That's another two months of parties, yes?"

"It will be wonderful to have you with us for such a long visit." Mary beamed up at him.

Mrs. Porcher cleared her throat again. "Peter, let us speak privately." He hastened to hold her chair and offered her his arm. As if to emphasize her ill health, she made slow progress out of the room. They crossed the hall and shut the study door behind them. When they returned, Mrs. Porcher paused in the dining room doorway. "Mary, come along. I require your assistance."

"Yes, Maman." Mary gave me another puzzled glance as she followed her mother upstairs.

Peter went to the sideboard, poured himself a cup of coffee, and stared at me for so long I felt I must break the silence.

"Would you care for some birthday cake?"

He shook his head as if to clear it. "Yes, of course. Thank you." He sank into a chair and accepted the plate I passed to him. "I cannot credit why Maman considers this a crisis of such magnitude that I must risk my life to attend to it. It's lucky I met no enemy patrols on the way here." He looked so tired, rumpled, and frustrated that I tried to explain.

"Her ambitions for Mary put strain on them both."

"Has it been so unpleasant for her?" He stabbed at the cake with his fork. "It's just a series of parties."

Did he not recall his own discomfort at the Christmas party? "How can it be anything else, with your mother hovering at her shoulder and counting the number of times she's asked to dance? The poor girl is so desperate I fear she will accept any man who proposes."

"Unmarried girls attend the Season to secure a proposal."

"Yes, but your sister has little experience with men. She needs guidance, not pressure."

"Whereas you have a great deal more."

His unexpected comment should have hurt my feelings, but instead it raised a flicker of the passion I'd felt for him on Christmas. I lowered my voice to a whisper. "I daresay you enjoyed kissing a woman with some experience. Did you not?"

I was baiting him, and I half expected him to respond by taking me in his arms, but instead he looked as if I'd slapped him. He pushed his plate away and stood. "I'm too weary to discuss this now. Good night."

Hurt and confused, I watched him leave. Was it fatigue or something else that made him so eager to get away from me?

15

Peter maintained a cool distance, spending most of his time in town, taking his meals out, and sequestering himself in the study when he was at home. The one evening he ate supper with us, I caught him staring at me like he was trying to read my thoughts. I would have paid a pretty penny for insights into his.

I could not deny the connection forged by our first kiss, and whether I wanted to or not, I felt the pull of attraction whenever he was near. Was I like Mary, mooning after someone who would only hurt me in the end?

Two days of heavy rain and high winds forced the cancellation of the St. Valentine's ball. The four of us gathered in the parlor, where Mrs. Porcher and Mary played cribbage and Peter sat in an armchair before the fire, a glass of port on the stand beside him and a book open in his lap as he stared at the flickering flames on the hearth.

It was my first opportunity to speak with him in a long while. "What are you reading?"

He raised the book so I could see the title.

"*The Wealth of Nations.* Isn't that what you were reading the day we met?"

"I saw it in a shop a few days ago and bought it so we'd have a copy here. It is an important work, and I hope its principles are used to pave

127

the way forward for the United States." Though the hour was still early, he closed the book and rose. "Good night, everyone."

The next week the weather cleared, and the parties resumed. As we prepared to leave for our next evening out, Mary showed me a small cut-paper heart. "I fashioned this for Mister McCall. Do you think he will like it?"

"Oh, I'm sure he will."

"I meant to give it to him on Saint Valentine's Day. It's a week late." She tucked it into her reticule and I followed her downstairs.

Peter awaited us in the foyer, dressed in an indigo wool coat and knee breeches and a yellow silk waistcoat. His stock was expertly tied, the ruffle starched. He greeted us with a formal bow and soberly helped us on with our cloaks before shepherding us out to the carriage.

I did not know what to expect from his company, but his dour demeanor of the previous two weeks transformed on the ride to the hall. He surprised me with one of his hoarded smiles as I alighted from the carriage, and greeted several people in the vestibule while we waited to leave our wraps.

"Henderson!" He threw a brotherly arm around one young man's shoulders and drew him along with us as we went into the ballroom. "Allow me to present my sister, Mary—" he paused and turned to me, "—and Eliza Wilkinson."

Mr. Henderson blushed and stammered a greeting, his eyes fixed on Mary.

I shot her a pointed glance and she asked, "Where is your home, Mister Henderson?"

He gulped. "Peter and I are neighbors. Not extremely close, mind you. My place is along the Savannah River, on the Georgia side."

"I see. How long will you be in Charles Town?"

"Through the remainder of the Season, I should think."

It was Peter's turn to give Mr. Henderson a pointed look over Mary's head. The young man stammered again, bowed to Mary, and extended his hand. "I—that is, would you care to dance, Miss Porcher?"

She put her hand in his, but as he led her away I saw her shoot a longing glance at Hext, who stared after them with surprise and curiosity on his face. Then he made a beeline for me.

"By all the saints–" Peter muttered the oath under his breath and then turned to me. "Eliza, may I have the pleasure?" That stopped Hext in his tracks.

"Yes, of course." As he escorted me past Hext, I realized it was the first time he'd called me by my given name.

Peter avoided the dancing at the Christmas party, so I assumed he either did not know how or did not care to. We joined a group of three other couples for the contredanse, and when the music began, he surprised me by moving through the figures with ease. Whenever we touched, the surge of feeling was so swift and powerful I might have been the key on the kite string in one of Dr. Franklin's electricity experiments.

He had to feel it too.

As the evening progressed, we danced so often that men who had engaged me at earlier parties stayed away, but it was clear his focus was on Mary and her welfare. Once again I made an effort to draw him out. "I know that you and Mr. Henderson are neighbors, but I know nothing else about your home."

He considered for a moment before he responded. "I live near Black Swamp. It is not unlike other places you have seen. Figure to yourself houses, gardens, fields, and woods."

"A bog, too, I imagine?"

"I prefer rivulet over bog. People unfamiliar with that country assume it is naught but mud, mosquitos, and malaria, but it is a land of evergreen pine, partridge and deer in abundance, bordered by a shimmering river."

Charmed by the way his face lit up when he described his home, I ventured, "Perhaps the name Black Swamp was chosen to keep people away. As you describe it, I would be eager to visit. That is, if I ever received an invitation."

"I would not want you to see it now, for my home is unfit for habitation, let alone to welcome guests." His expression hardened. "After Savannah fell, the Redcoats plagued our district with raids and skirmishes. Last April, partisans attacked a guard post very near my home, where they captured six of my comrades and burned the buildings. That, and the attacks on my home and the homes of my neighbors left me with an insatiable desire to oust every last one of them from this continent."

"I have also suffered at the hands of the Redcoats. They plundered my house and then burned it after the Battle of Stono Ferry. They threatened to kill my elderly father, and my brothers narrowly escaped capture when a squad came ashore at my father's house unexpectedly. Each episode haunts me, but none more than the captain who vowed he would return to claim me. I revile him, and my papa is too ill to offer real protection. The best way to protect myself was to leave. That is why I attended the Christmas party."

The concern on his face touched me. "What was the blackguard's name? Did he return?"

"His name was Sandford. He had not returned before I left for Charles Town. I reckoned there would be plenty of Continentals here to stand between me and him, but after hearing rumors that troops have come ashore to move against Charles Town, I'd feel better if more militia came in to help defend the city."

Peter shook his head. "The militia should not come here. Those men defend the outlying districts where their farms and houses will be plundered and their servants taken off if they're not keeping a sharp eye."

"With so many Redcoats and Loyalist militia in the sea islands, they'll likely be plundered regardless."

"Be that as it may, there's also the matter of smallpox. Some men fear that disease more than they do the Redcoats."

"Smallpox could just as well strike in the countryside. Here lies the greatest need, and the militia should reinforce the Regulars, so the city doesn't fall."

His gaze shifted from my face to over my shoulder. "Excuse me." He strode away and returned with a red-faced Mary in tow. He kept his voice low, but I overheard him say, "I forbid you to spend time in his company."

She clutched the love token she'd made. "I didn't have a chance to give it to him. Maman said–"

"You will obey me now, not Maman. Come. We're leaving."

As I followed them out of the hall, Hext caught my eye and smirked.

Peter's decision to bring Mary home from the dance early threw Mrs. Porcher into near-hysterics. When they all began shouting at each other in French, I fled to my chamber, and had long since retired when Mary and Mrs. Porcher came up. It was very late when Peter's tread on the stairs disturbed my wakeful sleep.

Driving rain and gray skies reflected the mood in the Porcher house. Some people believed the hurricane winds that battered the city were God's hand keeping the Redcoats from advancing, but as March came in like a lion, British forces struck, seizing Johns Island and Stono Ferry. Days later, they took control of James Island and Wappoo Cut. One by one, the roads and waterways between Charles Town and Yonge's Island fell into enemy hands, and Governor Rutledge sent out another desperate summons to militia units from the sea islands and the backcountry.

With Charles Town's militia and the Continentals called to man the ramparts and fortifications on the Neck day and night, women now outnumbered the men at parties. Hext was always surrounded by a crowd of girls, which only served to increase Mary's desperation.

Peter refused to reverse his stance on Hext, ignoring his mother's scolding and his sister's tears. After a few weeks of sulking, Mary's spirits improved and she and her mother began to brave the cold weather to go out shopping two or three afternoons each week.

Despite Peter's watchfulness, I often noticed Hext trying to catch Mary's eye, but I told myself he could inflict no real harm. She was always in the company of at least one of us.

One morning as Jennie and I hurried down Archdale Street toward the hospital, heads down against the wind and rain, Hext hurried to hold his umbrella so it sheltered me. "My dear, I hardly recognized you! Are these your country togs?" He lowered his voice. "Or perhaps you are in disguise because you are meeting a lucky gentleman for some clandestine pleasure?"

"We are on our way to do charity work at the hospital."

He affected a hurt expression. "Why must you be so cold, my dear? I was only jesting."

"How can I be anything but cold in this awful weather? Let us pass so we can get indoors."

"Yes, do hurry along. The garrison just announced a half-nine curfew for civilians, so you mustn't be late to McCrady's this evening. It has been too long since I've had the pleasure of a dance, and the revelry must end at such an unfashionable hour."

When I did not answer, he stepped aside with a sweeping gesture and departed.

Once inside the hospital, Jennie and I shook out our wet cloaks and hung them up. Before we could go about our separate assignments, Dr. Chapman, who was in charge of the smallpox ward, asked to speak with me. We left Jennie in the hall and I followed him into the doctors' study.

"Your slave woman is a quick learner, and well-versed in herbal and natural remedies. You said your husband gave her some training?"

"Yes, that is correct."

"Would you be willing to introduce her to more European medical practices? You would not be violating any anti-literacy laws if all you do is read to her."

When I nodded, he collected a textbook and some pamphlets. "This will increase her value, now and if you choose to part with her in the future."

How could he praise her intellect, yet see her as a possession whose worth could be measured in dollars? I held my anger in check as I took the materials. "Thank you, Doctor."

We returned to the hall, and as he and Jennie headed off toward the smallpox ward, I hoped the additional study would fulfill her enough to keep her frustrations at bay. I put the books in our basket and donned an apron, trying not to be jealous that she, who possessed the affinity for healing, was being noticed for her skills, while I spent my shift flirting with soldiers and holding a bloody basin.

It was nearly time to leave when Polly Brewton blocked my path as I carried a basket of soiled linens to the laundry. I sighed. "Let me pass so I can put these down."

"What are you playing at?"

"I might ask you the same thing." I tried to sidestep her, but she was too quick.

"You're a society widow, here to do the Season and find a husband."

"What business is that of yours? Have I done something to offend you?"

She fixed me with a penetrating stare. "You could be entertaining a suitor or two before a blazing fire, yet you're in this cold, drafty hospital with the sick and the wounded." She chuckled in a maddening way. "James said the two of us were alike."

"I daresay he couldn't be more wrong."

"I don't want a husband. I think you don't either. Why are you here?"

Just like Dr. Chapman, who did not see Jennie for all that she was, this woman seemed determined to reduce me to a caricature of a society belle. I kept silent. What I wanted was none of her business.

"I'll ask again: why are you here?" This time it was not an accusation. The change in her demeanor caught me off guard and the words poured forth.

"If you must know, I managed one of my papa's places until the Redcoats burned the place last June. He sold the land and bid me to find a new husband, with no consideration for what I wanted. I am staying with a friend who has a capricious and interfering mother. I became reacquainted with a childhood friend who professes love for me, yet he flirts with every girl in the room. I met another man I thought I could love, but he doesn't feel the same. The parties hold no charms for me. I hoped I might find respite, peace, and a sense of purpose in Christian good works. That's why I'm here." I stopped, breathless, as Polly stared at me with raised eyebrows.

"My goodness." She held out her arms to take my basket. "I daresay you'll feel better now that you've unburdened yourself." She left me staring after her, unsure whether I'd made a friend or committed social suicide.

16

Jennie and I arrived home from the hospital wet and shivering. In my chamber, she stirred up the fire and helped me out of my work dress. "I'll take it down to be laundered. It's warm in the kitchen with the ovens going, you know."

"Yes, I'm sure it is. You're the lucky one today. After I go back out in the cold you can spend the evening with your books. Please fill the warming pan before you leave?" When she obliged, I burrowed under the counterpane and stretched my icy toes toward its warmth. "I'm going to stay here until it's time to get ready for the party."

I had just started to feel comfortable when Mary let herself in and crawled under the covers with me. "I need to speak with you."

"Of course. What is it?"

"Liberty is a good thing, yes?"

"That's what our statesmen envision for the citizens of the United States. It's what our soldiers hope to gain by defeating the British."

She considered this. "So if liberty is good, is 'granting a liberty' good?"

"Mary, to whom would you grant a liberty?" I was afraid I already knew the answer.

Her voice dropped to a whisper. "Mister McCall. He is very keen on the idea, but I don't know what a liberty is."

"I thought Peter forbade you to speak to Hext."

She raised up on one elbow. "Maman has been taking me to meet him in the afternoons. She thinks Peter is being too protective."

I fought to keep my anger under control. Did that foolish woman mean to allow her own daughter to be compromised? "Does she leave you unchaperoned?"

"Never for very long."

"Has she not spoken to you of–"

"Of liberties? No. I can't ask her. That's why I came to you."

I chose my words with care. "Mothers keep such knowledge from innocent girls. Granting liberties is the reverse of virtue and modesty, and best left for, well, for when you're married and you trust the other person with your heart." Even as I spoke I recalled my Christmas night encounter with Peter, and blushed at my hypocrisy.

"Oh, Eliza, Mister McCall speaks of nothing else. He begs I grant him a small liberty to prove my affections are sincere. Then I daresay he will propose."

The depth of her naivete astounded me. With no idea of what Hext was asking of her, she would be unprepared to defend herself.

"Mary, refuse him."

"But why?"

"Refusing is the best way to assure he respects your feelings. Do you understand?"

She sighed. "Society is so very complicated, isn't it?"

"Yes, it is, and so is family. I think you should make peace with Peter."

She sat up. "I'll go speak to him now."

As I watched her leave, I recalled the days of my engagement to Joseph. While we waited for the reading of the banns that announced our intent to wed, I granted what could be called little liberties whenever we found ourselves without a chaperone. Allowing those kisses and caresses awakened my curiosity for what awaited me in the marriage bed without making me feel coerced. I shuddered to think what Mary would experience should Hext get her alone.

Late in the afternoon the rain stopped, and with clear skies came another significant temperature drop. It was hard to leave my bed.

I wore my indigo, and Mary appeared in the yellow she'd worn to the first event of the Season. When Peter joined us, he smiled at his sister and bestowed a gentle kiss on her forehead, and there was real warmth in his smile as he brought my gloved hand to his lips. "You look radiant, Eliza." He offered his arm, and before we left the house he laid his other hand over mine. "I know you spoke with Mary today, and I want to thank you for advising her. You have been a steadfast friend to this family despite my unpleasantness. It cannot have been easy for you."

His changed demeanor made the ride to the tavern so companionable that I forgot my earlier encounter with Hext, who was waiting for us when we entered the main hall. When Peter let go of my arm and took a protective step in front of Mary, Hext countered by approaching me.

"Eliza, you promised me a dance when we were together this morning."

"The lady is already spoken for." Peter put out a hand to check him, but Hext brushed it away.

"The proprieties dictate she cannot refuse me and then accept an invitation from you."

"I extended my invitation first."

Hext sputtered angrily. "The hell you say!"

"Will you both stop talking about me as if I'm unable to answer for myself?" I addressed Hext. "I must refuse, as I've already accepted Mister Porcher's invitation."

He fixed me with a hard look. "Dear, dear Eliza. We could have had such fun, you and I." He purposely bumped against Peter as he left us.

Peter shook his head as he watched Hext shove his way through the crowd. "This is why I avoid society. The plotting and scheming that goes on in Charles Town's ballrooms is more complex than strategies devised by generals." His tone turned apologetic. "I regret I that I could not discern truth from lies. I judged you unfairly and I humbly beg your forgiveness."

"What lies do you speak of? Did Hext say something about me?"

He looked away for a moment, and then he met my eyes. "Revealing your detractor would not excuse my behavior. Please, Eliza. May we forget what has passed between us since I arrived and begin anew?"

That was all I wanted, and he looked so hopeful that I forgave him without reservation, but I pretended I was still considering his apology. At length I said, "You really *are* terrible at silly games—for what could be sillier than society gossip? Perhaps we could begin anew with a minuet?"

His face relaxed into a smile, and he leaned close as we joined the waiting couples. "If it's not too bold to suggest, might we revisit that which we began on Christmas night?"

"You mustn't assume my forgiveness extends that far, sir."

"Indeed?" He dropped his voice to a whisper. "Do I gain no additional favor for rescuing you from Hext McCall?"

I couldn't help smiling. "I don't need to be watched over. I'm not your little sister."

"Trust me. That's not how I think of you."

When it was our turn, we moved through the figures of the dance as if we'd done so countless times before. We both bowed low when the music ended, but instead of escorting me away, he froze, his gaze fixed over my shoulder. I turned to see Hext and Mary waiting their turn among the other couples. Hext whispered in her ear, and her smile faltered. I took hold of Peter's arm to coax him away. "Come, don't embarrass her in front of everyone."

He followed, muttering, "What is she thinking? Why did she not do as she promised?"

We joined the other spectators as Hext led Mary out and made an ostentatious bow. He stood poised until the music started, and then he turned on his heel and strode away, leaving her alone under the gaze of every eye in the room.

A shocked murmur went through the crowd, and the musicians stopped. Tears welled in Mary's eyes and her chin began to tremble.

Peter tensed beside me, but before he could go to her aid, Mr. Henderson stepped into Hext's empty place and bowed to her. The musicians started again, and I watched every step and transition, willing them to finish without a mistake. Henderson was not a gifted terpsichorean, but he made a valiant effort to spare Mary more embarrassment, and when the final note faded, it seemed that the room itself breathed a sigh of relief. I turned to see Peter's reaction, but he was gone.

Knnowing Hext's cruel trick would bring the acrimony between the two men to a head, I picked up my skirts and hurried after them. They were not in the taproom, so I continued downstairs and into the dimly lit courtyard. The sounds of a struggle drew my attention to the shadows on the far side of the yard, and as I hurried over, I saw Hext, too intoxicated to be a dangerous opponent, swing his fist, miss, and catch hold of Peter's shirt to keep from falling. Peter shook him off, set his stance, and delivered a blow that spun Hext around on his feet. His knees buckled and he fell to the muddy bricks, where he stirred and groaned, but did not rise.

Together we stared down at him, and Peter scoffed as he flexed his hand. "He's so far into his cups he won't remember why he took that beating." He picked up his coat, brushed it off, and shrugged into it.

"I, on the other hand, will treasure the memory." He gave Hext a last, contemptuous glance and strode toward the tavern.

I ran to keep up, and when he slowed I grasped his arm to focus his attention. "We should take leave. I'll find Mary."

He nodded. "I'll call the carriage and meet you in front."

Inside, I soon spotted her in Mr. Henderson's company, face flushed with excitement. "Oh, Eliza! Where's Peter? Did he see us dance?"

"We both did." I bestowed a smile of thanks on Mr. Henderson before turning back to Mary. "Peter called for the carriage and asked us to meet him outside. We don't want to miss curfew."

Emboldened by his triumph on the dance floor, Mr. Henderson asked, "May I accompany you ladies to the carriage stand?"

Mary answered for both of us. "Please."

We collected our cloaks, and once we were out on the wet cobblestones we each took one of Mr. Henderson's arms and held up our skirts to avoid the puddles. At the carriage stand Mr. Henderson drew Mary aside. I turned my back so they would have a little privacy, but I heard every word.

His usually mild voice was charged with indignation. "If I may say so, that lout McCall had no regard for your feelings whatsoever—it was a singular display of bad manners. Had it been me—"

Mary replied, "It was you who rescued me."

"What I mean to say is, when I ask you to dance, I will always see the commitment through." He spoke in a rush. "Next time we will be most familiar partners."

"Yes, we will."

The carriage pulled up and Peter, unaware he was interrupting, stepped out. He extended his hand to Mary, but she gave hers to Mr. Henderson instead.

"Good night, Miss Porcher."

"Good night, Mister Henderson."

Peter wore a satisfied smile as he echoed Mary's farewell to his friend.

He helped me in, and as he sat beside me I murmured, "You handled this evening's intrigue well. There may be hope for you yet."

"Is that so?" He settled his shoulder against mine.

"Without a doubt."

As the carriage pulled away from the curb, I mulled over everything I'd learned about Peter that evening. He could admit when he was wrong and ask forgiveness, and he did not shrink from protecting and defending his loved ones. I felt as if I'd discovered his most closely guarded secret: he was an admirable man.

17

The carriage pulled away from the curb and Peter leaned out the window to speak to the coachman. "Toby, could you drive us past the Orangerie before turning for home?"

I glanced over at him, silhouetted against the carriage window. "You want to go past the Orange Garden? At this hour?"

He shrugged. "If we arrive at home early, Maman will demand an explanation. To avoid further discord, we're taking the long way."

"I daresay the weather's too cold for orange blossoms, but in a few weeks, it will be pleasant to go walking among the trees, won't it, Mary?"

The question startled her from her thoughts. "What? Oh, yes. Lovely."

Moonlight glistened on puddles as the carriage rumbled over the uneven cobblestones. We turned onto Orange Street, and as I glanced up at the house on the corner, a figure silhouetted against one of the second-story windows plunged from that great height, and a man's roar of pain echoed off the garden walls.

"Did you see that?" I pounded on the carriage wall. "Toby, stop here, please!"

I opened the door, climbed out of the carriage, and ran toward the garden with Peter and Mary at my heels. The moonlight that streamed through the trees fell upon a uniformed man sprawled on the muddy ground, one leg bent beneath him.

I held up my skirts and picked my way through the muck, but Peter reached the man's side first and knelt beside him. "Colonel? How may I assist you?"

The man roared again in pain and frustration. "Outrageous! Locking the doors, of all things!"

Peter grasped his arm, and the officer did a double take.

"Porcher, is it? From Savannah?"

"Yes sir. Can you stand?"

He tried to straighten his leg. "Blast! My ankle may be broken. I require assistance." He waved vaguely toward the house. "Get my adjutant." Then he threw his head back and bellowed, "McQueen!"

"Right away, sir." He said to Mary and me, "I'll find McQueen. See if you can make him more comfortable." He skidded in the mud, but stayed on his feet as he hurried out through the gate.

Mary and I each took one of the colonel's arms, and when we pulled she slipped and landed on her bottom. I almost lost my own footing as I helped her up.

The officer continued to mutter, mostly to himself. "Who ever heard of allowing the enemy to entrench before you fight him?" He wrinkled his hooked nose and wiped his hands on his trousers. "I daresay the men have used this garden for a latrine. Doing their occasions—" He sputtered and went on. "I suppose it's to be expected. Negligence toward duty destroys discipline."

I tried to distract him. "Sir, what happened? How did you fall from the window?"

"Fall? Bah! I jumped. I despise the social tyranny of these infernal entertainments. It's McQueen's fault for locking the doors."

"I'm afraid I don't understand. Why did he lock the doors?"

"Thunderation! Where's that lout? He's slower than Lincoln and d'Estaing. It'll be a wonder if the British don't catch us completely unprepared!"

As he raved on, I began to wonder if he'd hit his head and concussed himself. "The fools. The fools! Why drink to victories we have not yet won?"

What was keeping Peter? I glanced toward the gate, but then a shrill burst of feminine laughter drew my attention upwards. People crowded every rear-facing window of the house and stared down at us. A moment later, Peter and four officers ran into the garden. They helped the colonel up and supported him back to the house.

Peter wiped his muddy hands on his breeches and brought a clean handkerchief out of his pocket. "I don't know how much good this will do you—"

"Give it to Mary." I followed his example and wiped my hands on my mud-spattered petticoat.

She took the handkerchief and scrubbed at her soiled gown. "Oh, I hope Maman is asleep when we get home. I don't believe I've ever been this filthy in my life."

"Don't worry. I'm sure it can be cleaned." In the carriage, I helped Mary turn her cloak inside out to help keep mud off the upholstery. Before I could attend to my own, Peter spread his overcoat on my seat for me.

As I settled in, I asked, "Who was that?"

"Lieutenant Colonel Francis Marion. I was under his command at the Siege of Savannah. He's particular about—well, everything."

"He jumped from the window. Why would he do such a thing?"

"From what I could surmise, McQueen declared no one would leave the party until all the wine and spirits were drunk, and proceeded to lock everyone in. I had to pound on the front door for a long time before anyone answered. Marion does not partake, and I suppose he got tired of being stuck in there."

I recalled the dangerous height. "That's madness."

"That's Marion." Peter chuckled.

I started to giggle, and then Mary joined in. Our hilarity fed upon itself as we passed through town, but we hushed each other before the carriage turned onto Society Street. We came in on tiptoe to find Mrs. Porcher had already retired. Mary, eager to find Letty and attend to her soiled cloak and gown, bid us goodnight and hurried upstairs.

Peter followed me into the parlor, where I held out my skirts to inspect the mud spatters. "Oh, dear. I'm a mess."

"A most charming and disarming mess." He swept me into his arms. After holding ourselves in check all evening, this kiss was a thousand times more thrilling than the one we'd shared on Christmas night. His gentle caresses, those of a hopeful lover, soon gave over to the heat and passion of a victorious warrior. At length he paused and gazed down at me. "I want you, Eliza, and if you feel the same, I vow that I will endeavor to be the generous companion you desire."

"Did Mary tell you about that?"

He smiled. "A good spy gives one the advantage."

"Do you need an advantage? Are you among those who liken courtship to warfare between the sexes?"

"I've been in battle." His lips trailed down the side of my neck, sending a pleasant shiver along my spine. "This is nothing like war, though the possibility of surrender intrigues me."

The double entendre took us another step beyond the boundaries of propriety. "My generous companion would not expect to capture my heart. But if he gave me his, whole and entire, I would joyfully exchange."

He drew me down beside him on the settee and as his lips took mine, he wove his fingers through my swept-up hair until it came loose from its pins and tumbled in raven waves down my back. His caresses grew bolder, and as our excitement built, the fear, loss, and disappointments that had brought me to this moment fell away, leaving me free to begin anew.

With a word, I could have all of him and the physical intimacy I longed for, but this was not a proper wedding night, and I lacked the reckless courage to forge ahead and hang the consequences.

When we broke apart, his breathing was ragged. "I did not believe it could be more difficult to part from you than it was on Christmas." He traced my swollen lips with his thumb. "How can I bid you good-night when everything I want–" His face fell, and his words turned bitter. "So much time wasted. If I had trusted my own heart from the beginning, I should have begged to exchange it away long ago."

"I daresay you did not expect to make a match during the Season."

"Don't be so certain of that." He kissed me on both cheeks, and then on the lips. "*Bon nuit, mon cher.* I vow I shall not sleep unless it is to dream of you."

When I tiptoed into my chamber, shoes in hand, I found Jennie curled up in the armchair, engrossed in Dr. Chapman's medical text.

She looked up from the page and rose in alarm. "What happened to you?"

"I'm fine."

She lit more tapers. "You look like you been compromised. Your hair's a rat's nest, your bodice is half-open, and there's mud all over your gown."

"It was an eventful evening."

She heaved a sigh of relief. "When I first saw you I thought Mist' Hext had got you alone." She helped me pick the hairpins out of my tangled hair.

"I've been with Peter." When she did not respond, I felt I had to defend him. "I know we started off wrong when he arrived on my birthday, but that was a misunderstanding. All is well between us now."

She nodded. "On your birthday, I saw his face when he come in, and I could tell he was bustin' to see you, cause ain' no man that excited to visit his mama and his sister. But then he changed. I seen him watchin' you like you somethin' he want but can't have."

"That's behind us now, and when he asks for my hand, I will accept him."

I waited for her reaction as she undid the hooks on my gown and helped me out of it. Finally she said, "If you want that man enough to put up with his mama, he must fire your blood."

We both burst into giggles and climbed into bed together, where I recounted almost everything that had happened that night. The remaining memories I kept to savor as I lay awake, listening to him toss and turn in his chamber across the hall.

Jennie was gone when I awoke the next morning. Giddy with anticipation, I sang as I dressed and arranged my hair. *"Only while we love we live, love alone can pleasure give."*

I fairly danced downstairs, but my good humor faded when I reached the dining room and found Peter's seat empty. While Letty served the meal, I asked in what I hoped was a casual tone, "Where is Mister Porcher this morning?"

"A message come for him just after dawn. He left right away, din' even eat."

I told myself it was not unusual for Peter to attend to business in the city. When I finished eating and excused myself from the table, Letty followed me into the hall. She looked around to make sure we were alone, and then whispered, "Mist' Peter say to give this to you in private." She handed me a sealed letter and hurried back to the kitchen.

As soon as she was gone I unfolded the single sheet of parchment. He had written in bold strokes, *In the book I was reading when first we met, underlined on page 7.*

Intrigued, I searched the parlor bookshelves until I located *The Wealth of Nations*. The passage read:

Whoever offers to another a bargain of any kind, proposes to do this. Give me that which I want, and you shall have that which you want, is the meaning of every such offer; and it is in this manner that we obtain from one another the far greater part.

A passage extolling mutually beneficial relationships touched my heart a thousand times more than the meaningless compliments men often employed when wooing a girl. I clasped the book to my chest. Peter, who claimed to have no skill at games, had played a master stroke.

Yet he did not return that day.

We were scheduled to attend a card party that evening, and when I claimed to have a headache and begged to be excused, Mrs. Porcher and Mary departed without me. I spent the evening with a book open in front of me, reading the same page over and over without comprehending.

Near curfew, Peter came in the front door and hurried past the parlor without seeing me. He took the stairs two at a bound and soon I heard him moving around in his chamber. I was waiting for him in the foyer when he came down dressed in a fringed buckskin hunting frock, leggings, and a black cocked hat. There was a haversack slung over his shoulder, and he carried a rifle.

He pulled up short, a guilty look on his face. "Eliza. I didn't think you'd be at home. Did Letty give you my note?"

"She did, but it seems you had no intention of honoring it, or anything you said last night. You were going to leave without saying goodbye."

He shifted uncomfortably. "General Lincoln ordered all officers without assignments out of the city."

"You're not an officer. You're not even with your militia unit. I nearly surrendered all to you—"

"If I had known what this day would bring, I would have been a gentleman last night and spared us both." He leaned his rifle against the wall. "There is so much I am not at liberty to explain, but I can tell you this: after dark, people and provisions move in and out of Charles Town on the Cooper River. Today British ships came over the sandbar and invaded the harbor, and I must leave before the Redcoats cut the last route out of the city."

He looked down at me for a long moment and then reached into his haversack and handed me a folded piece of parchment. "I was going to leave this for you."

My anger flared. "Another note?"

"Please read it. I care for you, Eliza, more than I know how to express. I would not leave you if I had a choice." When he leaned in to kiss me goodbye I abandoned my pride and clung to him, but he pulled away. "Say nothing to Maman or Mary. It's better no one knows what I'm about, and Maman could not keep a secret if my life depended on it."

He picked up his rifle and left without looking back. As soon as the door closed behind him, I read what he'd written.

Eliza,

Last night as I lay awake, unable to banish you from my thoughts even for a moment, I chose the passage from Smith as my response to your proposed exchange of hearts. Now I regretfully pen this note to inform you of my departure. I cannot tell you where I am bound, or why. If I have the opportunity to write I will use a code: clusters of three numbers which correspond to a page, line, and word in that book with which we are familiar.

Yours,

Peter

The postscript was a series of numbers, but I had neither the time nor the patience to puzzle it out. As I stood alone in the foyer, fear for his safety and for the inevitable, coming conflict took hold of me. Charles Town was no longer a haven. It was a powder keg set to blow, a trap from which there was no escape. In one wild moment I decided to run after him, for it did not matter where I was when danger was everywhere. I grabbed my cloak off its peg, and as I hooked the clasp, I heard footsteps outside. Had he returned? Joy and relief bubbled out of me in a half-sob as I threw open the door.

Instead of Peter, I came face to face with Mary, who embraced me the moment she stepped over the threshold. "I can't believe you weren't there!" She held up her left hand to display a ring whose sizable central diamond was surrounded by a cluster of sapphires and rubies. "Mister Henderson proposed! It took the whole evening for him to get up his courage. Silly man! He already knew I would accept."

Mrs. Porcher was right behind her, and in their giddy enthusiasm, they swept me along to the parlor and rang for Letty. Mrs. Porcher wiped away a tear. "Bring the best Madeira! Miss Mary is to be wed!"

"Right away, missus." Letty hurried away.

I was still wearing my cloak, and when I removed it, my hostess regarded me with curiosity. "Where were you off to?"

"Nowhere." I laid it over the back of a chair and changed the subject. "You must be overjoyed."

"Yes, indeed, a most suitable match! The Hendersons are an illustrious family. My husband is sure to approve." She turned to Mary. "We must send a note to Missus Thompson in the morning and schedule a consultation for your wedding gown, dearest."

"Yes, of course, Maman."

Letty brought the wine and glasses on a tray, and as I took one, my throat constricted and tears clouded my eyes. That was all it took for Mary's tears of happiness to flow. "Oh, Eliza, we're both overcome! You're sweet to be so happy for me. The Season is almost at a close, but there is still time for you to find happiness. Is Peter home? I can't wait to tell him."

"He's not here." I set my full glass aside. "Forgive me, Mary. My headache is worse. I believe I shall go to bed."

She looked sympathetic. "Of course, dear. Sleep well."

They were so caught up that neither noticed me take Peter's book from the shelf before I left the room. Alone in my chamber, I transcribed the message.

duty calls know I will treasure each moment spent with you

A lump formed in my throat, but as much as I wanted to give vent to my disappointment, the tears would not come. I cursed the Fates that had brought us together, only to rend us apart.

18

Peter was right about the threat posed by the British warships in the harbor. The day after he departed, word spread that General Moultrie had ordered the guns from American warships taken out and mounted at the fort, and the ships scuttled to reinforce the boom that blocked the entrance to the channel.

When the first explosion went off, Jennie and I walked to the end of Broad Street and joined the growing crowd of onlookers on the piers. Six ships sat at anchor in a line that stretched from the Exchange Battery to the opposite shore. Sailors boarded one and opened the seacocks to allow water to flood the hull. With kegs of explosives placed where they would best weaken the structure of the vessel, they set fire to the ship and evacuated into a rowboat.

The crowd waited in anticipation, and when the powder ignited, the force of the blast nearly knocked me off my feet. Ears ringing, I covered my head as splintered wood and flaming debris rained all around us. The woman next to me brushed some red-hot embers off my skirt, and Jennie checked to make sure neither of us was smoldering. Within minutes, the ship listed in the shallow water, creaking and groaning as what remained of the hull slipped below the surface. The protruding masts remained as a warning of the wreck.

If destroying half a dozen serviceable vessels was the best way to defend our harbor, I reckoned Charles Town must be destined to fall—and every civilian within range of the British artillery pieces would be in constant danger, whether they lived in a mansion house or one of the refugee tents.

The distant thunder of guns we'd heard during the battle at Stono Ferry had only lasted an hour. If siege was imminent, we could be under fire for days or even weeks. As I walked on, my resentment simmered. Peter had left us to contend with the danger alone.

At St. Philips, a woman in the food line whom I'd met the week before looked pale and glassy-eyed, and held her infant in a grip so slack I feared she would drop him. Her little daughter coughed as she clutched her mother's skirts.

"You're Missus Turner, aren't you? I'm Missus Wilkinson."

When the woman nodded, I guided her out of the line. "You should go to the hospital."

She coughed tiredly. "I have no money for a doctor."

"It's an indigent hospital." When I picked up her daughter, the poor thing sagged against my shoulder. "I promise they will have beds for you."

Just then the girl raised her head and gave a mighty sneeze, and I wiped her spittle off my face with my sleeve. "It's going to be all right, sweetheart."

It was a short walk, but Mrs. Turner paused to rest so often that we made slow progress. Once she stumbled and I feared she would drop the baby. "Let me take him so you don't tire yourself." As she handed him over, I noticed a rash on her arm.

She scratched at it. "Fleas. They're everywhere in the refugee camp."

When we reached the hospital, I stayed to help with the little ones until they were assigned cots on the women's ward.

Most of the muffled feeling in my ears had gone, and when I started home, the ringing of the noon bells hurt. Polly Brewton was out, in the company of a tall soldier in a mended Continental uniform. She beckoned me over and introduced us. "Eliza Wilkinson, meet Corporal Thomas Foster. He's one of the brave lads of the Virginia Line who marched all the way here from North Carolina."

"Your servant, madam." He offered me his other arm. "Won't you take a turn around the bay with us?"

Polly winked. "It's your duty as a patriot, Eliza."

I took his arm, and as we began our promenade, he said to me, "Every man in my unit would relish a chance to go walking with a lady as pretty as you, madam. Shall I bring one along next time?"

Still too disconsolate over Peter's departure to warm to the corporal's flattery, I shrugged.

Despite the row of sunken ships, the British naval vessels easily took control of the harbor, and General Clinton's forces moved into position above the city. In a single night, his men dug a siege line a thousand yards from the defense works at the Neck. Both sides launched intermittent sorties, and as the Redcoats advanced, digging trenches closer and closer, our riflemen took places on the ramparts and picked off anyone who dared to show himself.

The tension between the two armies hung over the city like a massive storm cloud on the horizon. Mrs. Porcher and Mary, who had been so happily caught up in wedding preparations, now cowered inside the house, afraid to go out.

The first time a shell exploded close to the house, I feared Mrs. Porcher would lose her reason. After days of listening to her exhorted prayers, tears, and angry criticism of General Lincoln, a letter arrived from her husband.

She clasped it to her bosom. "Père has sent for us, Mary. Now we'll get away from this place and all will be well." Hands shaking, she broke the seal and read aloud:

> *"Madam: Under no circumstances are you to leave Charles Town, where you are under the protection of our army. The roads and waterways that lie between us are infested with the enemy and highwaymen dressing as soldiers and robbing unsuspecting travelers, especially unprotected women.*
>
> *I am, Madam,*
>
> *Your devoted husband,*
>
> *SP"*

Mr. Porcher's order to stay in Charles Town brought more dramatic, blubbering tears and irrational behavior from my hostess.

Though it was only mid-April, summer-like heat and humidity settled over the city, yet Mrs. Porcher insisted we keep the windows closed and the drapes drawn, as if this would somehow shelter us from the raining artillery shells.

Plagued by headaches that I attributed to the oppressive heat inside the house, I escaped to the shady garden whenever I could. At night I lay awake with my windows open in defiance of my hostess's wishes, hoping for a cool breeze as the bombardment continued, unrelenting, into the wee hours.

One morning the shelling stopped. We were so accustomed to hearing an explosion every few minutes that we all fell silent, waiting, until Mary asked, "Is it over?"

None of us had an answer. Minutes passed, and still we heard nothing.

"Praise be!" cried Mrs. Porcher. "I'm going back to bed."

"So am I!" Mary pushed back her chair.

I felt none of their jubilation, only worry about what this change portended. While I assisted Dr. Mosse that day, I overheard another doctor say that the ceasefire meant terms of surrender were under consideration. The thought of surrendering to the British turned my stomach, and I was almost relieved when the bombardment resumed the following afternoon.

British troops and partisan militia roamed the countryside at will, stealing from the farmers who normally supplied the city markets, and by the third week of April, food and supplies ran short. Even as we worried about how to feed ourselves, those of us on the St. Philips committee went house to house to beg for donations for the poor.

Desperate to feed his troops, Lincoln ordered his men to force their way into civilian homes and take whatever they could find. This sparked panic and resentment among the already beleaguered citizens. The solidarity we felt with our defenders when the siege began soured as they, too, threatened our survival.

In the midst of this Governor Rutledge fled the city. The Privy Council members who remained behind instructed Lincoln not to surrender, claiming the citizens of Charles Town were prepared to fight to the last man.

The bombardment continued, Mrs. Porcher and Mary grew so overwrought that Jennie began lacing their evening drinks with laudanum so they would sleep.

I allowed myself no such indulgence, and doggedly kept up my committee work. After another afternoon spent in futile attempts to procure food and supplies, I was carrying my empty market basket home, head pounding, when Corporal Foster fell into step with me. "You must allow me to escort you home, Missus Wilkinson."

He was so friendly that I made the effort to smile as I took his arm. "I had no fewer than four doors shut in my face today while foraging." We'd only gone a block when I had to stop. "Could we rest here a moment? It's so hot."

His look changed to one of concern. "I lived most of my life in Plymouth, Massachusetts, and I don't care for the winters there, though I'm not sure I'd trade them for your summers. I should think you'd be used to the heat."

"It doesn't usually bother me." The words were barely out of my mouth when I felt dizzy and my stomach heaved. I pulled away from him, dropped my basket, and vomited into the gutter.

He supported me until nothing more would come up. I was so mortified to have done such a thing on the street that I stifled a sob and heaved again.

"Steady, now. Can you walk the rest of the way home or shall I carry you?"

"I can walk. I'm sorry to be such a ninny." Eager to prove I was fine, I stood up, but when he let go of me to retrieve my basket the world tilted. I made a desperate grab for his arm, missed, and the brick pavement rushed to meet me. Then everything went black.

19

A roar a hundred times louder than thunder jerked me from sleep, shaking the house until the windows rattled in their frames. Disoriented, I blinked in the darkness. Church bells began to ring in a muted, discordant cacophony.

"Jennie!" My voice sounded faint and raspy. When she did not appear I tried to sit up and the room spun, reminiscent of the time I drank too much rum punch at a party. I sank back against the pillows and waited for the dizziness to pass.

As my eyes adjusted, I made out thin strips of light peeking in near each window. Mustering all my strength, I pushed back the covers and put my feet on the floor one at a time. I clung to the bedpost until I was certain my unsteady legs would support me, and then walked a drunken man's path to the nearest window, where the simple task of drawing back the portieres sapped my strength. I sagged against the wall and squinted in the bright sunlight as I looked outside, where black smoke billowed in the air on the Ashley River side of the city.

"What are you doin' out of bed?"

I turned from the window, a hand pressed to my throbbing forehead. "The British have fired the town! Help me dress. We must evacuate."

"No'm, Letty just come in from the market. Folks says the British soldiers done blow up the magazine in Harleston." She supported me back to the bed.

"There are Redcoats in Harleston?"

"Yes'm. Redcoats occupy Charles Town now."

"When did we surrender?" Tears welled in my eyes. "What's the matter with me? Why am I so weak?"

"You got smallpox." Though her voice betrayed nothing, I saw the worry etched on her tired face.

I touched the clusters of sores on my face and choked back a sob. "Will you bring me a looking glass?"

"No'm. You don't need no lookin' glass." She covered the one that hung over my dressing table with a towel and closed the drapes, plunging the room back into darkness. "I been puttin' goldenseal poultices on your face and arms every day, so you healin' up real good. Now just rest."

"What day is it?"

"May sixteenth."

"I've been insensible for more than two weeks?"

As I wrestled with this new information, Mrs. Porcher came to the open doorway, breathless with excitement. "Oh! You're awake! Have you heard? Hundreds of people were blown to bits! It's a terrible tragedy."

I turned my head toward her and that small movement set the room spinning again.

She went on. "They say the charred arms and legs of the unfortunate dead are scattered for blocks."

Jennie cleared her throat, but my hostess was too eager to be deterred.

"The workhouse, the jail, and the barracks near the magazine were all destroyed." She paused. "One of the brothels, too, good riddance."

I draped an arm over my eyes. "I don't understand. How could that happen?"

Jennie spoke up. "Letty say the Redcoats brought our soldiers' muskets to the magazine and piled them up in the yard—mos' of them was still loaded."

"Yes!" Mrs. Porcher agreed. "One musket discharged and ignited the powder, and set off the rest of them. The force of the explosion flung a man against the steeple at St. Michaels, and they say you can see where his body dented the copper cladding."

A sob escaped my lips, and Jennie put her hands on her hips and faced Mrs. Porcher. "That's enough. You upsetting Miz Eliza and she need to rest now, ma'am. Please leave her be."

Mrs. Porcher harumphed, but she did as Jennie asked. When she was gone I asked, "I must know. Is there any news of Peter?"

"No'm, not that I heard."

"When he left, he didn't tell me where he was going. Now I have no idea how to get news of him. If he cared for me as much as he claimed–" my voice trailed off.

"Everybody got secrets. I 'spect if he could've told you he would. Anyway, ain' nobody got word of their men yet."

I sighed. "Thank you for tending me."

She stroked my hair as if I was a child. "Hush. You know I won't let anything happen to you." She shut the door behind her, and I closed my eyes.

Just as before the siege, rumors ran rampant through the city in the wake of the capitulation. The next day I sent Jennie to Lucretia Sarrazin with a note begging her to visit. I trusted her to tell me what transpired while I was ill, and feared I'd go mad if I had to hear all the news from Mrs. Porcher.

Jennie set a chair near my bed for Lucretia and brought up a tray with a pot of hyperion tea and cakes.

I reached out to my friend. "It's good of you to come."

"Not to worry, dear. I was inoculated a few years ago, so there's no danger. We have been praying for your speedy recovery."

As soon as Lucretia took a sip of tea, I began to pepper her with questions. "Where are the rest of the Continentals and the militia? When are they coming to liberate us?"

"I'm afraid the whole of the Continental Army has been captured. General Lincoln was paroled to his home in Massachusetts, and Congress gave General Gates command of the southern theater."

"But if we have no army, who does General Gates command?"

"Soldiers remain in the north, dear, but there are almost none nearby. The *Gazette* said over five thousand were captured in Charles Town, the most in any battle of this war. The Redcoats have garrisoned the city, and can you imagine–General Clinton and Lord Cornwallis are using Rebecca Motte's house as their headquarters." She shook her head. "Our defeat left the rest of the state vulnerable. Loyalist newspapers report British troops have subdued all the rebel strongholds in the backcountry."

"What does that mean? Have we lost the war?" I could not bear the thought of the Union Jack flying over Charles Town where the Stars and Stripes should be.

"I daresay our war has just begun. Our conquerors agreed to recognize our men as prisoners of war, but still they treat them horribly–crowded conditions and spoiled rations. Those on the prison ships in the harbor have the worst lot of all. We hope things will get better after the militia are paroled and released outside the city."

"When are they to be released? I must go." If either of my brothers or Peter were among the captured, there was a chance I might be able to see them and speak to them.

"You ain't goin' nowhere." Jennie was firm.

I turned to Lucretia. "Will you go and take Jennie with you? Please. She is the only one who will recognize my brothers and my–that is to say, the son of my hosts–if they are among the parolees."

"Of course I will, dear." She rose and patted my hand. "I hope we will bring back news of your loved ones."

On the afternoon of the militia's release, I waited impatiently for Jennie's return, and when she came to my chamber I demanded, "Tell me! Did you see anyone we know?"

"I din' see your brothers or Mist' Peter—but I saw Mist' McCall."

"Hext? You saw him in the crowd?"

"No'm. He done go out with the militia. Most of the men looked tired and sad, but he was wavin' to folks and grinnin' from ear to ear."

"After he disdained to serve in the militia, he used them to flee the city."

"I'm sorry, Eliza. Can I bring you anything?"

I shook my head.

"All right, then. Doctor Chapman 'spectin' me at the hospital."

As she left I stifled a sob, too weak to fight the waves of resentment and worry that crashed over me. Hext had walked away from the occupied city with a wink and a smile while worthier men, perhaps even Peter, my brothers, and the soldiers I'd befriended during the Season, either paid with their blood or languished as prisoners of war.

And what of my father? I had not received a single letter from my family in these many months.

As I lay there brooding, Mary came to the doorway. "I'll keep you company for a while if you like." Without waiting for a response, she shut the door and sat in the wing chair across the room. "I wanted you to know I've taken over your shifts at Saint Philips."

"Has your mother changed her mind about charity work?"

She gave an uncharacteristic scoff. "Of course not. I told her of my intentions, and Mister Henderson assured her he would escort me to the church and back, so Maman could not object.We don't have as many people to feed as you did before the siege. Lucretia says many of the new refugees are Loyalists, and they tend to seek aid from the British authorities."

"Mister Henderson is not in any danger at present?"

"No, for he was not involved in the fighting, and owns no property in Charles Town. As a private citizen, he was paroled immediately. Now there's only the matter of the wedding. Maman cannot decide whether to have the ceremony at the French Protestant Church here or to wait until it is safe to travel and have it at home."

"What do you and Mister Henderson want?"

She blushed. "We don't care about the details. We only want to begin our life together. The planning is more for Maman's pleasure than for ours."

"I'm truly happy for you, Mary." She and I had come to Charles Town for the same purpose, both harboring our own fears and reservations. She had triumphed, whereas once again my life was in ruins.

20

❧

In the days that followed, melancholy took hold of me and most of the time I feigned sleep so I wouldn't have to speak to anyone. After the last of my pustules scabbed over, Jennie refused to let me wallow any further. She prodded me out of bed and into the chair for short periods, but still I was slow to recover. Then one morning she brought my breakfast tray and opened the portieres, flooding the room with sunlight.

I squinted. "I'm not hungry."

"Yes you is." She patted her apron pocket. "A letter come for you this morning."

I felt my first surge of hope and pushed myself up to sit. Peter had promised to write if he could, or maybe a letter from my family had somehow made it into the garrisoned city. "Give it to me now, please. I promise I'll eat." I opened it and read the single, tattered page.

May 1780

*Aboard the Pack Horse, also known as
Willful Murder*

Friend Eliza,

165

Please accept our hearty well wishes as you recover from the smallpox.

As soon as you are able, we invite you to join us for tea. You may find us in good accommodations, aboard the finest prison hulk in the harbor.

We will be pleased to entertain you and any congenial ladies who care to accompany you, though we do not lack for companionship if you count the rats, bedbugs, and lice.

How does Charles Town fare? We beg to know the state of the war. Since we were taken we have heard that Philadelphia has fallen, our troops in the north have laid down arms and surrendered, and General Washington has been killed. Doubtless the Redcoats are telling us stretchers to break our will, but we cannot be sure what is truth and what is falsehood.

Despite it all, we have no serious ailments and count our blessings that no one is shelling us at the moment.

Come with all haste!

Our kindest regards,

*James Kennan, Henry Kennan, Samuel
Ash, Edward Hall, Esquires*

My friends were alive, and their letter's light-hearted tone cheered and shamed me in equal measure. Imprisoned soldiers needed the company of friends to cheer their gloomy hours, and I would honor their request to visit without delay.

When Jennie returned to my chamber to take the tray, she found my plate scraped clean and me half-dressed, clutching the back of a chair for support.

"What do you think you're doing?"

I regarded her with defiance. "I've been invited to tea on one of the prison ships."

"You still too weak to walk across the room by yourself. You ain't leaving this house to go visitin' on no prison ship."

Too spent from exertion to argue, I let her help me back to bed, but the desire to see my friends revived my spirits. My appetite returned, and as I grew stronger I took short walks in the garden. On the day Jennie judged me fit to make a trip to the harbor, I sent a note to Lucretia. If anyone would know how to arrange such a visit, it was she.

The following afternoon, I was out of bed, dressed, and reading in my chamber when I heard someone outside call my name. From my window I saw Lucretia and Polly in the Sarrazins' phaeton. Polly was dressed in widow's weeds.

I leaned on the sill and called down. "You're welcome to come up to the house."

Polly waved a piece of parchment at me. "Hurry Eliza, and come out! We have a pass to visit the *Pack Horse*."

"I'll be ready in two shakes." I turned from the window to find Mrs. Porcher standing behind me.

"What in the world is that young woman about, shouting in the street when she is in mourning? She has no sense of decorum. You may not go anywhere with her."

"Indeed I shall. They are my ride to the harbor." I ignored her sputtering indignation and pulled the towel away from the looking glass. The redness and scars on my face gave me an unpleasant start, but I was not so vain that they destroyed my confidence. I stared at my reflection. "My nose is honored with thirteen spots. As much as I revere the number, I hope they won't pit, for I would not choose to have such a conspicuous mark." I tied my hat under my chin and turned to go. "I'll be home before supper."

In truth, Mrs. Porcher was not wrong to criticize Polly's lack of decorum. Not content to ride quietly to the harbor, she waved her handkerchief and called greetings to people she knew, and when we passed Redcoats on the street, she threw pignuts at them. She had surprisingly good aim, and I giggled when one hit a soldier sharply on the back of the neck, and he slapped the spot as if he'd been bitten by a mosquito.

"Fix your viz!" Polly hissed.

"What?"

"Fix your visage, child. Don't give me away and spoil my fun." She kept a serious, haughty expression on her face as she hit another soldier on the leg.

"Polly, that's enough." Lucretia turned to me. "We are not visiting the prison ship on a lark, Eliza. We are taking on an important Christian duty. Our army's commissary department found it difficult to supply troops in the field, and procuring rations and clothing for the prisoners is an insurmountable task, so women's relief committees are stepping in to help. Ours will bring comfort to those incarcerated on the *Pack Horse*. As soon as you are completely recovered, I hope you will become a regular member."

"Of course."

When we arrived at the wharf we alighted from the phaeton and joined a group of a dozen women, some of them with servants carrying baskets, jugs, and hampers.

Lucretia addressed the group. "Ladies, though we mourn the state of our beloved city and her defenders, let it not be with despair. We must wish our soldiers well, sweeten their hours of sorrow, and arm them with resolve."

She presented our pass to a sentry, who inspected it minutely and then handed it back. "There is room for you ladies on the provisions barge that's headed out soon."

While we waited to go aboard, I asked Polly, "What became of Corporal Foster? Do you know where he is?"

"Yes, he's fine, and I am able to see him. Do you know he carried you home when you fainted on the street? It looks as though you are recovering well."

"Please thank him for me. He was very kind."

She pulled a handkerchief from her pocket and handed it to me. It was heavily scented with vanilla and orange blossoms. "Take this. You'll need it to help mask the odors when we go below."

I tucked it into the front of my gown as I joined the end of the line. One by one we climbed down the short ladder from the dock, grasped the ensign's hand, and stepped aboard the barge. When I sat on a wooden plank seat, one of the women passed me an earthenware jug of hot coffee wrapped in towels. The soldiers pulled at the oars, and I heard the clink of china in Lucretia's hamper as we bobbed in the choppy harbor.

The breeze was not cooling enough to make the trip comfortable. The barge smelled of the rotting provisions meant to feed our soldiers, and I fought back waves of nausea while the women with parasols struggled to keep them from blowing overboard.

The prison ships in the harbor were easy to identify, for the rudders, sails, and rigging were removed and iron bars put over the gunports and ventilation holes. When we came upon the *Pack Horse's* starboard side, the stench of damp, disease, and human waste wafted from the hulk. The ensign tied up the barge and stepped onto a small, floating dock, offering a hand to each of us in turn. Other soldiers offloaded the provisions, using a net on a rope and pulley to lift the crates and barrels to the ship's deck.

As I followed the other women up the steep gangplank, the smell from below was a thousand times worse than the rotting food on the barge, worse even than the pigs I'd kept in my chamber. It was a blend of every terrible smell I ever smelled with several new and awful smells besides. I gagged and shifted my grip on the coffee jug so I could bring the perfumed handkerchief to my nose.

Seagulls soared overhead, their hoarse cries giving voice to the sadness and outrage I felt for the prisoners held in this horrible place.

The sentries, who seemed used to the smell, took their time inspecting the contents of our baskets, taking whatever they fancied and stuffing some of the food into their mouths in front of us. When one of them pocketed some jerked beef, Lucretia spoke up. "'Be mindful of prisoners as if sharing their imprisonment. Hebrews thirteen, three.'"

When he lacked the good grace to look contrite, she scolded both of them like naughty children. "Your army holds these men in deplorable conditions. It is our Christian duty to feed the hungry, clothe the naked, and console the prisoners. The Bible does not say anything about feeding their jailers. Now, I'll thank you to leave those baskets alone and step aside so we can be about our work."

One of them took hold of her basket's handle. "We inspect everything brought on board." He plunged his hand into the basket, shoving the coffee cups about roughly.

When the sentries were satisfied, one of them opened a latticed hatch in the deck and gestured toward the ladder that led below. "You have an hour."

The stench on deck was merely a prelude to the horrors below.

The stifling heat inside the hold was made worse by the pervasive damp. As I climbed down the ladder I could already feel beads of sweat running from my armpits and down my back.

As my eyes adjusted to the dim light, I saw scores of captive soldiers crowded into the hold, the lucky ones perching on crates, barrels, hammocks, and benches. In the darker recesses, more men moaned in delirium.

None of them wore a full suit of clothes. Most were barefoot, and the gentle rocking of the boat sloshed a noisome mixture of bilge water and waste back and forth under a network of planks that served as walkways. Mosquitos kept up an unending whine as they swarmed over us all.

I could not imagine allowing any living creature to exist in such filthy surroundings. I breathed through the handkerchief until the smells from the ship became almost bearable.

Just weeks ago, these men had fought valiantly to defend Charles Town. Now, though they were living in steamy misery, covered in dirt and filth with matted beards and lank hair, not one looked discouraged. But oh, how it hurt my heart to see friends in this deplorable state!

As we moved among the prisoners to distribute the food and drink, I heard a familiar voice.

"Eliza! You're here!" I looked around, and saw two men waving me over. It wasn't until I drew near that I recognized the unkempt scarecrows as fun-loving Samuel Ash and Edward Hall.

I reached out to shake their hands, but Edward pulled away. "For God's sake don't touch us! We're crawling with lice." He jerked his thumb at the men perched on a nearby crate. "Especially those two."

"James! Henry! It's so good to see you." The Kennan brothers' red hair made them easier to recognize.

James winked at me. "Don't worry about the lice. How about a kiss?"

When I hesitated, they all roared with laughter, and after a moment I joined in.

"Please, sit." Samuel scooted over and offered me a crate to myself. I perched on the edge and tried not to cringe as the dirty water sloshed over my hems and shoes.

"Quite a step down from the Assembly Room, eh?" Henry asked.

"Oh, I don't know. Isn't it the company that matters most?" I looked around. "Though you were hardly exaggerating when you called this place the *Willful Murder!*"

All the men near me laughed.

As we chatted, the women who carried earthenware jugs of coffee poured servings into the men's tin cups.

"Sugar?" Lucretia followed with dainty silver tongs, and broke generous portions from a sugar cone to drop into each cup.

"Here, Miz Eliza." Her maid filled a cup from the tea service for me.

The men acted as though the lukewarm coffee was a rare treat. "This," said Edward, "is the nectar of the gods. We only get whatever's left over from the Redcoats' rations. Peas, rice, some watery soup, and dirty drinking water."

Samuel added, "They let us up on deck for an hour each day, and shore duty is a plum assignment. We draw straws to see who will go fetch water."

Dr. Mosse inched along the boards to join us. "'Tis a fine thing it is to behold you, lass. I see you prevailed over the smallpox."

"Yes, I'm much mended, though I still tire easily. I didn't realize you were on board, sir."

"We're lucky to have the doctor with us." Samuel pulled a rip in his tattered shirt together. "Tell the truth. Have we lost the war?"

"No, of course not." I was glad to be able to dispel that rumor. "The British hold Charles Town, Savannah, and New York, but Philadelphia remains liberated, and Washington lives."

He breathed a sigh of relief. "That's good news. I try to believe there's a higher purpose to our suffering."

Dr. Mosse asked, "How do you all fare in town?"

I was determined to downplay our hardships too. "The Redcoats treat civilians well enough. They've realized they can't intimidate us and force our allegiance. Our dedication to the Cause, and to you, will never waver."

Another group of women moved through the ship handing a few pieces of scrip to each man. Henry saw me looking on curiously. "A peddler woman rows out every few days and sells sundries to us through the bars on the portholes." He gave the notes a rueful glance. "I never thought I'd see the day when I'd accept charity to buy tobacco and writing paper."

"I'll bring you some." I looked around. "You all must want for everything. Tell me what you need most, and we'll try to get it for you."

From above, one of the sentries rapped on the deck with the butt of his musket. "Time's up!"

I lingered while the men made hasty requests, trying to commit everything to memory, until I was the last visitor left.

"Come back soon, Eliza."

"I will, boys. As soon as I can."

My arms and legs shook with fatigue as I climbed out of the hold. On deck, I drew in great gulps of fresh air and then vomited over the railing.

Mrs. Porcher was waiting for me in the parlor, but she put up a hand to stop me from going farther than the doorway. "I can smell you from here, miss. I don't know why you persist—" She took a good look at me. "Gracious! That gown is practically new, and it's wet to the knees from being on that filthy ship! Have your girl take it straight to the laundry tub." She waved me away, but I stood my ground.

"The state of my gown is the least of my worries, ma'am. If I refused to go on board the prison ship to render aid to our prisoners, wouldn't I be complicit if they died from want of food or medicine? Aren't you concerned for the welfare of our men when your own son could be among them?"

"Peter left me a letter saying he was returning home to attend to the rebuilding of his house. He is well away from Charles Town. Those men are none of my concern." She waved a dismissive hand. "Hurry along and freshen up. Mister Henderson is coming for supper."

Whatever Peter had written to his mother was likely meant to spare her from worry, and I took comfort in knowing he'd trusted me with as much truth as he could share. From the way he was dressed when he departed, I suspected he was headed for the backcountry, where rebel skirmishes with Loyalist militia were said to be fierce. If tragedy befell him there, I might never learn his fate.

21

Ahead of our second visit to the *Pack Horse,* we collected the heartiest foods we could find for the men. We brought potted and smoked meats, rice and peas, and some garden truck someone's maid bought at the market in our baskets, along with honey and fruit preserves. But the sentry at the dock merely glanced at our passes before handing them back. "These are no good. Expired."

"I beg your pardon, sir, but they are not." The stormy look on Polly's face portended a tongue-lashing for the sentry, but Lucretia put a hand on her arm to silence her. We stood as one behind them, confident Lucretia would sweet-talk our way onto the barge.

She affected a look that was puzzled and hurt. "What harm can a visit from our ladies' committee do? We only seek to comfort the men and raise their spirits."

"Let's see the baskets, then."

The ladies at the fore surrendered theirs willingly, and the sentry sneered as he dumped the contents on the ground. "We're not doing our jobs properly unless those bastards die as fast as they used to desert."

A woman whose husband was on board gave a strangled cry, and the sentry smirked.

Lucretia put an arm around the distraught woman and faced the sentries. "The Lord will judge you for your actions." Then she addressed the group. "Come along, ladies. We shall return another day."

Polly fumed as she marched back to the carriage, and Lucretia attempted to soothe her. "Getting angry does no good. We shall prevail." Before the group parted ways, she spoke to the group. "Now we see the obstacles before us and can take steps to circumvent them. Ladies, if you come to my home in three days' time at nine in the morning, we shall prepare to make our next visit."

Polly and Lucretia were silent on the ride home. Lucretia's head was bowed in prayer, but Polly looked as though she was plotting mischief.

As I alighted from the phaeton, Polly said, "Be sure to wear something with a full skirt and plenty of flounces when next we meet."

After our first visit to the *Pack Horse*, I warmed to Polly, and realized her brash manner was simply fearlessness and a lack of care for what others thought of her. That drew my admiration, and now I could scarce contain my curiosity. What was she plotting–and what could a committee of women in party gowns do against the power wielded by the occupying British?

On the appointed day, I arrived at the Sarrazin home on Hasell Street to find the committee members gathered in the parlor amid laundry baskets and food hampers. All of us were dressed in gowns too elaborate for the dirty circumstances that awaited us.

Polly was missing, but Lucretia called the room to order. "The Redcoats can turn us away for any reason. If we bring too much food, they will steal it. If we bring nothing, we are also suspect." As she set her cup down with a delicate clink, someone gasped.

I turned to see Polly enter the room, clad in just her underthings. She gave a saucy grin and made a slow turn in place.

She had on wire-framed side panniers under her petticoats, which made her hips look much wider than her natural figure. She made an exaggerated pose with her hands on her hips, tilting the panniers in a way that brought giggles from everyone in the room, but when she spoke, she was serious. "Those sentries are just pups. Likely they have no idea what's under a woman's skirts, so they'll never guess how much we can squirrel away." She lifted the outer layers to reveal a row of canvas pockets sewn into the wires of the hoop, and a second tier secured with twine that hung at varying heights down to her knees. "It took a long time to balance the weight of the food inside the panniers."

She waved a hand toward a laundry basket filled with men's shirts, and said with mock seriousness, "It's startling how many households put shirts on their peg lines and then leave them unattended for hours at a time. It's no wonder a great many blow away and are lost."

One of the other women rolled a shirt into a small, tight bundle and tied it with twine, and Polly motioned to me. "Eliza's polonaise will do nicely. Come here and we will demonstrate how easy it is to conceal shirts in your overskirt."

I stood with my back to her as she pinned the bundle in place under one of the poufs and fluffed the fabric. "*Voila!*"

One of the women I didn't know clapped her hands. "Polly is devilishly clever, isn't she? I wouldn't miss this for the world."

Soon we were all employed in secreting food and clothing for the prisoners inside our gowns. Some strung twine through shirt sleeves from cuff to cuff, gathering them to fashion underpetticoats. Other women stepped into men's breeches, buttoning each new pair over the one beneath. Lucretia's maid ripped a small opening in the seam of her straw bonnet's lining, and hid muslin-wrapped bottles of medicine in the space.

When as many shirts as could be were concealed within the folds of my overskirt, I was too nervous to sit, lest some of them come loose.

I heard Lucretia ask Polly, "Which sentry will be on post?"

She replied, "I daresay the one who gave us trouble has since landed in the brig for fighting. He won't be a problem."

"How do you know?"

"I just do." Polly winked.

As she predicted, a different sentry accepted our passes and waved us aboard the barge. The smell was no less abominable than our first trip out, but this time all my awareness was focused on the contraband we carried for the men and the importance of delivering it without detection.

As we drew alongside the floating dock, Polly turned to the group. "Fix your vizzes, ladies."

I tried to look demure and empty-headed.

Lucretia, the first up the gangplank, handed a cloth-wrapped bundle to the sentry with a smile. "Some ginger cookies for you, young man."

He opened it eagerly and stuffed two into his mouth while the other sentry crowded in. "Shares! Give me some." As the young men wolfed down the treat, we formed a queue and filed slowly past. Those of us with baskets held them open for inspection, showing only small amounts of food.

In the week since our last visit, the prisoners looked thinner, and many of them coughed continually.

When we had all descended the ladder, Polly teetered along one of the planks and swung her skirts like a bell until the men near her leaned back to get out of the way. When she had everyone's attention, she raised them to reveal the bags of smuggled food, giving the men a scandalous peek all the way up to the garters tied above her knees. "That's as much as you'll see of me! Turn your backs, boys!"

The men obeyed, chuckling, and we all set about retrieving shirts, breeches, and food from each other's clothing.

With my arms full of the bundled shirts, I moved through the crowded hold, passing them out to any man who lacked one. I found my friends sitting together near one of the barred gunports, where the breeze off the water stirred the air.

Dr. Mosse, pale and glassy-eyed, looked as ill and exhausted as the rest of the men, and I suspected he was forgoing his own needs to tend to them. As soon as he saw me, he came over and asked, "Were you able to procure the tinctures I asked for?"

"Yes, along with some opium." I motioned to Lucretia, who untied her bonnet and brought several vials out of the lining.

"Thank you, madam." He drew me aside. "The men are dying at the rate of seven or eight a day. Many more will follow if our conditions here do not change. Can you not come more often, lass?"

"The sentry turned us away three days ago, or we would have been back sooner. We've brought a great deal of food this time and we'll do our best to get the medicines you need, sir."

"You can never smuggle in enough, lass. The men are growing weaker, and some are resigned to their fate. The Redcoats force us to carry our dead comrades up on the forecastle and leave them where the birds pick at their flesh. Once daily they dump them on shore, where a detail digs a shallow grave on the bank and hove all the corpses in together. It's indecent, unchristian."

James, who had been listening, added grimly, "Despite all that, shore duty is still a plum assignment. It gets us off the ship for a spell."

"I'd sooner stay on this ship than be forced to bear arms against my countrymen," retorted Henry.

"The Redcoats save that detail for men they think they can persuade to take an oath of allegiance, but we've vowed not to." Edward had dark circles under his eyes and his skin looked pale in the dim light, but he squared his thin shoulders in one of the new shirts. "We thank you for your favor, Eliza."

"Your country has not forgotten you, and we will not forsake you."

Samuel wore one of the smuggled pairs of breeches with his torn shirt. "You ladies may not have forgotten us, but I daresay the Redcoats believe they have us licked. Why should Congress care what happens to us?"

"Take heart, man." James glanced at his companions before he spoke. "We must hold firm, but Samuel is right. We won't survive if we wait for Congress to help us. During the siege, we vowed to escape if we were taken. We want to join Marion. We hear he's in the backcountry trying to drive the Redcoats out."

Edward agreed. "None of us want to take the oath. If I could get a few hearty meals under my belt, I'd be ready to get back in the fight. If we were being held in the barracks near the Horn, we'd be long gone, but we can't get off this ship without help."

"Tell me." I leaned in. "What have you reckoned?"

James said, "First off, the guards have no idea how many of us there are. They never come below, and they never call roll."

Henry nodded. "Every morning, they call, 'Rebels, turn out your dead!' and I thought to play possum and get carried ashore. Then I'd wait until their backs were turned, make a run for the tree line, and lose myself in the swamps."

"Trying to escape one at a time is no good," said Samuel. "They'll give chase, and if you get away, they'll make the rest of us suffer for it."

Henry gestured toward the iron bars on the gunport. "A healthy man who can swim could steal away on a moonless night. If we had the proper tools, we could loosen the bars and let ourselves out. I've been chipping away at the wood with a nail I found, but the work would go a lot faster with a couple of iron crows."

I nodded. "The drop to the waterline is just a few feet. Can you remove the bars without the guards hearing?"

"I could work on it at night. The ship creaks, and so many men groan with fever that it's never quiet down here."

One of the sentries walked heavily across the deck and my eyes fell on the lattice cover over the hold. He called, "Time's up!"

As we sailed back on the barge, I was so busy forging a plan I hardly noticed the beating sun or the stench of the putrefied food.

I wanted to know more about how Polly brought off her schemes, so once we were In the carriage I asked, "Where did you really get all those shirts? There must have been twenty."

"Twenty-five, actually. I stole ten of them off clotheslines. The rest I took from the home of a friend that was commandeered for a garrison storehouse."

"How did you dare?"

"How could I not? There are no rules of engagement in this fight, Eliza. The Redcoats have no concern for our men, and they make fun of our sense of Christian charity. I won't ask forgiveness for anything I do in the name of the Cause. If stealing a few shirts is the worst sin I commit before this war is over, I will thank God for sparing me."

"I don't judge you." I put a hand on her arm. "I want to do more, and I believe I know a way to help the men escape from the ship."

She put a hand over my mouth even though there was no chance of being overheard. "This is not a game. There are people involved who risk far more than we do. If you take rash action, you could ruin all— not just for you and me, but for untold others. Do you understand?"

I didn't, not fully. But I could not let that hold me back. I explained the plan, finishing with, "I don't know when it should come off, though."

Just then we passed a printer's apprentice posting a broadside announcing a celebration in honor of the king's birthday.

"Look at that." I pointed, but the carriage passed too quickly. "Oh, bother. Can we turn around?"

Polly shook her head. "Never mind, there's another up ahead."

This time, Polly asked her driver to stop, and I said aloud, "Fireworks and a flotilla. On June fourth."

22

I was right to trust Polly with my idea. She took charge of the planning and brought together individuals who could help us. Once she
revealed the extent of the operation, it was hard to quell my excitement as I worked my shifts at St. Philips and the hospital. One afternoon I returned home to find a note inviting me to tea at the Sarrazin
home. I'd spent the morning with Lucretia, and it was odd that she had
not mentioned anything about it.

I hurried upstairs to freshen up and change my gown, and when
I arrived at the Sarrazin house, a maid showed me into the parlor.
Lucretia, Kitty, and Polly were already there, in the company of an
older lady and gentleman.

Lucretia rose to greet me. "Eliza, this is our eldest sister, Marguerite, and our brother, Jonathan."

I bowed. "It's a pleasure to meet you both."

Polly patted the seat next to her.

Jonathan, a stocky, white-haired gentleman who wore spectacles
and a heavy watch chain on his waistcoat, cleared his throat and stee-
pled his fingers as he addressed me. "My dear, we invited you into our
circle today because you are privy to some plans that are soon to be
put in motion, yes?"

I nodded.

"Before we proceed, we felt it prudent to discuss recent events that may impact those plans. Have you heard of the slaughter of patriots at the Battle of Waxhaws?"

"No, I'm afraid I have not. What happened?"

"The Tory newspapers tout it as Banastre Tarleton's great victory over the rebels."

"My hostess will not allow any Tory newspapers in the house, and with the Whig-leaning papers completely suppressed, I'm afraid I am uninformed."

He looked at me over his spectacles. "I see. In the future, I recommend you find ways to stay current. Perhaps stop at a coffee house and read the paper there."

"Yes, sir. I will." His gentle reproach stung.

"We received a dispatch from outside the city that tells the truth of what happened." He unfolded a tattered piece of parchment, and began to read.

"'A detachment of three hundred fifty men of the Third Virginia Regiment commanded by Colonel Abraham Buford marched from Virginia for the relief of Charles Town in May. When Buford received word of the capitulation, he turned back to the north. He and his troops were pursued to Waxhaws by Banastre Tarleton, who had under his command six hundred cavalry and infantry.'" He looked up from the page. "Nearly two onto one."

He continued to read. "'Tarleton demanded surrender on the terms granted to the garrison in Charleston, which Buford refused. Tarleton attacked Buford's rear guard, and Buford ordered a flag of surrender raised and arms grounded. He expected the treatment sanctioned by civilized warfare. Instead, the ensign who advanced with the flag was fired upon and cut down.

"'Before Buford's men could ready their arms, Tarleton's forces fell upon them and hacked them to pieces with sabers and bayonets. Their pleas for quarter were in vain. Not a man was spared.'" He laid the paper aside, took off his spectacles and wiped his eyes with his handkerchief.

Marguerite also dabbed at her tears. "Once an army abandons the rules of engagement on the battlefield, what is to stop them from executing prisoners or butchering civilians?"

"Tarleton and his men slaughtered unarmed opponents." Jonathan looked at each of us in turn. "We have a duty to help as many of our imprisoned countrymen as possible to escape so they can return to the field of battle and continue to support the Cause. However, should we be detected, I fear the reprisal will be harsh for both soldiers and civilians. So I must ask you all. Do we proceed?"

Polly squared her shoulders. "The least among us are the least suspect. Charles Town's women must continue to resist." She turned to Jonathan. "I say we carry on."

I looked around the room at the other nodding heads. The horror of the British atrocities and the reprisals we could expect for daring to resist had not led the other women to despair. Instead, it raised their fighting blood and determination. I gave my assent as well.

True to my promise to Jonathan, I added visits to different coffee houses to my daily rounds to I could keep up with news in the Tory papers.

On our next visit to the prison ship, we brought food and plenty of scrip for the peddler's boat. Lucretia brought more cookies for the sentries, but they seemed wary of us and refused the treat.

"Very well." Polly took back the bundle of cookies and ate one in front of the men. "They're not poisoned." She put the rest in her basket.

When we descended, the sentries followed us into the hold, something none of them had done before.

While the other committee members distributed the food and scrip, Lucretia planted herself before the sentries and lifted her voice in prayer. Polly led the other women in exhorting along with her while

I made my way to our friends. I'd hidden a note in a stack of scrip, and pretended I was praying over James as I handed it to him. "Read the instructions. Be ready in three days."

On the day before the king's birthday celebration, Lucretia sent another note inviting me to tea. Understanding this was code for a clandestine meeting, I hastened over to their house, wondering what news would be shared.

As before, Jonathan presided over the group. "I presume you've heard of General Clinton's recent proclamation. It nullifies all paroles granted in Charles Town and requires everyone to sign an oath of allegiance to the Crown."

This time I nodded along with everyone else.

"What happens if one takes the oath?" asked Kitty.

"Those who take it can be forced to fight on the British side. Those who refuse to take it may be imprisoned and have their property confiscated."

I went cold inside. "Every one of our soldiers could be forced to take up arms against America?"

"Theoretically, yes. I believe that's the intent—to bring the war to an end by forcing our men to fight against the Cause they pledged to die for."

Marguerite added, "Many avowed patriots with illustrious family names I will not mention have taken the oath to protect their homes and property from confiscation."

Polly scoffed and crossed her arms on her chest. "You mean the Skirvings and some of the Pinkneys. I don't respect anyone who took that oath without intending to break it."

Lucretia asked, "Civilians are considered paroled prisoners too, are we not?"

"Yes," said Jonathan, "but the proclamation says civilians will not be forced to take the oath unless they are arrested for seditious activity."

"It's just for men, not women," added Polly.

"Do not take this lightly," Jonathan warned. "Though we are civilians, we could be arrested and lose our homes and property. I caution you all—even you, Polly—to be especially circumspect. Now, if there's nothing else, let's enjoy our tea and be about our business."

In my note to the men on the *Pack Horse*, I'd told them to expect us late in the day, and we arrived at the dock just in time to board the barge that made afternoon stops at the prison ships. "Hurry now," shouted the captain, "else we'll leave you behind!"

"We apologize. Our tardiness could not be avoided." Lucretia spoke in a serene tone while the rest of us boarded the barge at an unhurried pace. "We thank you for allowing us to continue our good works."

When we reached the floating dock, I was first up the gangplank, where one of the sentries waited to inspect our baskets. As I stepped onto the ship's deck, I heard a woman scream, and turned in time to see Polly fall off the dock in a flash of underpetticoats and garters.

"Oh, dear! Quickly! Help her!" Lucretia cried. The sentry on the dock knelt and reached for Polly while the other women, who were in various stages of disembarking from the barge, fluttered and lamented and got in the way. Polly splashed and sputtered, skirts billowing in the water, just out of the sentry's reach.

"Young man! You must render assistance else she will drown!" Kitty beckoned to the sentry who was on deck with me. With a muttered curse, he hurried down the steep gangplank, but I moved faster. Bending over the lattice hold cover, I shoved the two cloth-wrapped crowbars I'd hidden in my basket through and Henry, who was waiting below, caught them. Then I pulled a vial from my pocket and poured a few drops of opium into the pewter tankards from which the sentries drank their ale.

When I returned to the railing, Polly stopped flailing, caught hold of the sentries' outstretched hands, and let them haul her up on the dock. Her wet clothing clung to her body, and as the sentries gawped at her half-exposed bosom, she pushed her wet hair off her face and gave them a radiant smile. "Thank you, gentlemen, for saving my life. The water was actually quite refreshing."

Unable to take their eyes off her, neither of the sentries paid attention to the rest of the women who, still fluttering and clucking about the excitement, filed up the gangplank. Two of them helped me move the lattice cover aside so I could hand my basket down, and then replaced it.

One of the sentries came back to himself. "Hold! We must inspect your baskets!" He hurried back up the gangplank, and everyone on deck opened their baskets without protest.

Once we had permission to go below, I gave the opium vial to Dr. Mosse. Then I handed out the hard-boiled eggs in my basket to give the men strength for their swim.

The return of the supply barge ended our visit. When the sentries called down for us to take leave, I kissed each of my four friends and Dr. Mosse. I lingered a moment longer with James, knowing it could be the last time we saw each other. He was a good, kind man, and if I'd never met Peter, I might have been able to love him. "I am sorry I was capricious during the Season. I did not mean to hurt you. I'll be praying for you."

"All is forgiven. After tonight, I shall always be in your debt."

As soon as we boarded Polly went to the rail that faced the mainland, something small and silver in her hand. She held it at chest height and slowly rotated her wrist several times before putting the silver object in her pocket.

In the carriage on the way home, I asked Polly, "What happens next?"

She shrugged. "There have been dozens of escapes since the surrender, yet the Redcoats claim the city is subdued and there is no resistance. We give them the lie and carry on as though we are none the wiser."

"What if the sentries suspect we assisted them?"

"They won't. They underestimate women. It's hardest to reconcile that we may never know if our efforts were successful, or what became of those men."

I changed the subject. "Have you seen Corporal Foster?"

She smiled. "Yes, I make time to visit with him often."

"How does he fare?"

"Same as ever. I warrant Thomas sees the whole war as a lark."

"And you don't? I daresay you enjoyed falling off the dock to distract the sentries."

"Of course I did." She laughed at the memory, and then grew serious. "The men who soldier suffer hardship, deprivation, and defeat, yet they will be the ones to drive the Redcoats from our shores. If I acquit myself well, no one will ever know what I've done to aid the Cause."

Later, as I sat on the Porcher's piazza in the darkness listening to the artillery salutes and watching the fireworks, I thought about what she said. It had been one year since my first encounter with the enemy. Their plunder of Plainsfield, great horror that it was, seemed like a matter of small moment when compared with the dire circumstances faced by our imprisoned soldiers.

The men who sought to escape from the *Pack Horse* could be even now making their way toward land. When I thought about the risks they were willing to take, I vowed to help as many of them as I could, and consider it a blessing if my actions on their behalf remained a secret for all of eternity.

23

Mary's wedding plans, halted during the uncertainty of the siege, now proceeded under full sail. Though she continued to do charity work at St. Philips, she and her mother spent the bulk of their time shopping and at dress fittings and we were rarely at home at the same time. Seeing the fabric swatches, lace samples, and bills of sale in the parlor forced me to contemplate how my own circumstances might have turned out differently, but there was no road back. All I could do was pray for Peter's safety and continue my own work within the city.

On our next visit to the *Pack Horse,* the three new sentries searched us so thoroughly I feared the authorities knew we had a hand in the escape. When I went below, I was shocked to find as many prisoners in the hold as before. I spied Dr. Mosse in the crowd and as I made my way to him, tears welled in my eyes, for he looked thinner and sicker than before. "I had not thought to see you again, sir."

"Och, lass. I had to stay and tend to the weakest prisoners. As you see, they transferred more men from the barracks." He glanced around and dropped his voice to a whisper. "One of the sentries drank his ration of ale after you left and fell insensible. When he would not wake, the other grew suspicious and came down in the hold. The prisoners overpowered him and held him while I dosed him with enough opium to put him out. I dosed them again in the night, and neither man could recall what transpired when their relief arrived in the morning.

"Soon as 'twas dark, the Kennan brothers loosened the bars on the portholes, and the men who could swim let themselves into the water. Sure and it was a grand sight, dozens of them drifting away, clinging to barrels that someone put in the water for them."

"Thank you for telling me."

"Mind, I can't say what became of them once they reached land. But we hope for the best, do we not?"

On the heels of General Clinton's proclamation came another blow: rebel property within the city would be confiscated. Mrs. Porcher took this news harder than the capitulation. She cried about losing her townhouse and declared she would not wait to be put out on the street. As soon as Mary's wedding gown was finished, they would go home. I supposed I must go too, though I worried about who would attend to the prisoners once all the rebels were driven out of the city.

I hoped I would have a few weeks before Mary's gown was finished, but just two days later, the servants were carrying baskets and crates to the foyer when I returned from an early hospital shift. I found Mary upstairs in her chamber, her trunks half-packed.

"Oh, thank goodness you're back, Eliza. Jennie is readying your things, and Letty is helping Maman. Mister Henderson has gone to his rooms to get his bags."

My words burst forth as if of their own volition. "I can't leave."

"Nonsense! You must."

"I have my committee work." I picked up one of her gowns and folded it.

"You can't stay alone with so many enemy soldiers in town, and I counted on you being at my wedding." She came around the bed to clasp my hand. "I never thanked you for everything you did for me during the Season. What a mistake I might have made! Instead, I have much to look forward to with my dear Mister Henderson—I mean, my dear Jeremiah."

"Peter will be so happy for you both."

"We're having the wedding at home, so he will be there. Are you sure you won't come?"

When I shook my head, she looked downcast. "I thought you'd want to see him, but I declare I hardly know you anymore."

To change the subject, I gestured toward the large, pasteboard box on the bed. "May I see your wedding gown?"

"Yes, of course. It arrived just after breakfast." She brightened as she lifted the cover off and folded back the tissue paper to reveal a creamy, embroidered silk, simple and elegant in its design. "I convinced Maman that ribbons and bows look better on a young girl than a married woman."

"It's perfect. You'll be a radiant bride."

Letty came to the door. "Miss Mary, Mist' Henderson waitin' in the parlor."

"Thank you, Letty." She turned to me. "Would you keep him company while I finish?"

"Of course." I would have an opportunity to speak to him alone.

He rose when I entered the parlor. "Missus Wilkinson, how nice to see you."

"And you, Mister Henderson." I took a seat and went straight to the point. "Have you any word from Peter?"

"Not since he asked me to watch over his family in his absence."

"I see. Did he tell you where he was going?"

He paused before he answered. "Did he not tell you?"

"Not enough to satisfy my curiosity."

"I'm afraid what little I know would not satisfy either–only that he was summoned away on a matter of great import."

"Mary believes Peter is safe at home and will be there for your wedding."

He shook his head. "That is unlikely. I daresay he knew he'd be called away, just as he knew his sister and I would make an amiable match. It was he who prevailed upon me to come to Charles Town in February, you know. He mentioned you, too. Quite often, in fact. I more or less assumed you and he would—"

"They're bringing the trunks down." Mary came into the parlor and her face lit up at the sight of her intended.

He rose immediately and bent over her hand. "I shall see if I can be of assistance, my dear."

I stood, intending to follow him outside, but Mary put out a hand to stop me.

"If you don't come with us, where will you go?"

"To Polly Brewton's." The idea was new, but Mary need not know that.

Her face fell. "Please say we shall always be friends. I don't want anything to change between us."

"Of course we will. I promise I will write and tell you all, as soon as I can. You must write to me about the wedding." I could tell my answer did not satisfy her any more than Peter's had satisfied me.

Jennie came to the parlor door. "Miz Eliza, your gowns ain't all gon' fit in your trunk."

"It's all right. We just have a short journey to Miss Polly's." The second time I said it aloud, it sounded like a reasonable plan.

24

Mrs. Porcher insisted the servants pack more than could fit in the carriage, and the rest of us stood by as they rearranged the trunks, crates, and baskets until she was forced to choose what to leave behind. With the carriage full to bursting, she and Mary held the box containing the wedding gown across their laps, and she declared herself ready to leave. As Mr. Henderson swung into his saddle and the servants took their places, a momentary surge of panic threatened to overwhelm me. I pushed it away and waved goodbye as they departed, though I was losing my only link to Peter.

The carriage passed four Redcoats coming up the road on foot. When they reached the house, one of them consulted a sheet of parchment and asked me, "Is this the Samuel Porcher residence?"

"It is."

Another of them brazenly looked me up and down and said, "That's a lucky stroke for us."

All of them chuckled, and I felt clammy sweat start in my armpits. I took a deep breath and remembered to fix my viz.

The first one went on. "We've got orders from the billet master to quarter here, Missus Porcher."

I felt a pang when he called me by that name. "I am not Missus Porcher. I was a guest here, and I am also leaving."

195

Another of the group spoke up. "Shame, that. Why don't you stay?"

"No thank you." I turned to the soldier who held the written orders. "If you will please have your men wait here until my maid and I finish packing, I would be much obliged."

He shrugged. "Our captain will be along shortly. We'll wait a quarter hour, and if that don't suit, you can make your complaint to him."

I hurried inside, going first to the library for Peter's copy of *The Wealth of Nations* and then up to my chamber where Jennie gestured toward the pile of gowns on my bed.

"Keep the indigo and the day dresses and leave the rest."

We worked with all haste, cramming the trunk full and wrapping the things that didn't fit in sheets. Though the soldiers entered the house when the quarter hour elapsed, none of them offered to help bring my trunk downstairs.

Outside, we loaded everything in a barrow the servants sometimes used in the garden. I tried to take one handle and help but she brushed my hand away. "We ain't at Plainsfield no more, Miz Eliza. You gotta remember to treat me like folks do in the city."

Chastised, I left her to manage while I led the way down Society Street. As we turned north onto Meeting Street, more squads of Redcoats marched by. Carriages passed, some filled with refugees like the Porchers.

On the next block Jennie slowed. "Which house is Miz Polly's?"

"It's the red brick with the columns. Right there."

She glanced warily across the road, and the barrow struck a loose brick in the walk and tilted precariously.

"Let me help you."

She jerked the handle away from my outstretched hand and the bundles spilled.

"Oh, bother!" I started to pick one up.

"Eliza, stop!" Her sharp tone changed to one of contrition. "Don't help me." As she loaded them back in an untidy heap that was sure to spill again, a tear slipped down her cheek.

"Jennie, what's bothering you?"

She lowered her voice. "You forgot what you promised. What about your people from Plainsfield? You said you was gon' free them, and instead you spent money on clothes and went to fancy parties to catch a new husband, except you don' catch one. This is a waste of time."

"Joseph believed gaining independency would drive America toward abolishing slavery. One path leads to another, don't you see? None of the workers from Plainsfield are in mortal peril like the men in the hospitals and prisons here. We must stay and continue to aid the Cause, and I won't hear another word about it. Wait here while I speak to Polly."

Stung by her criticism, I marched up and knocked on the door. A plump, middle-aged maid admitted me, and Polly, looking distracted, came into the foyer.

"Who is it, Teena?" She stopped in surprise when she saw me.

"I'm sorry to come by unannounced. I need to ask a favor."

"What is it?" She glanced past me as though she was expecting someone else.

A wave of self-consciousness engulfed me. "My hosts refugeed out of the city today. My maid and I need a place to stay."

"Why didn't you go with them?"

It surprised me that she would ask. "I wanted to continue my committee work."

"You should have gone. The Redcoats could seize this house tomorrow." She stared off into space for a moment as if making a decision. "You can't sleep on the street. Do you need help bringing in your things?"

"No, we can manage."

"If you do need help, ask Teena or Abbey. The guest chamber is upstairs, first on the left. I have something I must attend to." As she hurried back into the room she'd come from, I saw an untidy stack of papers on a card table before she shut the door.

This was off to a terrible start. I had not guessed living with Polly could be more uncomfortable than with Mrs. Porcher. I went outside, only to find Jennie and the barrow gone. I called her name, heading to the end of the block first in one direction and then the other, but there was no sign of her. Perhaps it would be easier to look for the barrow's tracks. I bent to examine them, and then followed them into the garden at the rear of the house. There Jennie sat, knees drawn up to her chin.

"Didn't you hear me call you?"

"Yes'm."

"I'll help you bring everything inside."

She rose reluctantly, and when I tapped on the rear door, another aging maid answered.

"Good afternoon. I am Missus Wilkinson, and this is my maid, Jennie. I'm going to be a guest of your mistress for the time being."

"I'm Abbey, missus." She dropped a brief curtsey and fixed her gaze on Jennie, who stayed half-hidden behind me.

I forged ahead as though I had not noticed. "Very nice to meet you, Abbey. We'll take up our things."

As we carried the trunk upstairs, I asked, "Do you know her?"

Her expression revealed nothing. "I think I might. From a long time ago."

The chamber, though large and comfortably furnished, had of course not been prepared for a guest's arrival. When we opened the windows, dust motes swirled.

I tried to smooth things over with her. "The room needs to air. Go down and get reacquainted if you wish. I'll fetch the bundles, and you can put things away later."

I left her there and went back outside, where movement at the corner of the house caught my eye. I peered around in time to see a hunched, filthy-looking man in a ragged suit of clothes open the street-level door and go in.

Though I knew there were vagrants about the city, as well as the ragged street sweepers known as scavengers who were employed by the British town sergeant, it shocked me to see one bold enough to enter a gentleman's home. I must warn Polly of the intruder.

Inside all was silent as I tiptoed down the hall. Then I heard Polly cry out and plead, "No, don't, I beg of you!"

A man's rumbling reply was unintelligible, and she cried out again.

I grabbed a heavy silver candlestick off a console table as I hurried to where I'd last seen her. Heart beating so I feared the interloper would hear it, I opened the door a crack and as I peeked inside I stifled a gasp.

The rogue held her in his clutches, his mouth fastened on hers. Polly struggled in his grip and struck his shoulder with her fist. My stomach churned with revulsion as I recalled my own terror and helplessness when the Redcoat corporal threatened me at Plainsfield. I raised the candlestick and charged, striking him on the back. "Leave her alone!"

In one swift motion he turned and pushed Polly behind him, and the papers stacked on the table scattered across the floor. I realized he was not stooped, but tall and powerful. My candlestick was a weak weapon against such a man, but I brandished it anyway.

Polly stared at me in surprise. "What in the world are you doing?"

I took another swing at him, and he had the audacity to laugh as he nimbly moved out of my reach.

"Eliza, stop! It's Corporal Foster."

As soon as she said his name, I recognized her beau in the tattered, dirty figure before me. I lowered the candlestick, too embarrassed to speak.

Foster grinned as he swept off his grimy hat. "I see you have completely recovered your health and strength, madam." He turned to

Polly. "I told you this disguise was a good one." As if to demonstrate, he slapped the tattered blanket he wore over one shoulder and raised a puff of dust.

She waved it away. "Thomas escaped from the barracks prison a few days after the surrender. He's been in hiding." She gave him a stern glance. "He's too much of a fool to leave the city."

He shrugged. "I have plenty of reasons to stay."

"It's an unnecessary risk."

"Soldiering was risky too. I would rather take bold and decisive action to liberate Charles Town from the inside."

As their words grew more heated, I turned my head first toward one and then the other, as though I was watching a game of shuttlecock.

She scoffed and folded her arms on her chest. "I daresay you over-estimate your skill. What you call bold and decisive is reckless and likely to end in disaster."

He responded with a cheeky laugh and took her in his arms. "You've never complained about my skill before, my girl."

She turned her face up to his. "So you'll heed what I said? We're in agreement?"

"Always. Now I must take leave." They kissed, and, certain they'd forgotten I was in the room, I slipped away to retrieve my bundles.

Polly met me at the door and helped me carry them upstairs. "Thomas has gone. We shouldn't have argued in front of you."

"I don't care about that. I want to know more about liberating Charles Town from the inside. Remember, the escape from the *Pack Horse* was my idea."

She set the bundle on the bed and settled in one of the overstuffed chairs before the hearth. "That was a one-time operation."

"But you do other such operations. You, Thomas–and the Sarra-zins?" The pieces of the puzzle came together in my mind, and I took the seat opposite her.

"We and a number of others, including my father." She gave me a thoughtful look. "The day we met at the hospital, Major Moore vouched for your character and your commitment to the Cause."

"He did?"

"Yes. I didn't see it at first, but you proved yourself by staying cool during the escape. It's one thing to be part of the network, but if you live in this house, you must understand it's more like a waystation than a home. People come and go at all hours. We'll have to train you to size up a situation so you don't attack any more operatives." She smiled to let me know it wasn't a criticism.

"So I may stay and be part of your network? Do you call it that because you catch Redcoats in it, like a fisherman's net or a spider's web?"

"I suppose so. First, tell me anything about you that could jeopardize what we do."

"I'm not sure what you mean."

"You told me about a Redcoat captain who was enamored with you."

"I can't believe you remember me telling you that. I haven't seen him since December, and I don't know where he is now. "

"Details are important. What about romantic liaisons?"

My face grew hot. "He left the city before the siege, in March."

"Now that your other hosts are gone, you are quite alone."

"Except for my maid, yes."

"Very well. I'll send word to Jonathan that we wish to see him tomorrow." She rose. "My father has a meeting this evening and won't be home for supper. You can summon your maid and finish settling in."

She left and shut the door behind her, and I breathed a long sigh of relief before I went in search of Jennie. On the main level, I wandered until I heard voices, and followed the sound into the dining room. I pushed open the swinging door to the butler's pantry, which smelled of the eucalyptus and rosemary bundles hung from the rafters to ward off insets. Jennie and Polly's maids sat around a worktable lit by a single candle, deep in conversation.

"They ain't been at they town house for more than a year. Maybe they dead." The door creaked on its hinges. Abbey stopped speaking, and they all looked up, startled.

"I didn't mean to burst in. Jennie, when you're through here may I speak with you?"

"Yes'm." Immediately she rose and followed me upstairs. As soon as we reached my chamber she apologized.

"Eliza, I'm sorry for what I said. You doin' your best. I think every-thing here gonna be fine."

Stunned by the change in her, I nodded. "I appreciate the apology, but you've always been free to speak your mind with me. I value your counsel."

"Yes'm." She sped around the room, putting away the last of our possessions. "Do you need help undressing? If not, I'll go now."

"I can manage. Goodnight."

I undressed and settled into the unfamiliar bed. Later, in my waking time between first and second sleep, I heard footsteps in the hall, and something bumped against the wall outside my chamber. I slipped out of bed and tiptoed to the door. As I opened it a crack, Polly's throaty laugh and Thomas's low response came from the dark-ened hall. My heart pounded as I watched one shadowy form become two. She took his hand, led him into her chamber, and closed the door.

I eased my own door shut, understanding all too well the need for comfort and companionship in uncertain times. If Peter was here now, I knew I would not turn him away. Loneliness and longing brought tears to my eyes as I returned to my solitary bed.

25

When Polly came downstairs for breakfast the next morning, it was clear that whatever transpired between her and Thomas in the wee hours had softened her usual hard edges. I smothered a knowing smile.

"What?" She looked at me over the rim of her teacup.

"Nothing. Will we hear from the group today?"

"I've already received word. We shall meet this afternoon."

Tea at the Sarrazins included the same group as before, with the addition of a young black man, who sat off to the side. Jonathan introduced him as his shop assistant. "Abraham is a valued part of our network and carries out a multitude of tasks. He is the one who released barrels into the harbor to aid the escapees from the *Pack Horse*."

"Pleased to meet you, Abraham. Doctor Mosse mentioned the barrels and how they helped the men float toward shore."

Jonathan turned to me. "If you wish to be one of us, *mon cher*, you take on responsibility for all of our safety. For this reason, you must agree to follow orders that may make no sense, and complete tasks that may seem mundane. You may not speak of what we do to anyone outside this room. Do you understand?"

"Yes, sir. I do."

"Very well. Charles Town is the main port for supply ships in the southern states, and it is the only place where cargo is allowed to be delivered during the occupation. It is valuable to the British, which makes it valuable to our side as well."

"How so?"

"Privateers capture enemy vessels, interrupt trade, and gain plunder and profit for the United States, while we observe the comings and goings of troops, ships, and individuals of interest. Our operatives keep watch for unusual occurrences or changes to routines which, combined with other intelligence, reveal a larger story. The information is then disseminated, verified, and dispatched to contacts inside and outside the city."

I nodded, and he went on.

"Do you know of Charles Town's Liberty Boys? Most of the original members were tradesmen and mechanics, for the taxes and restrictions levied by the British at the end of the French and Indian War affected our business. We staged protests and worked to keep peace in the city during those turbulent times. That set us apart from the Sons of Liberty in Boston, who are best known for daring exploits and sabotage."

He gestured toward Polly. "Captain Weyman is one of my most trusted compatriots. As a glazier, he can serve as eyes and ears as he repairs windows damaged during the bombardment. We also use ladies like yourself, who we find have an affinity for details."

"We can also move about the city without arousing suspicion," said Kitty.

Polly added, "No one gives women a second thought because we collect intelligence while doing what men expect us to do. We go shopping, to coffee houses, and take walks along the bay."

While she spoke, the parlor's double doors opened and a man entered the room behind her. Once again the change in Thomas Foster was so extreme that it took a moment before I recognized him. I'd first known him as a Continental soldier. Yesterday he was disguised as a dirty, hairy vagrant. Now he was clean-shaven and dressed in a gentleman's clothes, with his brown hair pulled back in a queue.

He sat next to Polly and poured himself coffee as though he hadn't a care in the world, and her eyes widened as she beheld him. "Thomas Foster! What are you about?"

Kitty exclaimed, "Corporal, I had quite forgotten what you looked like without your beard."

Lucretia added, "It will take weeks to grow it back."

"I don't need that disguise anymore. I took the oath of allegiance this morning. I am restored as a subject of the Crown."

Polly cried out in indignation. "Curse your stubbornness! After we agreed you would not!"

"I agreed to nothing of the kind."

"You did!"

Jonathan put up a hand for quiet. "*Pax*, Polly." He turned to Thomas. "Tell us more."

"It worked as we planned, sir—late last night I returned undetected to the barracks prison and this morning asked to be taken to the ranking officer on duty. My name was still on their roster–which suggests they have no idea how many Continentals have escaped since the capitulation.

"I declared my desire to help put down the rebellion and my willingness to do tasks none of the Regulars want, like guarding prisoners. The officer read me the oath, I signed it, and they released me." He put a hand on Polly's shoulder. "You were right. I can't stay in the city as a fugitive and risk being picked up by the patrols. I told the officer a convincing tale about how my heart had turned because I'd fallen in love with a Loyalist girl."

She crossed her arms on her chest and responded with an unladylike snort.

"I said I wanted to make Charles Town my home, marry that girl, and have lots of Tory babies." He paused. "Everything I said was true, except the Loyalist part."

Jonathan broke in. "Well done."

"They assigned me to stand sentry at the prison."

Polly punched his arm. "What happens when your superiors realize how many escapes happen on your watch?"

"I'll be discreet. Abraham and I have worked out several scenarios we can use to bring off escapes." He grinned. "You're out of sorts because you prefer me in the scavenger disguise. Don't worry, I'll roam the city as a half-mad vagrant on my nights off."

"Calling you half-mad is too generous."

He chuckled. "I return your sentiments, my dear. Now that I've made my report, I must be off." He rose, bowed to the room, and departed.

As soon as the door closed behind him, Polly rounded on Jonathan. "How dare you sanction such a risky plan! Did you two discuss this with my father?"

"Yes, we did. Over supper last night."

She grew more agitated. "So all of you stood against me?"

"We believed your judgement would be clouded by sentiment."

"Of course my judgement is clouded!" With an oath, she rose and stormed toward the door.

"Stop!" Jonathan's voice cut through the air like a whip. "We are not finished."

She whirled around. A mutinous look crossed her face, but she returned to the settee, and there was no anger in her voice when she spoke to me. "As I was saying before we were interrupted, you will be assigned routes to travel in within the city. Sometimes you will stop in a market or shop. Along the way you will pass sentries and guards. You must note their locations and when they change posts. Look for spots that could serve as escape routes into the tidal creeks and swamps beyond the Neck. See which ships come in and out of the harbor. Keep watch on the garrison storehouses and know the ones where security is lax."

"How do I record information without being observed?"

Jonathan answered, "Memorize everything, so if you are stopped and searched, you will possess nothing incriminating. Make a written report like this when you return home."

He produced a sheet of parchment for me to look over, and pointed out how to organize notes and use code names for designated observation points so operatives' reports could be compared against one another. "Do you understand, my dear?"

"I think so."

"Polly will accompany you the first few times and you will make your reports together. If that is all, let us be about our business."

When we left the Sarrazins' I linked arms with Polly, but we did not speak until we reached home. Then she slammed the front door to give vent to her frustration.

"Why do men ply us with sweet words and caresses and then think we'll overlook their foolishness? I daresay Thomas knows he can charm his way into anywhere, from my bed to a British prison. Jonathan encourages him."

Embarrassed by her admission and unsure how to offer comfort, I suggested, "Perhaps he charms you so he can shoulder the burden and spare you."

"I don't want to be spared! I was doing intelligence work long before I met him. I'm not content to sit at home and embroider while he fights for the Cause."

"I suspect he would not admire you as much if you stayed home and embroidered."

Polly chuckled. "It's a good thing. My first and only sampler was an absolute horror."

Over the next few days I integrated twice-daily walks into my schedule and learned the rhythm of the Weyman household. Abbey and Teena ran things without interference from Polly. Everyone followed their own schedule and attendance at any meal was optional, so I was surprised to come down to breakfast and find both Polly and a dark-haired, barrel-chested man in tradesman's clothes waiting for me.

"Allow me to present my father, Edward Weyman." After introductions, Polly laid an opened letter on the table. "This came into the city with other dispatches from our contacts."

My excitement surged when I recognized the writing. "That's for me, isn't it? It's from the man I told you about."

"Why is it written in code?" Captain Weyman regarded me with raised eyebrows.

I picked it up and blushed as I explained. "As a flirtation, and a way to keep the message safe from prying eyes. When he left before the siege, he said he would communicate in code if he had the opportunity to write. This is the first I've heard from him."

Captain Weyman did not look convinced. "This is most irregular. If you have played false with us—"

"I have done no such thing." My grip on the precious letter tightened. "You may read it after I transcribe it." I retrieved Peter's book and wrote out his message while they watched.

My love use caution thousand afford now intelligence Charles town

Peter

When I was done I read it aloud. "This is nonsense. What can he mean by it?"

Polly took the paper and studied it. "He could be using more than one code. The number sequences for the words *thousand* and *afford* are stacked atop one another. Has he done that before?"

"No. I cannot credit if it means anything."

Captain Weyman looked over Polly's shoulder. "Perhaps the words belong in a different order."

We rearranged the brief message a dozen times, but there was no revelation to be found. Peter's nonsensical message frustrated me to no end. If he was trying to convey something of import, I knew not what.

26

Polly and Captain Weyman's reactions to Peter's letter and its arrival through their intelligence channels left me frustrated and worried that I had lost their trust. Why, after all this time, had Peter wasted an opportunity to really communicate with me? Determined to prove myself loyal to the network, I resolved to study it again when Jennie and I returned from our morning walk.

Pleased by the way she'd taken to Abbey and Teena and our living situation, I suggested we visit some shops and the market while we were out. "I've never known you to spend your wages. If you take a liking to something, you should have it."

She considered that. "I ain' never thought about it, but I s'pose we could look."

"While we're here, you should learn to enjoy shopping."

We made the slow, now-familiar loop around the city, and on the way back, she stopped in front of a display window. "Could we go in here?"

"Of course."

Once inside the shop, we approached the clerk together, and Jennie asked, "May I see a lace fichu like the one in the window, please?"

The clerk glanced at me, but when I did not step in, he addressed Jennie. "Right away."

He laid it on the counter and as she picked it up, a smile played over her face. "It's so pretty, ain' it? I'll take it."

She brought scrip from her pocket, and the clerk made the sale and wrapped her package. As she accepted it, an older woman across the shop gave us a curious stare. I stood ready to defend Jennie's right to spend her own earnings, but the woman made no comment.

When we were back on the street, Jennie put the package in her basket. "I bought meat and vegetables at the market before, but this ain' the same thing at all, is it? It's better."

"It feels good to indulge every now and again. As I said, it's part of enjoying city life."

I had expected Polly and Captain Weyman to be out and about their business when we returned, but I heard heavy footsteps overhead. Curious, I went upstairs and found two Redcoats in my chamber. One was short and broad-shouldered. The other, who was tall and lanky, was still in his teens.

"What are you doing—" the question died in my throat as I saw their knapsacks and footlockers. They were moving in. As I stood in the hall, Polly came out of her own chamber and motioned to me.

"Eliza, could you please assist me?" I went to her and she shut the door behind us. My clothing, shoes, and personal items lay in a jumbled mess on her bed, with more draped over the back of a chair.

"They arrived with papers from the billet master an hour ago and demanded a room, so I moved your things in here. We can share for the time being. I sent Teena to Father with a message. He responded that we should not expect him for dinner tonight."

"Why?"

"The Redcoats claim they've subdued resistance inside the city, but in truth, they're still trying to stop it. They know Father's history of patriot activities. If they've placed those two here to spy, we must limit their access to him, and instead, we shall spy on them. I intend to search their things this evening."

"Can that wait until they are out of the house?"

"It is better done while they are here, downstairs and relaxed after a meal. Then they will not suspect."

This was an opportunity to prove my worth to the group. I recalled how Susannah had prevailed upon me to entertain Captain Sandford when his troops quartered at Island House, and I cast my eyes around Polly's chamber. When I spied a guitar standing in the corner, I went over and picked it up. "I can keep them occupied for a spell."

Polly took pains to make the billets feel as uncomfortable as possible at supper. She instructed Abbey and Teena to undercook the rice and burn the meat, and the maids took to the task so thoroughly that I resolved to visit the larder after the billets retired and find some more palatable food.

Corporal Shilley, the lanky youth, blushed whenever he looked at me. The other, Sergeant Blair, tried to draw Polly into conversation. "My condolences for your loss. Was it your husband, madam?"

"My husband has been dead for years, sir. I mourn for Charles Town and her temporary difficulties, and therefore I reject your condolences."

Her frosty response put him off, and Blair turned to me. "Where is our host this evening?"

I replied, "Captain Weyman has business with the Palmetto Society for the benefit of widows and orphans. Did you know he personally paid the funeral costs for more than fifty families this year?"

After that Blair lapsed into silence, and as the men picked at their food Polly gave me a surreptitious wink. When the meal was over, we put our plan into action. I rose first and went into the parlor. When Blair and Shilley heard me tuning the guitar, they came in and took seats.

I played and sang, and after each song Shilley applauded with enthusiasm. From time to time he exclaimed, "This is grand entertainment! You are quite musical, ma'am."

I sighed in a helpless, feminine way. "I must fill the time somehow. I could not safely go home after the social season, so here I remain in the midst of my enemies."

"Do not say enemies." Shilley looked distressed. "Every soldier in the garrison would protect and serve you."

Blair added, "Perhaps while we are here we shall convert you."

"That you never shall, for I am determined not to be converted."

He gave me an appraising glance. "It would be a shame to lose a lady as fine as yourself to the rebels."

Shilley tried to reclaim my attention. "Perhaps you shall convert me."

"I would not attempt to do so, sir. Now I bid you good night." I rose and left the room, guitar in hand. Polly was waiting for me in our chamber.

"I searched top to bottom and found nothing out of the ordinary, but I don't trust Sergeant Blair. Something about him rankles me. I daresay Shilley is sweet on you. Too bad he's such a simpleton."

I dismissed her observation. "I prefer men, not boys. He's far too young–and he's a Redcoat to boot. Where is Peter's book? I want to look at his message again."

She located it in the pile of my things on the bed, but when I opened it Peter's messages were not where I left them. I drew in a breath, and turned the pages until I found them at the very end of the book.

"What is it?" Polly asked.

"Nothing." She did not press me further. I set about transcribing the message on a fresh sheet of paper, but the result was no different.

That night I lay in the unfamiliar bed next to Polly, mulling over my suspicions. Someone in the Weyman household had handled the book and moved Peter's letters. Either Polly and her father did not trust me and had examined them without my knowledge, or the billets had searched our room and found them. Though I squirmed with embarrassment at the thought of Blair or Shilley reading what Peter had written to me, a love letter and a cryptic message I could not make sense of myself could be of no value to the enemy.

27

While I dressed to go out the next morning, I debated whether to leave the letters or carry them with me. If I was stopped, it would not look well to have coded messages with me, but neither did I want anyone in the household to take my only tangible links to Peter. In the end, I put them back in the book.

Jennie was due at the hospital, so Polly offered to accompany me. All was quiet in the house as we ate a hasty breakfast, but just as we put on our hats Shilley came downstairs.

"Going out, ladies?"

When Polly replied, "Only to take a little walk," he immediately turned around and ran upstairs.

I sighed. "As sure as you're alive, he is gone for his hat and sword and means to accompany us."

"Trust Corporal Shilley-shally to horn in where he isn't wanted," said Polly. "Let's be off before he returns."

We caught up our skirts and giggled like schoolgirls as we ran down Meeting Street. When we glanced back, we saw him walking at a great rate to overtake us.

"Come on!" Polly pulled on my arm. We turned the corner onto Tradd Street and ducked into Bedon's Alley, where we stopped to rest for a moment.

"Should we walk the assigned route if he's following us?"

She shook her head. "I say we go to the shops instead."

An hour later, we had a selection of yard goods and ribbons spread on the counter in a mercantile on King Street when he spotted us through the window and came inside. "There you are, Missus Wilkinson and Missus Brewton!"

He was so overjoyed to find us that I didn't have the heart to order him off, and as we left the shop he offered me his arm. "The pavements are uneven. You may get a fall."

"Thank you, but I don't need your assistance."

He looked hurt. "Must I turn rebel to escort you?"

Polly and I walked on without reply. Undeterred, he followed us into a dry goods shop where a group of soldiers loitered, some of them sitting on the counter kicking their heels. He did not speak to them, but took a post near the door.

I purchased some small items I wanted, and then I spied a roll of black-and-white striped ribbon on a high shelf. I asked the clerk, "Sir, please fetch that down and reckon if they are thirteen stripes."

A few of the soldiers who heard me scoffed.

The clerk plucked it off the shelf and handed it to me. "Yes, upon my word, madam, they are thirteen."

Upon close inspection, it was only a narrow black ribbon wound around a broad white one, and I shook my head. "It will not suit. You may put it back."

"Madam, you can tack them in stripes."

"By no means. I cannot have them tacked. I prefer my thirteen stripes firmly united."

My words rang out louder than I'd intended and every soldier in the shop fell silent, but the clerk laughed as he put the ribbon back on the shelf. As I signed for my purchase, the bell on the front door jingled, and all the soldiers snapped to attention.

"At ease."

A cold shiver crept up my spine when I heard the familiar voice. I squeezed Polly's arm to alert her to my distress and steeled myself before I turned to face Captain John Sandford.

His smile put me in mind of a hungry wolf. "Missus Wilkinson, it has been an age since our last meeting. I thought to reunite with you long before now."

"Captain." Surrounded by him and the other soldiers in the close confines of the shop, bile rose in my throat and the urge to flee grew so strong I had to fight to maintain my composure.

He looked past me at Polly. "This must be Missus Brewton."

She did not respond.

"Permit me to escort you ladies."

My mouth was so dry I had to swallow before I could speak. "I'm sure you would find the rest of our errands tedious, Captain. Corporal Shilley can see us home."

"Dismissed, Corporal." Sandford tossed the command over his shoulder and the lad departed in haste.

As Sandford demonstrated he could remove any obstacle between us, I summoned the clerk. "I've changed my mind. I shall take both the black and the white, if you please, in honor of the United States' alliance with France." The clerk made the sale and wrapped the ribbon for me, and then I faced Sandford. "Captain, when last we met you claimed to understand how royals think. Tell me, does it bother King George to face the rebellion of his former colonists and, at the same time, war with his ancient foes France and Spain?"

He opened the door and spoke through gritted teeth. "If you please." Once we were outside he offered his arm, but I drew away and kept my elbows close at my sides as we three proceeded down the walk.

Polly claimed to have errands in every shop on the block and we lingered in each one, debating our choices before making some small selections. Instead of becoming impatient and leaving us, Sandford hovered ever closer. When there were no more shops to visit, we had gone a short way toward home when my nerves prickled, sensing danger, and I realized I could not prevent him from learning where I lived.

I racked my brain for a way to be rid of him. As we passed the governor's house, he tried to draw me away from Polly and she stumbled, tearing her gown's crape ruffle on the wrought iron fence bordering the lawn. Rather than have the torn flounce trail behind her she pulled it free, tied it on the gate, and gave a dramatic sigh.

"Where are you, dear Governor? Surely the magnanimous Britons will not deem it a crime if your house as well as your friends mourns your absence!"

It was brash, even for Polly, and I expected the captain to react, but he held his peace until we reached home. As she took leave, Polly dropped a curtsey that had all the refinement of an eye roll. I started to follow her inside but Sandford put out his arm to stop me.

"A moment of your time, if you please." His smile did not match the coldness in his eyes. "It would give me great pleasure if you would accompany me to a supper at Frederick's Wednesday evening. There will be a musical program—"

"Pray do not continue. None of the ladies of my set fraternize with British soldiers."

His chest rose and fell, and his face twisted with displeasure. "It is in your best interest to treat me warmly, madam. I should think a widow, alone and with limited resources—"

"I am far from alone, sir. I'll thank you stay out of my business and let me pass."

He made as if he would leave, but before I could go in he turned back and produced a crumpled letter from his inside pocket. "I am billeted at a home on Society Street, once owned by the Porcher family. This arrived there some days ago. When you ordered me off, I nearly forgot to give it to you."

He made an about face and stalked down the stairs.

The letter was from my brother Frank. Unsurprised to find the wax seal broken, I shut the door and unfolded the single page.

May 5, 1780

To my dearest Sister,

It is with a sorrowful heart that I share painful news. Our beloved father, Francis Yonge, Sr., has entered his eternal rest, as ordained by Divine Providence.

He departed this life after bearing his suffering with grace and fortitude. We thank God that he passed peacefully in his bed, surrounded by family. May our Heavenly Father comfort us and provide strength to endure this loss.

With deepest affection,
Your loving brother,
Francis Yonge, Jr.

There was a postscript in our younger brother's spiky script.

Eliza, Papa's will says you now hold the note to Plainsfield and M. W. is to make future payments to you, so at least you

will have something. Unless you object, your
servants can stay at Susannah's until you
have a place for them.

Frank and me are near destitute. Pa's place
is broke down, and Frank's is near as bad. The
Redcoats came through again and burned our
crops.

Post here is suspended, and we don't know
when we'll meet someone who can carry this
letter. We've had no word from you since
you left in January. Write when you can to
establish yourself as a living heir.

Will

Tears blurred my vision as I crushed the letter in my fist.

"Oh, there you are." Polly came out of the parlor. "I was afraid I
was going to have to rescue you from your ardent suitor. You were
right. He's an absolute horror." Her teasing smile faded. "What's the
matter?"

"My father is dead. Word didn't reach me for two months." I
choked back a sob. "Sandford learned of it before I did." Then I began
to cry. "He knows where I live, and he's sure to come back. That could
jeopardize the network. Should I leave? Where will I go?"

"Hush." As she put an arm around my shoulders and led me into
the parlor I continued to sob.

"I wasn't with him when he passed. I haven't paid him the proper
respect. I should be in mourning clothes."

"If it makes you feel better, you may borrow a few of my gowns, but there are plenty of grieving women in Charles Town who either can't afford or refuse to buy imported fabrics for proper mourning clothes. You can show your bereavement with a ribbon or a necklace. Wearing colors doesn't mean you loved your father any less."

I sniffled. "That doesn't solve the other problem. I hoped to never lay eyes on Captain Sandford again. How do I avoid him?"

"Maybe you don't need to." She lowered her voice. "What if we turned the tables on him?"

"How?"

She thought for a moment and pulled an answer out of the air. "We could somehow trick him into passing false intelligence to the Redcoats and disgrace him."

"I wouldn't know how to do such a thing."

"We'll make him think he's stumbled upon a trove of intelligence by sending out dispatches that we want the British to intercept and prove that we're as capable as the men." She gave me a conspiratorial look. "Father says no one but the head of our network knows the name of the person who carries intelligence in and out of the city. I think it's someone the Redcoats would underestimate. Maybe it's even a woman."

"Do you think a woman would take such a risk?"

"Plenty. Rebecca Motte, my late husband's aunt, is one of the richest women in South Carolina—maybe the whole of the United States. All the wealth in the world means nothing without liberty. She could have taken the oath of allegiance, but instead she plays the genteel hostess while she and her maids collect intelligence to send to Colonel Marion."

As I considered this, another thought occurred. "The message from Peter came to me through the network. Can I send one to him?"

"You can't send a letter without knowing its destination." She changed the subject. "While we were out today a letter arrived today from Major Moore, inviting us to an Independence Day celebration at Haddrell's Point."

"They're going to celebrate Independence Day in an occupied city?"

"We haven't surrendered. 'This too shall pass.'"

"I don't know if I can bear to see Major Moore brought low in prison."

"You must! Think how it will cheer him to see us. July Fourth is no day for mourning. I believe I shall wear colors."

We spent the remainder of the afternoon fashioning black and white cockades from the ribbon I'd purchased and pinned them all to my indigo gown as a not-so-subtle symbol of defiance I could give the officers at the party.

I knew Polly was trying to keep me busy to take my mind off Papa and I blessed her for her effort, but nothing could distract me from the thought at the forefront of my mind.

Peter made contact with me through the network's channels. Therefore, why would a letter sent to him by the same method fail to reach him? After supper I went upstairs to write to him. It was harder than I expected to craft a coded message by searching for each word in the book, and I labored over the short lines for hours before I was satisfied.

Your house seized and family gone home. I remain in city safe for now. I understand why you left and long to see you again my love.

I put it in my pocket, intending to keep it under my control until it was on its way to him.

28

That night's sleep did not come easily and when at last I drifted off, fears I'd held at bay for months manifested in disjointed, nightmarish visions of Captain Sandford. I woke up drenched in sweat and afraid to go back to sleep and lay staring into the darkness while Polly slumbered peacefully beside me. At first light, I let my guard down and drifted off, and somewhere between waking and sleep I heard the click of a lock falling into place. I came awake in an instant.

Polly rose from the chair at her cluttered escritoire. "Good, you're awake. It's nearly ten, and we should leave in an hour to catch the ferry. Make haste."

I dressed in my indigo gown, which could have been a Mrs. Thompson creation, bedecked as it was with dozens of cockades. Downstairs in the dining room, I yawned as I poured myself coffee.

Sergeant Blair came to the doorway. "You ladies look especially festive today." His eyes lingered on Polly, who, instead of her customary black, wore a striped yellow gown.

I answered, "We're going to post a letter and pay a call."

"If you have correspondence to go out of town, I am bound to Columbia on assignment and would be honored to carry it for you."

Polly waved a dismissive hand. "No thank you, Sergeant. I don't want my letters read by Marion's Brigade. I understand their patrols have been attacking Redcoats traveling that road of late."

A look of uncertainty crossed the sergeant's face, but then he squared his shoulders. "I shall return in three days' time. Good day, ladies."

As soon as we heard the front door close, Polly chuckled. "The British fear Marion's men. I hope he falls prey to them."

The sky was clear and gulls rode the breeze as we made passage to the far side of the harbor, where we disembarked and walked through the village of Mount Pleasant. We soon spotted three brick buildings arranged in a U shape that looked much like the barracks near the Neck, and I wondered what kinds of conditions we would find there. Though I could imagine nothing worse than the plight of the men on the prison ships, would the British not punish the leaders of a rebellion even more harshly?

Before long we spied Major Moore watching for us at the edge of the village. He hurried to greet us. "Welcome! A happy Independence Day to you both!" Seeing him hale, dressed in a clean uniform, and free to move about outdoors dispelled my earlier assumption about how he was being treated. He kissed us each on the cheek and inquired after our fathers.

Polly spoke for both of us. "Mine is busy as ever and sends his regards. Eliza recently received sad tidings about her father's passing."

He took my hand. "My heartfelt condolences to you, my dear. Are your brothers still serving? Do you intend to return home?"

"Frank is dealing with estate matters at present. The news came so recently I have not made any plans."

As we drew near the officers' barracks it was clear their situation was far from the harsh and squalid conditions I expected. In the courtyard, some servants cooked over campfires, and a short distance away others stacked dried wood for the bonfires that would be lit at dusk. Several of the officers worked in shirtsleeves, carrying beds and chairs out of the barracks. Major Moore waved as we passed, and told us, "They're making room inside for dancing."

A round-faced officer passed by with his arms full of bottles. "The British haven't drunk their way through every wine cellar in Charles Town yet. My servants smuggled these in with my laundry."

Major Moore steered us away from the preparations. "Come, have a glass of lemonade and meet some of the officers' wives."

In a nearby shady grove, a group of women fanned themselves in the sultry heat, while the men played at quoits, ninepins, and cards. The atmosphere was more like a house party than any prison I had seen. After we took refreshment and exchanged pleasantries, he offered an arm to each of us. "Shall we walk along the creek?"

Though I took his arm, I thought of how the men on the *Pack Horse* suffered and starved, and my resentment grew until it threatened to bubble over.

Polly voiced what I was thinking. "Your circumstances are far better than the prisoners we visit, Major."

"The Redcoats separated us from our men to lessen the threat of revolt. Some of my cohort complain that the barracks are too small to accommodate all of us confined here, but I know it could be far worse. I daresay we have much to celebrate."

I spoke up. "The men on the prison hulks in the harbor think they have nothing to celebrate. They believe Congress and their country have forgotten them. Good men die on those ships every day for want of nourishing food and medicine."

"My dear, it is not within our power to intervene for our men. The British adhere to hierarchy of rank. They allow our servants to attend us, and to forage, fish, and hunt. A number of the officers imprisoned here have homes nearby, and so we also have the supplies left in their larders and wine cellars at our disposal."

I felt a twinge of guilt, but not enough to let the subject go. "We don't want you to suffer either, sir, but it's not fair. The enlisted men are held in such abominable conditions, and you get to have a picnic."

"We must meet each situation as we encounter it, and do what we can to make it better. Today, we celebrate America's independence, though we have yet to secure it. That comes tomorrow."

Polly added, "Tomorrow, we'll be back in the hospital or on a stinking prison ship, bringing aid to those who languish."

Moore looked sober. "We are lucky to have such dedicated and compassionate women as you to aid our soldiers. Believe me when I say there is not an officer here who would see his men suffer without cause. This is part of why we are fighting–so all men will have the same rights."

I understood we could not resolve this injustice today, so I changed the subject. "If I may beg your indulgence and I ask your advice on another matter, Major." We paused in a shady grove, and I told him of our encounter with Captain Sandford and Polly's plan.

He considered for a moment before he spoke. "I assume the captain has spent enough time with you to be aware of your saucy nature?"

"Yes. I never bothered to hide my disdain for him, and once I refused to kiss a miniature of the queen."

He chuckled. "Don't change your demeanor or you will raise his suspicions. Even though he wants to exercise control over you, he also wants to impress you. He shouldn't be difficult to manipulate." He smiled down at me. "Wanting liberty is woman's natural state, isn't that what you declared last year? With thousands of our soldiers imprisoned, it falls to women to fight for the Cause on our behalf."

"Eliza showed plenty of ginger when we encountered Captain Sandford." Polly relayed the story of the ribbon. "She was so bold that I decided I could not be outdone. I tied a strip of crape from my gown to the governor's gate in front of the captain."

"Is the trim on your gown fashioned from that ribbon?"

"Indeed." I removed a cockade.

He pinned it on his hat. "Thank you, my dear. What a capital idea."

Someone rang a bell to announce the meal, and we took seats at one of the tables in the courtyard. Servants brought platters of fried fish and oysters, bowls of rice and peas, and plenty of rum punch, brandy, and champagne.

When every glass was filled, the officer who had given the blessing called for a toast. "To General Moultrie and Independence."

Major Moore stood. "Life, liberty, and the pursuit of happiness!"

Still another rose and said, "The worthy palmetto tree." Some of the other officers laughed, but he retorted good-naturedly, "The Lobsters never had such a drubbing in their lives as they had at Sullivan's Island. Like the palmetto trees we used to construct the fort, we shall absorb the blows and resist the heaviest fire."

While we ate, the men at our table were eager to share their experiences. The one seated next to me said, "When they brought us here in May, their officers asked where our second division was. When we told them these were all the Continentals we had, except for our sick and wounded, they were surprised and admitted that for the numbers in our ranks, we made a gallant defense."

Another across the table agreed. "My men fought with heart, despite being outmanned and outgunned. I wish I knew how they fared."

After the meal, someone at another table clamored for entertainment.

A young officer stood and flung his jacket over his shoulders. "Did you regret missing the King's Birthday Ball? I shall endeavor to recreate it." He strutted around and performed an exaggerated minuet, bowing and posing as though he was dressed in a crown and ermine cape. Then he broke into a frenetic jig, and the other men roared with laughter and applauded.

"Let's have a tune," someone called from the rear of the crowd. "Music has charms to soothe the sore and angry heart."

Someone from near the barracks called, "I've a guitar. Does anyone care to play?"

"I will." He brought it to me. I took a moment to tune it and then strummed a few chords. "This guitar plays none but rebel songs."

Everyone laughed, and I sang,

Torn from a world of tyrants
Beneath this western sky
We formed a new dominion,
A land of libert-ay;
The world shall own we're freemen here,
And such will ever be,
Huzza, huzza, huzza, huzza
For free Ameri-cay.

When I finished, a cheer went up from the officers, who beat their tankards on the tables.

Major Moore said, "Missus Wilkinson is also going to favor us with cockades she has brought." He indicated the ribbon on his hat, and immediately a crowd formed around me. Polly helped me unpin and pass them along to the men.

Another officer spoke up. "What next?"

The one beside him drained his cup. "I say, nothing too proper! This is an antiroyal affair."

One of the officers began to sing *Yankee Doodle*, and as every voice joined in, some couples danced a lively polka.

When the sun went down, the bonfires and the scattered furniture outdoors evoked a scene from Captain Barth, as though we were castaways on an island. Music and candlelight spilled forth from the barracks, now filled with dancing revelers. A group of officers in the courtyard, all well into their cups, grew louder and more animated until one of them shouted, "Liberty!" He raised his pistol in the air and fired.

Another responded, "Or Death!" and more shots rang out.

"Huzzah for Free Ameri-kay!"

"Gentlemen!" A stern voice rose above the clamor, and everyone's attention turned toward General Moultrie. "Desist and calm yourselves, or I daresay this day will end with a visit from our oppressors."

The guilty parties subdued their merriment, but it was too late. In the distance, we saw bobbing lanterns moving about at the fort. Soon a squad of Redcoats arrived in a row-galley, came ashore, and marched on the barracks.

"Fall in." The officer in charge spoke in a condescending tone. "The women too." We stood in a line, and the soldiers trained their weapons on us while their officer took down the names of the guests present. Then he addressed us. "I am Captain Roberts, commander of Fort Arbuthnot. We did not object to you celebrating this day with music and illuminations, but discharging small arms is most irregular and improper."

"Captain." General Moultrie stepped out of the line to address Roberts. "The pistols fired in the course of our celebration were not meant as an outrage against you, but as a tribute to the cause which these officers have embraced, for which some of them bled, and for which all of them are now confined."

"General, I daresay it was naught but a pathetic attempt to glorify your defeated cause. I will leave it to you to keep order."

Moultrie nodded. "You have my word, Captain." He stood tall and proud, but it had to sting to be compelled to carry out an order from a lower-ranking officer.

The captain called his men to attention and at his command, they stepped off toward the shore and boarded the galley. As soon as they were away, someone sang softly, "*Huzzah, huzzah, huzzah, huzzah for Free Ameri-cay!*"

The party resumed without its earlier spirit of rebelliousness. When everyone grew tired of dancing we spent the rest of the night playing cards and talking.

The next morning, Major Moore yawned as he walked us to the edge of the village. "'Twas a rare evening indeed." He kissed each of us on the forehead in farewell.

Like a true Town lady, I retired to our chamber as soon as we arrived home, slept the day away, and woke to complete darkness. Disoriented, I fumbled to light a taper and then ventured into the hall. Captain Weyman and the billets' chambers were empty, but this was not unexpected for Blair was away and I recalled Shilley mentioning overnight sentry duty. As I proceeded downstairs the clock struck one. Polly, who was nowhere to be found, had likely gone to Thomas.

I was wide awake.

This was my opportunity to learn more about the network. I returned to our chamber and tried the escritoire's drawer. It was locked, but I imagined Polly would not let that stop her.

I worked on the lock, first with a hairpin and then a letter opener until I heard a click. In the drawer was a packet of letters tied with ribbon, all addressed to women. I heated the letter opener over the candle flame and used it to pry the seal off the letter on top.

The letter contained naught but chatty news and gossip, with the various parties' names redacted, as I was also wont to do when I sought to keep my correspondence private. Still, it was curious. I looked deeper into the drawer, under a stack of writing paper and some sealing wax, and found a piece of leather with small windows cut in it. As I held it in my hands, I saw bits of the open letter through the holes, and with a flash of realization, I lay it over the page and read the exposed words. A brief new message emerged.

What the message said was of little import to me, ignorant as I was of anything but my own observations on behalf of the network. I had found something far more valuable–a way to send my own letter out of the city where, presumably, it would move through channels to Peter.

My hands trembled as I resealed Polly's letter and inserted mine midway down the stack. Then I retied the ribbon, placed everything as I had found it, and used the letter opener to nudge the lock's bolt back into place.

29

After my late-night foray into Polly's locked drawer, I was too excited to return to sleep. I dozed off near dawn and slept until Jennie came to ask if I was ready to leave for the hospital. I rose, wooly-headed, and she helped me dress at top speed. As we dashed around gathering our things, there was a knock at the door. I opened it and came face to face with Captain Sandford.

"Missus Wilkinson, how lovely you look today." He pushed his way inside and shut the door.

"We were just leaving. We must go or we'll be late."

"This won't take long." He seized me by the arm, and I resisted as he pulled me toward the parlor.

I raised my voice. "Leave me alone!"

Jennie hurried into the foyer, but Sandford waved her away. "Go along, girl. I wish to speak to your mistress in private."

"Stay here, Jennie." I tried to pull my arm free. "Have they assigned you no duties in Charles Town, Captain? Else why are you free to pester me?"

"I only came to inquire after your well being, madam. You cannot know how it distressed me to learn you were arrested for inciting a riot."

"What?" I scoffed. "There is obviously some mistake."

"Do you deny you were at Haddrell's Point on July fourth?"

"I was there, but I wasn't arrested. I was visiting our imprisoned officers."

"I daresay I am concerned for your welfare, madam. You should consider the company you keep."

"I do, sir. That's why I prefer for you to go away."

He squared his shoulders. "I see I must protect you from yourself, just as I feared." He wheeled around and stormed out, slamming the door.

My shift at the hospital was uneventful, but the captain's parting words left me wondering what his next move would be.

On the way home, Jennie said, "Eliza, Abbey asked me to make a stop at the market. Pick up somethin' for her."

Jennie went to a market stall where two women were selling sweetgrass baskets. After a short exchange, Jennie produced a small package from her pocket and swapped it for a similar one. As I wondered what she was about, someone nearby shouted, "That's my mimba! Mimba!"

Confused, I looked around, thinking someone had been pickpocketed, but Jennie abandoned her own basket, ducked around the stall, and fled.

I had no idea what had just transpired, but driven by Jennie's panic, I sped home and burst in the front door, calling her name. She was not at the rear of the house so I started upstairs.

"I haven't seen her." Polly came into the hall, carrying an armful of clothing. Her voice sounded thick, and her eyes were red.

"Are you crying? What in the world are you doing?"

"I have four hours to pack a trunk before I sail with the tide this evening."

"What do you mean sail? Where are you going?"

"The commandant ordered me banished from Charles Town. I am being sent to Philadelphia."

"Whatever for?"

"Sedition." She gave a shaky laugh. "Jonathan and Lucretia warned me to watch my tongue. So did James. I knew better, and I shouldn't have let him bait me."

"Who?"

"Sandford. He had me arrested this morning, and claimed I'd made threats against a British officer. I demanded to know who, but he kept evading the question until finally I scoffed and said, 'Well, I daresay if Bloody Ban knows what's good for him, he'll always be looking over his shoulder,' and then Sandford smirked at me and said 'it was unseemly for a woman to know so much about men's business.'"

"Oh, Polly."

"There's more to my tale. They searched me and took a packet of letters I carried that contained false information. I was going let them fall into their hands, and I did it." Her chin trembled. "I said I was willing to sacrifice for the Cause, and I supposed I ended up sacrificing myself."

"Sandford came here this morning, too, and told me I should beware of the company I kept. He's banishing you to isolate me. What packet of letters are you talking about?"

Downstairs someone pounded on the front door. We both jumped out of our skin, and I forgot about the letters as I looked at the clock. "It's too soon."

We crept into the hall and I held my breath as one of the maids opened the door. We heard a man demand, "Where is she?" His heavy tread crossed the foyer. Heart pounding, I followed Polly to the head of the stairs and saw Thomas pause with his foot on the bottom step, as though steeling himself for what he would find. When caught sight of Polly, relief swept over his face, and he raced up.

She dropped the armful of clothes and stifled a sob as they clung together. "Are you mad? You can't be here. You're supposed to be a Tory now."

"Burgoyne for that." He cradled her face in his hands and kissed her. "I couldn't stay away once I heard."

"Will you get word to my father?"

"We're trying to find him."

"I thought it would be you, not me."

"Polly, I swear by all the saints—as soon as I can book passage I'll make my way to Philadelphia and marry you there."

Tears shone in her eyes. "That's the worst idea you've ever had."

"I don't care. How long until they come for you?"

"Less than three hours."

"Plenty of time for me to be gone." He swept her into his arms, carried her into our shared chamber, and kicked the door closed behind them.

Alone in the hall, the gravity of the situation washed over me, and I choked back a sob as I folded her gowns and left them in a neat pile. I clung to the bannister like an old woman as I descended the stairs. As I sank down on the parlor settee, fear and dread gripped my body, but my mind was racing.

Sandford had taken the packet of letters, which included mine to Peter. There was no point in telling Polly I'd planted my own message in the ones that were taken, for her fate was sealed.

Another knock sounded at the door, and my panic rose again, lest they find Thomas upstairs with Polly and arrest him too. If I did not answer, they would break the door down. Knees quaking, I went into the foyer and answered the door.

Instead of a squad of soldiers, a thin, middle-aged woman stood before me. "You have my Mimba."

There was that strange word again. My brain was so taxed by the strain that I struggled to comprehend. "I beg your pardon, your what? I don't understand."

"You were at the market with Mimba—we called her Chloe, but when they run, you know, they go back to using their country names.

I followed you here. See for yourself." She handed me a broadsheet offering a reward for the return of a female slave. "She absconded in January of seventeen seventy-four. We want her back. My husband will pay the reward for her return."

This news felt like a physical blow, and I wavered on my feet before I answered, "My girl can't be your missing servant."

"I'm certain it is her. She was uncommon pretty, even for a—"

I looked her in the eyes and lied. "I've had her since the spring of 'seventy-three."

"Perhaps you misremember the date."

"She was a wedding gift, so I'm not likely to forget when she came into my household. I regret that I cannot help you. Good day." I shut the door and sagged against it.

"Eliza?" Jennie came furtively into the foyer. I could tell by her expression she'd heard.

"I think it's time for you to tell me everything." I shepherded her into the parlor, where we took chairs facing one another.

She wrung her hands in her lap. "I lied to Mist' Joseph when I said I was a free woman. He was a good man. He trusted me, and I felt so bad about lyin' to him that on the morning of your wedding I confessed and tol' him I was a runaway. He said it didn't matter. I was safe in his household, and he'd keep my secret."

"He never told me."

"I lied to you too. Remember you asked me did I know what happens between men and women on wedding nights, and I said no?" Tears rolled down her cheeks and her voice broke. "When my master forced himself on me it wasn' no wedding night, and I could never tell anyone, least of all you, 'bout the evils he did to me. They lived right across the road, and when you say Miz Polly live here, I think, I can' do it, I can't pass they house every day without them seeing me. But then Teena tell me the house jus' sittin' empty for a year, and maybe they dead. But they come back."

"If you'd just told me."

"I couldn't." She swiped at her tears. "You got your life. Maybe you marry Mist' Peter someday, maybe you won't, but right now you doin' good work for the Cause. You can have liberty, but even if we win the war, there ain't gon' be liberty for me in Charles Town, maybe not anywhere. I'll be lookin' over my shoulder for the rest of my life."

She hung her head in despair, but I saw a way forward. "Philadelphia." The city seemed mythical—bound up in my Before. It was the birthplace of Joseph's convictions, the cradle of liberty—and home to Quakers. Abolitionist Quakers.

Jennie was also part of my Before. Together we weathered heartbreak, loss, an invading army, the intrigue of the social season, and the fall of the city. I thought I was her friend, yet she'd kept so much from me. I could not let her go back to a cruel, abusive master.

"What about it?"

"You must go to Philadelphia with Polly. You'll have a better chance for a good life there." We rose as one and as we embraced, I felt her trembling. "Hurry and collect your things so you'll be ready when they come for her."

As she hurried away toward the rear of the house, a loud thump in the upstairs hall made me jump out of my skin. My heart was still pounding when Thomas came downstairs carrying Polly's trunk and set it in the foyer. I followed him back upstairs to explain to Polly how she'd come to acquire an excellent maid. Then I took my reticule and left them to their goodbyes.

When Jennie returned with her bundle I handed her half of what remained from the Plainsfield money. "God go with you. I pray that you find happiness. Maybe you'll find a Quaker physician who will take you on as an assistant."

"What about you, Eliza? What will you do now?"

I could see she was already considering what her life in the north could be. "I'll stay with the Sarrazins. You can write to me in care of them." I smiled to give her courage, but my stomach churned until I feared I would be ill at the thought of losing her.

When the hour for Polly's departure drew nigh she came downstairs alone, eyes red-rimmed from crying. We embraced, and it seemed hardly a moment passed before a squad of soldiers was at the door. She stepped away from me and drew a deep breath. "Tell my father I'll write when I can."

In short order, they escorted Polly and Jennie to a closed carriage that waited in the street and loaded in their possessions. As they drove away I closed the door, sank to the floor, and wept.

30

Wallowing in misery on the foyer rug was a luxury I could not afford. Blair or Shilley could return any time and they must not discover Thomas in the house. I found him sitting on the rumpled bed, head in his hands.

He looked up as I came in and wiped his eyes. "I couldn't stop them from taking her."

"No, you couldn't. You must leave before our billets return."

He nodded slowly, and as he got to his feet I heard rapid footsteps on the stairs that did not belong to either of Polly's maids. I hurried into the hall and met Jonathan's assistant Abraham.

He paused to catch his breath before he spoke. "Soldiers arrested Mist' Sarrazin at the shop. I been all over town trying to find Cap'n Weyman. I thought he migh' be at home."

Thomas joined us in the hall. "Weyman's not here. Polly's been banished to Philadelphia."

We all stared at each other for a long moment before I asked, "Are we undone? Will they come for the rest of us now?"

Thomas swore. "What if the Redcoats have arrested Weyman too?"

Tears welled in my eyes again and I blinked them back. "I'll go to the sisters. They may know something."

The men followed me downstairs and I saw them out the rear door. Then I ran the short blocks to the Sarrazin home.

Their front door stood ajar, and my heart pounded as I tiptoed inside and closed it. The scene in the parlor proved our circle of operatives had been targeted. Furniture was tipped over, rugs pulled up, dishes smashed, and papers strewn everywhere, but the sisters worked together with quiet efficiency. While Marguerite collected the scattered papers and stacked them on Jonathan's desk, Kitty replaced books on the shelves, and Lucretia swept up shards of broken china.

Marguerite noticed me in the doorway. "Come in, dear. As you can see, we've had a visit from the Redcoats."

"So have we." I picked up a chair and set it on its feet. "Polly's been banished from Charles Town, and it seems Captain Weyman is missing."

Lucretia nodded. "We were aware of the risks."

"Yes, but what do we do now?"

Kitty smiled sadly. "We lean on our faith, Eliza, and believe our Cause is a righteous one."

Without warning the front door burst open with such force it slammed against the wall. We stifled cries of alarm as the town sergeant strode into the parlor, accompanied by a squad of Hessian soldiers with muskets at the ready.

He announced, "Margerite, Katherine, and Lucretia Sarrazin, you are under arrest."

"On what charge?" Marguerite's tight-lipped dignity caused him to falter before he replied.

"A treasonable offense against his majesty's government." As the soldiers took the sisters into custody, the sergeant's gaze fell on me. "Who might you be, missus?"

"Eliza Wilkinson."

A slow smile spread over his face. "I also have a warrant for you." Before I could protest, one of the soldiers took me by the arm and we followed the others to a closed carriage identical to the one that had taken Polly and Jennie away.

The four of us huddled together on the bench seats as the carriage rumbled through the streets. When we arrived at the Exchange, the soldiers pulled us out roughly and forced us down the slick, stone stairs that led to the dungeon. They shoved us through the doorway one by one, and we sprawled in the filthy hay that covered the brick floor.

The noisome liquid under the hay seeped through my clothing, and I scrambled to my feet. Lucretia and I helped Kitty and Marguerite right themselves, and we clung to one another as I took stock of our situation.

An inadequate number of candles barely pierced the darkness, but when my eyes adjusted I could make out a rib-vaulted ceiling that made the dungeon feel cave-like. The stench and the humidity were unpleasant, but far better than on the prison ship.

From the shadows, the clank of irons and incessant coughing gave an indication of how many people occupied the space. Then, like something from a nightmare, several shadowy forms shuffled toward us.

As they closed in, Kitty cried out and fell against me. Unwelcome hands groped at my skirts, and I shoved and slapped them away. Another shadowy form caught me around the waist and grabbed a handful of my hair. He pressed up against me, and as I fought to push him away, he muttered close to my ear, "You're a live one, ain't you? Fancy going sailing on a man o' war?"

His breath stank of whiskey and putrefaction. Terrified, I beat his chest and shoulder with my fists and shouted for help. Raucous laughter from the other prisoners mocked my distress, and someone called out, "Ain't no help coming, missy."

Then to my surprise the man sagged against me and his grip slackened. I wrenched myself out of his grasp, and he pitched face forward onto the ground where he lay, snoring.

I choked back a sob and heard Marguerite call softly, "Over here, dear."

The sisters huddled away from the unsavory crowd near a lantern hung on the wall. We were all smeared with filth, and I could still smell the rank odor of my attacker. A few feet away, a man undid his trousers and defecated on the ground with no regard for decency or for privacy. Revulsion overwhelmed me, and I bent double and vomited on the floor.

"How long do you think they mean to keep us here?" I wiped my mouth with the back of my hand.

Lucretia whispered, "There is no way to know."

We clung together for what might have been hours or days until a guard clumped down the stairs, unlocked the door, and shouted, "Sarrazin! Wilkinson! Present yourselves."

It was dark outside, and I heard a clock strike five as he prodded us up the stairs and conducted us into a room on the main floor of the Exchange. Then he took his post at the door as if he was guarding dangerous criminals instead of four frightened women. My face flushed with the humiliation of being brought before the British commandant while covered in muck, and I clasped my hands to keep them from trembling.

Colonel Nisbet Balfour, a ruddy, barrel-chested Scot, came into the room. He picked up a document from his desk and glanced at it. "How do you answer the charges against you?"

Marguerite looked quite unafraid. "We demand to know what offense we have committed."

He scoffed. "You stand accused of inciting the people of Charles Town to reject British rule."

Lucretia spoke up. "They have already rejected British rule. Tell me, sir, how does one convince people who have tasted independence to return to the reduced status of subjects? It is not by violating their rights and allowing common soldiers to plunder their homes."

"It is no secret we mourn for our City and decry its oppressors." Marguerite fixed him with a look of disapproval. "From the beginning, your army was unwilling to feed and care for our sick and wounded soldiers, and it fell to women to do what you would not. We organized relief committees. We visited the hospitals, barracks, and prison ships to offer comfort, as is our Christian duty."

"Christian duty?" The commandant narrowed his eyes. "You are doing far more than comforting those treasonous wretches. You are spies, are you not?"

"It is also no secret the British army is cruel to its captives." Kitty spoke with the same coolness as her sister. "'Bear ye one another's burdens and so fulfil the law of Christ.' Galatians six, verse two."

Lucretia chimed in, "'Remember them that are in bonds, *and* them which suffer adversity.' Hebrews thirteen, verse three."

Before Balfour could interrupt, the sisters fired off more verses like volleys of artillery fire.

"'I was naked, and ye clothed me: I was sick, and ye visited me: I was in prison, and ye came unto me.' Matthew twenty-five verse thirty-six."

"'He hath sent me to heal the brokenhearted, to preach deliverance to the captives.' Luke four, verse eighteen."

"'Verily I say unto you, inasmuch as ye have done it unto one of the least of these my brethren, ye have done it unto me.' Matthew twenty-five, verse forty."

I cast my eyes down so I would not be tempted to smile.

"Enough!" The commandant lost his composure and slapped the table with his palm. "Your brother is a member of the Liberty Boys and a spy for the rebels. I will ask you again. Are you also spies?"

We stood mute.

"You may be nothing more than ladies who speak their minds on matters which do not concern them. But mark me—if you show any hint of treasonous activity, you will be dealt with harshly. Please step out." The guard opened the door, and as I started to follow the sisters, Balfour said, "Missus Wilkinson, remain here."

As soon as the sisters departed, Captain Sandford stepped into the room. My insides quailed as Balfour and the guard went out and closed the door behind them, but I raised my chin, refusing to let him see I was afraid.

"Wallowing with swine again?" Sandford smirked as he sat on the edge of the desk. "Now that we are alone, how do you answer the charges?"

I stayed silent.

His laugh was derisive. "You are all guilty as sin and you know it."

"If we have made some offense, Captain, why did the commandant release us?"

"Who says anyone has been released?" He rose and approached me. "I often think about the day we met on your idyllic island."

"Indeed?" My heart thudded in my ears until it nearly drowned out his voice.

"To see you was to fall in love with you. I believed you possessed a sweet and womanly reserve, but time has revealed your calculating and duplicitous nature." He sneered. "My, how you have come down."

I shrugged. "My sentiments about you have not changed."

His eyes narrowed. "You may despise me, but you care about the Sarrazin ladies, so consider my proposition. They go free if you take the oath of allegiance, come under my protection, and use your connections to spy for me."

I feigned confusion. "I work only for the relief and comfort of our soldiers. I have no connections and can do nothing to help you."

"You know nothing of clandestine meetings of the Liberty Boys? You are unaware of escapes from the barracks and prison ships? You have no idea that someone in Charles Town is sending intelligence reports to rebels outside the city?"

I did not answer.

"Wouldn't it be terrible for those spinster ladies to languish in the dungeon with the miscreants and the whores?" He walked around behind me and laid heavy hands on my shoulders. I squirmed away, but he spun me around to face him. "Don't play the innocent, Eliza. Plenty of so-called patriot women welcome the enemy to their beds. I daresay many of them like it."

What would get me out of this situation? I could not admit to spying or I could be imprisoned or hanged. Neither could I bear the thought of becoming his paramour. As if from another lifetime, I envisioned Hext smirking as he held out my garnet earbob, believing he could win my affections by coersion. Yet it was I who emerged the victor in that battle.

"Goodness, Captain. My disdain for you is well known among your subordinates, is it not?" I laughed. "If I welcomed your attention, I would become suspect, and therefore of no value to you."

"You are in no position to negotiate terms. Tell me, what do you know about this?" He tossed my letter to Peter on the desk, and then laid one addressed to me in his hand on top of it. I was not quick enough to fix my viz.

"Ah, so you recognize them. That's intriguing, since you insist you are not a spy."

"A friend and I correspond in code, to keep our messages safe from prying eyes. Since Redcoats garrisoned the city, the post is often tampered with."

"These were intercepted with some rebel communiques. They've been transcribed using a book that I believe was in your possession. Would you like me to read them to you?" He slammed his palm on the desk. "Tell me again you are not a spy while the evidence against you mounts."

I squared my shoulders. "Very well. I will take the oath, and receive instruction on how to spy for you, but I reject your offer of protection."

"You need not fear me, Eliza." He studied me for a long moment. "In time, you will come to appreciate everything I can offer you."

As he ran his hand over my bodice and cupped one of my breasts, I gave no sign I felt anything at all.

He scoffed as he withdrew his hand. "I do not wish to have you now. You smell of the dungeon."

The revulsion I felt at his touch paled beside having to raise my right hand and read, *I, Eliza Wilkinson, do solemnly promise in the presence of Almighty God to bear faith and true Allegiance to his sacred Majesty George the Third and will to the utmost of my power and Ability support maintain and defend his Crown and dignity against all traitorous Attempts and Conspiracies whatsoever. So help me God.*

As soon as I'd signed my name to the paper, he opened the door and stood aside. "I shall send for you."

I fled from the room, and the first rays of the morning sun dazzled my eyes as I stumbled into the street. With the words of the hated oath ringing in my ears, I picked up my skirts and ran up East Bay Street.

31

I arrived at Polly's house gasping, loath for anyone to see me in my filthy, disheveled state, but Abbey and Teena made no comment, and took my appearance as a matter of course.

"Has Captain Weyman come home?"

Abbey said, "No, miss."

"What about the billets?"

Teena replied, "They out, miss."

"Could you please prepare the tub for a bath and fix me something to eat?"

They ambled out to the pump to draw water and I hurried to my chamber to shed my filthy clothes.

My mind whirled as I undid the fastening on the front of my gown. I could not contact the Sarrazins without risking their arrest. I was adrift, with only Thomas and Abraham to turn to, and I could easily jeopardize them as well.

Something tapped at the French doors that led to the piazza. Uncertain what I'd heard, I pulled back the portieres to reveal Thomas waiting there. I unlocked the door so he could step into the room, holding my gown closed with one hand. "How did you get out there? Why didn't you come to the door?"

"Trust me–I know every way into this chamber." He wrinkled his nose. "God in heaven, do you know how badly you reek?"

"Of course I do." I retreated to the far side of the room.

"Abraham told me you and the Sarrazins were arrested. Did you see Jonathan or Captain Weyman there?"

"No."

"What did you tell the Redcoats?"

"Nothing."

"A number of patriots were arrested overnight."

"It wasn't because of me. I didn't betray us." My voice shook as I told him of my encounter with Sandford.

"You had a harrowing night. Clean up and get some sleep if you can. I'll try to learn more about the arrests." He climbed down the trellis, and I locked the doors before I went downstairs.

When at last I sank into the hot bath in a corner of the kitchen, I took up the soap and scrubbed until no hint of the dungeon remained. I put on a clean shift and my wrapper and ate at the worktable in the larder.

Though my eyes were gritty from lack of sleep, I was too agitated to rest. I dressed in one of Polly's mourning gowns, an appropriate choice given all I had lost. I was combing the tangles from my hair when there was a discreet knock on the door.

"Missus Wilkinson?" The knock sounded again. "It's Corporal Shilley. May I presume to speak with you?" When I did not answer, he continued to speak through the door. "Please. You teased me to turn rebel, but what you do not know is you've turned my heart and my sensibilities. Not just for you, but for the Cause."

I opened the door a crack. "Corporal, you forget yourself. What if Sergeant Blair hears you say such things?"

He pushed past me into the room, shut the door, and spoke in a whisper. "You, Captain Weyman, and Missus Brewton are good and decent people. I feel the utmost concern for you all in your hour of need, and I understand the terror under which you live.

"The day after I escorted you and Missus Brewton to the shops, Captain Sandford called me before the provost, and I was given ten lashes for dereliction of duty. Afterward, he warned me if I spoke to you again, it would be twenty." He pulled off his neckcloth and shrugged his shirt off his shoulders to show me the marks left by the whip.

"I believe his obsession with you has clouded his reason, and I quail at the thought of you at his mercy. You are alone in this house now, with no male protector. Perhaps if you knew the fate of Captain Weyman you could petition for his release."

"Go on."

"I have evening sentry duty outside the commandant's residence. Yesterday I saw Captain Weyman brought to Balfour's office in the company of other prisoners. A short time later, they were taken away. I don't know where they are now, but if they stand accused of treason, they could hang.

"Tonight, the commandant will sup at a tavern at half seven, and plans to attend an entertainment after. If you come to his residence, I can admit you to his study, where there may be papers that can assist you."

"I am a helpless woman, Corporal. I know nothing of the kind of intrigue you suggest."

"Do you know the commandant's residence? It is on East Bay Street, just north of Market."

"I know which house it is, though I have never been inside."

"I beg of you, Missus Wilkinson, go there tonight. This may be your last chance to help Captain Weyman."

"I can promise nothing."

"Consider what I have said. I must report for roll call soon." His sweet, youthful face seemed lit from within as he brought both my hands to his lips. "I would do *anything* to help you."

I shut the door behind him and leaned against it. I could not let Polly's father languish. But dare I search the commandant's residence for information that might help save him?

I couldn't. Not alone. I put up my hair, took Polly's black tricorn hat and a veil from the clothespress and headed for the silversmith shop.

A sign on the front door said the shop was closed, but I went around to the door off the alley and Abraham answered my knock and admitted me to his quarters, where Thomas sat at the table, a half-empty bottle of rum in front of him.

I told them both of Corporal Shilley's plan. "I dare not attempt this alone."

"You sound like you willing to try." Abraham went into the store-front and when he returned, he carried a silver candlestick.

I looked at Thomas. "If this is a joke, I fail to see the humor."

Abraham handed it to him, and he grinned as he hefted it. "This is more than a weapon." He removed the top, which had a cork stopper that fitted into the candlestick's hollow shaft. "It's a watertight place to hide papers." He gave it to me. "You can strap it to your leg, like a dagger."

Abraham gave me a tinder box, some candle stubs, a ring of keys, and a small round mirror in a silver frame. "You never know what you gonna need." I put the lot in my pocket.

We spent the rest of the afternoon working out a plan. It was some comfort, knowing both of them would be nearby to support me.

Abraham rummaged through a box and brought back a black pair of knee breeches, a striped shirt, and a gray waistcoat. "Women opera-tives get overlooked, unless they seem out of place. You should take these clothes with you."

I held up the shirt and waistcoat to my front. They were large enough to make me look like a young boy in ill-fitting clothes.

"Around soldiers, you attract less attention dressed as a boy. I don' know how you gonna carry them, though."

"This is how we smuggled clothing onto the prison ship." I stepped into the breeches, pulled them up under my petticoats, and buttoned the flap. Then I put the arms of the shirt through the waistcoat's armholes so I could put them on as one, and hiked up my skirts to tie the shirt's arms around my waist.

I walked about, testing the feel of the extra layers. "This is easier than smuggling in a dozen shirts. Now, as to the Pinkney residence—I told Shilley I'd never been inside, but I went to a card party there once. I remember which room is the study." I described the location of the room and we agreed upon two signals–one for success, and one for distress.

Abraham said, "Now all that's left is for Thomas and me to get ready. But first, we need to fill our stomachs."

He set out a simple meal of bread, cheese, and ale, and when we were finished eating Thomas and Abraham changed into their disguises and departed. I went over the plan again and again in my mind while I waited for nightfall. It seemed we had left nothing to chance, except what I might find in the commandant's office.

Gulls wheeled overhead as I left the shop, diving in like small artillery fire to pick at the rubbish and scraps in the gutters. Their cries muffled my footsteps as I crossed the cobblestone street, and once I was away from the streetlamps, I moved like a wraith among the shadows.

No one was about on the streets near the commandant's residence save a scavenger pushing a small haywagon and a lamplighter whose cart was filled with jugs of whale oil.

Shilley stood in front of the commandant's residence, musket on his shoulder and eyes fixed ahead. When he caught sight of me, he beckoned with a subtle movement of his hand. I ran lightly across the street and followed him into the house, where he opened the colonel's study door to admit me. Inside, a taper on the desk gave enough light to see the stacks of papers and ledgers piled on. It flickered as he closed the door and left me alone.

It took only a moment to find the arrest warrant. I skimmed the page, murmuring the words aloud.

...citizens of Charleston, that by the articles of capitulation are considered as prisoners of war on parole... accused of conspiring to burn the town in an act of defiance...

I gasped. Could that be the false intelligence Polly created? Or had rebels truly intended to burn the city?

On Sunday instant, early in the morning...arrested and carried to the Exchange...after, on board the Sandwich guard-ship near Fort Johnson; and from thence, to be put on board a transport.

A transport to where? I scrabbled through the pages until I came to a list of names, headed by a notation from Balfour himself.

...orders for the seizure of estates, both real and personal, of those persons whose names are under mentioned...

I ran my finger down the list and noted familiar names. I was acquainted with Thomas Heyward and Arthur Middleton, who had both signed the Declaration of Independence. My heart sank as I read further and saw the names Jonathan Sarrazin, Edward Weyman, and Morton Wilkinson.

There was no time to copy the warrant, so I rolled it up with the list of names and stuffed them into the candlestick's hollow core. Then I scanned every paper on Balfour's desk until an order from General Cornwallis caught my attention.

By the time I finished reading it, my heart was pounding so loudly I feared someone would hear it in the hall. I dared not take time to extract the other papers from the candlestick and roll them up together, so I shoved the order into my stays. I secured the candlestick to my leg beneath the overlarge breeches, and then set the lighted taper on the windowsill. I passed my hand in front of it three times, the agreed-upon signal for success, and then stealthily turned the doorknob.

The door would not open. Willing myself not to panic, I waited a few moments and tried again.

This time it opened easily, but my sigh of relief turned to a gasp when the dim light revealed Captain Sandford, not Corporal Shilley, waiting in the corridor.

I backed away as he advanced into the office and shut the door behind him. "I assume you found the information you sought, Eliza? Did you think Corporal Shilley was too simple and guileless for intelligence work? He's been your shadow for some time."

"Captain—"

He raised an eyebrow. "I'd prefer if you called me John." As he took a step forward to close the distance between us, I knew the desperation of one who had gone too far down a dangerous path to turn back.

"Tell me, what will you say to the commandant when he learns you were discovered stealing confidential papers from his office?"

I tossed my head dismissively as I attempted to regain my poise. "Am I not supposed to be working for you? Perhaps you should tell him why you asked me to meet you here."

He smirked. "An admirable effort, but Balfour receives my reports."

I tried a different tack. "My friends are arrested, in exile, or otherwise removed from me. Under the circumstances, I must be pragmatic."

"Indeed?" He dropped his coat across the back of the chair and loosened his neckcloth. "What do you propose?"

"Why, learn to spy for you, as I agreed. I've already taken the oath. Will you have me kiss the queen's picture to prove my renewed loyalty?"

"That won't be necessary."

"You know my situation, Captain. I am a widow. I could not find safe transport home during the siege, and I have been an unwilling resident of the city ever since. My father, old and infirm, died with me far from his side. As a balm to my grief, I occupied myself as the other ladies of my set do—by feeding the indigent and tending to the sick and wounded. That is all I have done to aid the Americans."

He took another step toward me and I flinched. "It is one thing to do womanly tasks, but it is quite another to use your wiles to gather intelligence and pass it to the rebels. Though your lines of communication are broken, I daresay there are plenty of enemy spies left in the city. After I uncovered the plot to burn the town and massacre loyal subjects, Balfour charged me with subduing the resistance. You will help me root them out."

He'd taken the bait, but it could not bring about his undoing in time to save me. I was aware of each passing second as I waited for Thomas and Abraham to intervene, but help did not come.

"It's time to prove your loyalty, Eliza." He took my arm in a tight grip, threw open the door, and forced me down the darkened hallway. Terrified by his rough treatment, I resisted. With a growl, he grabbed me around the waist, half-carried me up the stairs, and shoved me into a chamber.

When he shut the door, the darkness was so absolute I could not get my bearings, and he was on me in a heartbeat. He clawed at my bodice and I felt the fastenings give way.

Then, faintly, someone on the street shouted, "Fire!" and a tremendous explosion rattled the windows in their frames. Sandford's grip on me slackened.

The house, silent and presumably unoccupied a moment ago, came to life. Doors opened and slammed shut. Rapid footsteps pounded down the stairs, and shouts for water came from below.

Sandford gave me a shove that sent me sprawling. "We are not finished." A sliver of light fell across me as he opened the door, and then the darkness engulfed me again and I heard him turn the key in the lock.

Staggering to my feet, I fished the tinder box out of my pocket and struck the flint. With a bit of touch paper, I captured the flame and used it to light the stub of a candle from my pocket.

I was in an officer's bedchamber. Setting the candle on the mantel, I opened the French doors that led to the second-floor piazza, where I could smell smoke from the nearby flames. I looked over the railing, but drew back from the dizzying height. There was no trellis or other means to climb down. I remembered Marion's plunge from the window on Tradd Street and knew I could never make such a leap.

Two more explosions went off in rapid succession, so close by that I ducked and covered my ears. Inside, the candle flickered as I ran past, mind whirling. Perhaps I could get out the way I came in. I tried each key on the ring Abraham gave me, but none of them fit the lock.

I might have minutes or hours before Sandford returned, and I vowed not to leave my fate to his whims. I shed my torn dress and the hat and veil. I wriggled into the shirt and waistcoat and used my black fichu to tie up my hair, in an approximation of Jennie's turban. Near the door, a uniform coat hung on a peg, and I put it on. It was so large the coattails hung almost to my heels.

Pushing back the cuffs, I transferred the contents of my pocket, the veil, and the candlestick into a haversack I found hanging behind the coat, slung the strap over my shoulder, and put on Polly's hat.

With my transformation complete, I went back to the piazza and leaned over the railing. I could just make out the scene on the street, which was now illuminated by lanterns and flaming torches. Soldiers hurried about carrying buckets of water while the officers barked orders.

Gratifying as it was to witness the disorder, I needed a means of escape. I ran back inside and pressed my ear to the keyhole again. This time I heard footsteps in the hall.

Whether it was Sanford returning or another officer mattered not; I dashed across the room and blew out the candle, dropped to the floor, and crawled under the bed. As a key turned in the lock, I made myself small and tried to take slow, shallow breaths.

Even in the dark with my eyes squeezed shut, I knew it was a man who came into the room, for I could feel his weight in the vibrations of his tread. I heard him strike a flint and when I opened one eye, I could see his boots in the circle of light shed by the candle. After a moment, he crossed the room to the open piazza door. He swore loudly, and as he ran back into the room, he stumbled over my gown and bent to pick it up.

There was a long moment of silence, and then he screamed, a sound so primal and full of rage that the hair stood up on the back of my neck.

I watched his boots stagger across the room to the clothes-press, where he pulled open the doors and flung the contents on the floor. Next came a resounding crash, and bits of broken porcelain bounced under the bed and ricocheted off my body. I pictured him sweeping his arm along the mantel and bookshelves, knocking the Pinkney family's possessions to the floor.

As he tore the counterpane off the bed, he trod so close to my hiding place that the toe of his boot grazed my arm, and I shrank back farther.

Then another man's voice rang out. "See here! What are you doing in the colonel's bedchamber?" There was an indignant gasp. "Good God, man—what is the meaning of this?"

I watched the boot heels click together as Sandford snapped to attention, and my gown fell to the floor at his feet. His voice, so menacing a short while ago, sounded confused and contrite. "I—that is to say—"

The other man barked, "This is breaking and entering, conduct unbecoming an officer and a gentleman, and rank debauchery! I'm not even going to inquire as to what you were doing with that gown,

Captain. You can explain that to the commandant. Until then, it's off to the brig with the likes of you."

As the officer escorted Sandford away, I breathed a long, slow sigh of relief.

32

Thomas did a double take when I joined him at our rendezvous point. "I'd about given you up for lost."

"So had I."

"Here—swap jackets with me. No one who sees you will believe you're a soldier."

I shrugged out of it. "It's Balfour's."

He handed me his and inspected the one I'd stolen. "Good, it's his field coat. No insignia that gives away rank." He chuckled as he put it on. "Redcoat officers started going into battle in plain coats because our sharpshooters were picking them off too easily."

"Don't you want to hear what I discovered?"

"Of course."

"Weyman, Jonathan, and dozens of others are being held on the *Sandwich* in the harbor. They're to be transported, but the papers I found didn't say when or to where."

"The *Sandwich*, you say? I watched her sail out with the tide about an hour ago."

My laugh came out as a half-sob. "They're gone? Everything I went through and we can't save them?"

"Don't worry. It's never all for naught."

I felt the crackle of Corwallis's order in my stays. "You're right. We have another problem we must attend to."

Thomas took my hand and led the way back to the silversmith shop through the darkness, keeping mostly to back gardens and alleys. As I followed, my thoughts whirled. Dozens of our city's most influential patriots were arrested and transported to some unknown destination. Our web was decimated. My beloved Plainsfield was the property of the Crown, and as I would receive no more payments on the note, I was now homeless and destitute.

We let ourselves in the back of the shop. "I wonder what's keeping Abraham," Thomas mused. "He should have been back by now."

My skin crawled as I regarded the dark shadows in the farther reaches of the room, and I used the single lit taper to light a second one before I collapsed in the nearest chair.

Thomas shrugged out of Balfour's coat and gave it a disdainful look as he tossed it aside. He sat and stretched his long legs out in front of him. "What happened? You signaled success."

"I signaled too soon. It's quite a tale, but I shan't share it with you now." I plunged my hand down my front and pulled out the orders from Cornwallis. "Look at this. 'Muster troops to report to Tarleton in Camden and quell the harassment to supply lines.' It calls for eight hundred men to march within days. We must warn Colonel Marion."

"You'll do nothing of the kind." Corporal Shilley entered the room and raised his musket. "You're bound for the dungeon in the Provost." He motioned for us to rise, but before we could obey, Abraham rushed in from the darkened shopfront and struck Shilley in the head with a candlestick. The first blow stunned him, and the second rendered him senseless. He dropped his musket and slumped to the floor.

Thomas pointed. "Take note, Eliza. That's the way it's done." To Abraham he said, "Good man."

Abraham grinned. "I seen him followin' you, so I laid in wait. We gotta mind the time."

Thomas asked me, "How do we get word to Marion, now that our communication lines are broken?"

"I don't know, but there must be a way. Were they broken when we failed to get the intelligence to Gates in time to warn him about Camden?"

Thomas snorted. "Ample warning would not have prevented that defeat. Gates made the cowardly choice to leave his men in the field and retreat into North Carolina on his own. If Tarleton gets those reinforcements and the Redcoats bring Marion's men and the other backwoods militia to ruin, the resistance in South Carolina will be reduced to nothing."

While I waited for one of the men to suggest a plan, I thought about what Polly would do. Then it came to me. "The only way word will reach Colonel Marion in time is if we take it ourselves. I spent weeks walking the area around the Horn, and I know the escape routes so well I can picture them in my mind. We can make our way in the dark. The only thing I haven't reckoned is how to find Marion once we're outside enemy lines."

Thomas said, half to himself, "If you head north and find a road leading to Camden—"

Abraham broke in. "Or you could hook on with the others."

Both men looked pensive, and Thomas shook his head. "I don't know if we dare alter the plan. It increases the risk for all."

"Ain't much time to think it through," Abraham replied.

I was ready to take action. "The information needs to reach Marion right away! You said yourself, he and his men are the only resistance left in South Carolina."

"All right," Thomas decided. "We'll help you get out, but we can't go with you."

That was not what I expected to hear. "But I can't go alone, and you're the only ones I know in the network."

"You won't be alone," Thomas answered. "There's an escape planned for tonight. You can wait at the tidal creek near the barracks and join them."

"You scared of gators?"

"Isn't everyone?"

Abraham chuckled. "Redcoats don' want no truck with gators. If you get away in the night, ain't no chance the soldiers'll follow you into the swamps." His words were small comfort. As if the matter was settled, he nudged Corporal Shilley with his foot. "We got our distraction righ' here. This'll be less suspicious than two haywagon fires in one night."

Thomas shrugged. "I suppose so. It's always good to expand our repertoire." He stepped over Shilley and took my hand to raise me to my feet. "Eliza, I'm going to say farewell now, before we make him ready, for it's not a pretty sight." He kissed me on the forehead and smiled down at me. "I know we'll meet again. Bring my coat and that bottle of rum, will you?"

The men picked up Shilley's limp body and carried him out to the alley behind the shop. I followed, bottle in hand, and watched as they dropped him in the gutter and rolled him over until he was covered in all the distasteful things that end up in gutters.

When they dragged him back up he smelled so much like the Provost dungeon that I gagged, but Thomas seemed to be enjoying himself. "Faugh, that's vile. Bottle, please."

The curfew bell rang as I handed it over. Abraham held Shilley's head while Thomas poured rum into his mouth and slopped a good deal more over his front.

Then he raised the bottle to his own lips and drained it. Together he and Abraham loaded Shilley onto the haycart that stood by the rear door and each took one handle. My heart pounded along with the rumbling cart as we started on a surreptitious route to the barracks at the Horn.

The barracks were three brick warehouses surrounded by a stockade fence. Thomas murmured, "The brickwork is unfinished in places.

After the capitulation, the prisoners hid the breaches and dug out more mortar until there were holes large enough to escape through. That's how I got out."

As we drew nearer, the night sounds of cicadas, crickets, and frogs from the marsh grew loud enough to drown out our footsteps and the rumble of the cart. About a block from the gate, the men hefted Shilley out of the cart and carried him between them, the toes of his boots barely brushing the crushed oyster-shell path. I followed them and kept to the shadows.

They were just out of sight of the barracks gate when Thomas took on Shilley by himself. Abraham hurried back to me and pointed at the tall grasses along the stockade fence, motioning that I should go. I nodded, and before I had time to thank him, he was gone.

I heard Thomas yell at the sentry. "You! Help me with this sorry excuse for a soldier!"

"Who goes there?"

"A disgrace to the uniform."

"What's the matter with him? Is he hurt?"

Thomas laughed. "Intoxicated, more like. I found him in the gutter while I was on patrol."

"I'll call the ranking officer." The sentry gagged, and when their conversation grew indistinct I started along the stockade fence. Within moments, mosquitoes swarmed over me, and I paused to take the black veil from the haversack and wrap it around my head and neck. I moved farther into the marsh to seek a good place to wait for the escapees and tried to ignore the smells of decaying flesh and human waste that overpowered the briny smell of the water.

33

Crouched in the gently swaying grasses, I watched the waning moon slowly move higher in the sky. Its soft light shimmered on the gentle waves that lapped against the bank and rolled away as the tide receded. I brought the candlestick out of my haversack, removed the cork, and worked with my fingers until the spiral of parchment came out of the hollow core. Then I fished the Cornwallis order out of my stays, rolled it with the other papers and stowed them all in the watertight space.

The bells at St. Michaels rang each quarter hour, and six chimes later, I saw movement from the corner of the fence. I peered into the darkness and counted twenty shadowy forms moving quietly into the shallow water. I hung onto handfuls of grass as I let myself down the bank and trailed after them at a distance while trying not to think about Redcoats, snakes, alligators, or the quicksand-like pluff mud I might encounter.

Soon the twelve-foot tabby wall of the city's fortifications rose before us, gleaming in the faint light. I had never seen beyond it, and now I followed the men as they headed through a gap and across an open field studded with the abatis our soldiers had fashioned from sharpened saplings before the siege.

Though it had been years since I'd climbed trees and roamed the woods with my brothers, I was nimble enough to keep up. I rolled across a tree trunk that rested a few feet off the ground. The canal ditch, fed during the siege by tidal creeks that flowed in and out of both rivers, had since been drained. I dropped the four feet to its muddy bottom, squished across it and scrambled out the other side. Next, I encountered the rolling hills of the redoubts and the siege line ditches, the furthest of which I had heard was a mile and a half from the city gate. After we'd passed it the group stopped to rest. I looked back toward Charles Town, which was nothing but a few specks of light in the distance.

The mosquito bites on my hands itched so badly I could have scratched my skin raw. The wet shirt chafed my skin, and the soaked breeches hung low on my hips, but there was nothing to do now but carry on. When the men resumed walking, so did I. The water's depth varied from inches to waist high, and I lost count of how many times I stumbled and sank.

An alligator's bellow rose above the cacophony of cicada, cricket, and frog calls, and a shiver ran down my spine when others bellowed in answer. I was more vulnerable alone. I must close the distance between me and the group.

Weakened by their months in prison, the men moved so slowly that I caught up with little trouble. One who had lagged behind the others seemed to be struggling, and I realized he was mired down in a patch of pluff mud. When I drew near I could see the desperation on his sunken face. I grasped his hands and pulled with all my might, but the quicksand held him fast.

Knowing how voices carry across the water, I spoke in a normal tone. "Someone help." Immediately the night creatures fell silent, and I added, "This man's stuck in the mud."

The men's surprised murmurs came back to me. "Who be that? A boy or a woman?"

"There were no boys in the prison. No women neither."

Two who were close to the mired-down man sloshed over to us. They each grasped an arm and pulled him free, supporting him until he was clear of the hazard.

Even as I breathed a sigh of relief, one of the men came toward me, brandishing the tree branch he used as a walking stick. He hissed, "We came out of the prison twenty men. Where have you come from? If you're a Tory spy, I'll drown you myself."

"Here," said the man who had been stuck in the mud. "The lassie revealed herself when she came to my aid. Why would she do that if she was a spy?"

The man with the stick was not convinced. "How did you come to be in our company?"

"I needed to leave the city undetected, so I waited outside the prison until I could join you."

"How did you know about our escape?"

"I am acquainted with the men who facilitated it."

"So you say. How can we be sure you're not out to betray us?"

I slapped a mosquito. "If I intended to betray you, I would have done so without coming into this miserable situation."

A few of them chuckled, and the man with the walking stick said, "You make a fair point. Let's all step lively."

Near dawn, we halted to rest in a grove of trees where the underbrush was thick enough to conceal us. I sat down, not intending to fall asleep, but the next thing I knew someone kicked my foot and startled me awake.

The man with the walking stick, the one who'd been stuck in the mud, and the two who had pulled him free stood before me. "We want to speak with you."

As I came fully awake, I felt the aches, itching, and empty belly that served as reminders of my previous night's flight. I got stiffly to my feet and followed them away from the other sleeping men to where a small fire burned in a pit about a foot deep, with a vent hole dug upwind from the main fire. "This is clever." I held my hands over the subterranean flames.

One of them said, "Never seen a stealth fire before, eh? You don't know much about surviving in the wilderness for a fact, do you?"

"No, I never had to, sir."

His companion said, "Some of the men think it bodes ill that a woman was able to find us and track us. They wanted to leave you where you lay sleeping."

"I vouched for you," said the man who'd been stuck in the mud. He indicated the other three men. "So did they."

"Thank you—"

"Private Caleb Smith." He held out his hand and I shook it.

The man with the walking stick followed suit. "Corporal Reuben Stone, missy."

"Where do you all intend to go?"

Stone answered, "Some of the men want to head for North Carolina. The British ain't got that state under their boot heels yet. Others of us figure we'll find some irregulars or militia and hook on with them. Where are you bound?"

"I'm not entirely sure." I decided not to tell them of the intelligence I carried. "I seek Colonel Francis Marion."

All four men chuckled and Smith replied, "'Twould be easier if Marion was seeking you. I hear tell no one finds him unless he allows it."

Despite knowing some of the escapees welcomed my company, I found it hard to relax enough to sleep in the heat of the day. That night, the moon provided enough light to see by as we traveled along a road headed north through fields and forests toward the Santee country. Though it was easier going on land, the men moved slowly, stumbling and staggering into one another. I wondered how much longer they could continue without sustenance.

About an hour before dawn, one of the men at the fore signaled for quiet. "Hear that? Sounds like half a company on the move."

We stood in silence as a shadowy party of eight horsemen rode up, followed by dozens of men on foot. As they halted, I heard them raise their weapons.

"Present yourselves!" commanded one of the mounted soldiers.

Corporal Stone answered, "We might ask the same of you. We're unarmed, and want no trouble."

The soldier tried again. "State your regiment."

"We've men from Virginia and Carolina." Stone hesitated before he added, "Escaped from the barracks prison in Charles Town two nights hence."

"We've come from Nelson's Ferry, where we liberated a hundred and fifty Maryland Continentals who were captured at Camden. These–" the soldier indicated the men on foot behind the horsemen "—are about half of their number."

"Who's your commanding officer?" asked Stone.

"General Marion."

My heart leapt at the news, but some of the men near me seemed disappointed. "Militia, eh?" one of them scoffed.

The mounted soldier shrugged. "Some of our number have served in the Continental Line. There are precious few of us left to stand against the enemy in South Carolina."

Another of our party asked, "We believed we were traveling north. Are we mistaken?"

Some of the men around me groaned at the thought that we'd been going the wrong way, while others muttered wearily.

One of the Maryland soldiers traveling on foot responded. "You're headed in the right direction. It's we who are bound for Charles Town."

Corporal Stone asked, "Whatever for?"

The Marylander replied, "We don't want to fight the Redcoats any-more, and we don't want to take the oath and be forced to fight against our own. We thought to go to the garrison, turn ourselves in, and take our chances in prison."

One of our party swore. "Are you daft, man? Look at us. We've been in the barracks prison since the surrender. We were willing to die trying to escape."

Private Smith added, "You're fools to trust your lives to the British guards."

"We appreciate your honesty, and I'll be honest too. Some of us chose not to follow Colonel Marion. We feel militia service is beneath us." The Maryland soldier scratched the back of his neck. "How far is it to Charles Town?"

With directions given, he addressed the men on horseback. "There's no need to accompany us further. If we meet a party of Redcoats we'll surrender." The men bound for Charles Town formed columns and stepped off just as the first rays of sunlight peeked over the horizon.

Incredulous, I watched them go.

Corporal Stone gave them a dismissive glance and then addressed the mounted soldiers. "There are those among us who'd be proud to serve under Marion's command. If you can provide us with vittles and a day's rest, we'd like to join up with your outfit."

"Aye." Most of the other escapees gathered around, nodding.

Another of the buckskin-clad men on horseback chuckled. "It may take more than that until you're fit for service. Those of you who wish to join us, come along. Those who would take your chances against the British patrols on this road, on your own heads be it."

As a few of the escapees headed off across the field, Private Smith spoke up again. "Begging your pardon, could you spare a horse so our lady can ride? She's walked as far as we."

"Your lady?" The horseman scanned our group, disbelief evident in his voice, and when I stepped forward, they murmured in surprise.

A young, sandy-haired man with a tan that was mostly freckles edged his horse forward. "She can ride with me." Corporal Stone gave me a hand up behind the soldier's saddle, and soon we were away. My new traveling companion introduced himself. "Your servant, madam. I'm Private Malcom McFarlane."

"Pleased to make your acquaintance, sir. I am Missus Wilkinson."

"You must have one whale of a story. How did you fall in with those men?"

"I joined them during their flight from the city. I have a message for Colonel Marion that is of the utmost urgency. When we arrive, will you help me gain an audience with him?"

"I'll do what I can—and mind, if you seek his favor, call him General."

"I'll remember that. We've only traveled at night. Isn't it risky to be on the roads by day?"

"Don't worry. We have good scouts, and we know this area better than the Redcoats."

After a time the land grew swampy, and we splashed through shallow water and along narrow paths under trees that dripped with swaying moss. Though the mounted soldiers walked their horses, the pace pushed the weary escaped prisoners to keep up. When we stopped to rest, Marion's soldiers shared provisions with us, but the salted meat made me unbearably thirsty. Even out of the sun, the heat and humidity were oppressive. My damp clothing clung to my skin, and I could think of nothing but a cool drink.

At length, we came into a clearing and the riders in the lead halted. At first I thought we were stopping to rest again, but then I spotted a rough log structure through a gap in the trees. The desolate place came alive with men dressed to blend in with the landscape.

The escapees sank wearily to the ground as Marion's soldiers dismounted. Private McFarlane helped me down and handed his horse's reins to one of the other men. "If you'll wait here, Missus, I'll go speak to the general."

34

While I waited, the soldiers in the clearing regarded me with such curiosity that I presumed they'd never seen a lady who'd traversed a swamp before. Their stares made me self-conscious, but before I could do more than brush some dried mud off my breeches, Private McFarlane returned.

"This way, please."

Inside, it took a moment for my eyes to adjust to the semidarkness. The intermittent rays of sunlight that pierced the spaces between the logs revealed what looked like a storehouse appropriated for meeting space. Sacks of provisions, barrels, blankets, and some saddles were pushed toward the walls to accommodate the mismatched chairs and rough table in the center of the room, where a single candle burned.

The men who occupied the chairs looked dangerous and alert even when in repose, but there was no doubt which of them was in charge.

I pulled the candlestick from my haversack as I approached the table, and bowed to the slight figure at the center. "General Marion, sir. I bring intelligence from Charles Town. General Cornwallis has ordered eight hundred men to rendezvous with Banastre Tarleton at Camden and hunt for you and your men." I uncorked the candlestick, took out the papers, and laid them on the table before him.

He and the other men exchanged glances before he spoke. "How did you come by these documents?"

"I found them on Colonel Balfour's desk."

"You?"

"Yes sir. Many patriots in the city have been arrested, and others were banished. Our intelligence network in Charles Town is fractured, and I believe I am one of the last to remain."

"You made your way out of the city and just happened to find us on your own?"

"I traveled in the company of some soldiers who escaped from the barracks prison. It was fortunate that we met one of your patrols on the road."

When he rose, I realized I'd never seen him on his feet. He was no more than an inch taller than I, but he fixed me with a gaze so scrutinizing that I looked away.

"A fantastic tale, no doubt. You may have talked your way into this camp, miss, but as these documents did not come through regular channels, I will not act without time to review and corroborate them."

Disappointed and exhausted, I felt my whole body sag. One of the men shifted position in his chair, and the creaking sound grated on my frayed nerves. Every danger and hardship I'd endured flashed through my mind and raised my fighting blood. "It took me the better part of two days to reach you, sir, and I insist you take steps to protect your men. There's no time to lose."

As he came around the table toward me, I could tell his ankle still pained him greatly. "You may not know me, General, but I remember you well. I was in the garden with you the night you leapt from the window."

"Is that so? What is your name?"

Before I could reply, a man spoke behind me. "Eliza."

I drew in a breath and whirled around to face the figure silhouetted in the doorway. As he crossed the threshold, one of the shafts of sunlight fell across his face and made his red hair gleam.

"James!" Too moved by the sight of my friend to care about military protocol, I flew to him and threw myself into his arms. "I wondered and worried about you so often."

"We made it here, thanks to you." He released me and faced Marion. "Beg pardon, General, but there's a dozen men waiting to pay compliments to this lady when you're done speaking with her. She's as true a patriot as any of us, and we owe our lives to her." He smiled down at me and squeezed my hand. "We'll see you when you finish your business."

Marion motioned to one of the men, who rose and followed James as he departed. Then he unrolled the papers, spread them on the rough table, and moved the candle close. I watched in silence as he examined each page, but inside my excitement was near bubbling over. Finally he looked up. "Extraordinary. I assume you are able to remain here for the time being? You have no pressing business elsewhere?"

"I shall stay as long as you need me, sir."

"Very well. I'm sure your friends will see to your comfort while you wait."

"Thank you." I bowed low.

Outside, the men from the *Pack Horse* crowded around me, shaking my hand and all talking at once. No longer starving scarecrows, they looked as lean, tanned, and dangerous as the rest of Marion's soldiers.

"What became of the other escapees?"

James's brother Henry answered. "They scattered, but every man who left the ship that night made it to shore. We have you to thank for our freedom."

I smiled, even as tears welled in my eyes.

James reclaimed my attention. "Are you hungry? The fare here is a sight better than what they fed us on the prison ship."

All the men laughed, and I joined in. "I would love some food. Is there a place I can wash?"

Samuel asked, "Of course. Would you care to borrow clothes? Not that we have any for ladies, mind."

"Anything clean will do."

Some of the men dispersed on these errands, and James showed me to a smaller log structure a short distance from the clearing. He opened the door to reveal a space the size of my chamber at Polly's house, with more provisions stacked along the walls. He took some rough wool blankets and hung them over a drying line strung from the rafters. "Does this suit?"

"It's all the privacy I could want."

"More than we're used to. Shall I kindle a fire to heat water?"

"I don't require that kind of luxury." I clutched his arm. "James, the general must prepare for the coming attack. There could be hundreds of Redcoats on the way here." A thought occurred to me. "I suppose whatever he decides will affect me as well."

"Don't worry, Eliza. We trust General Marion with our lives."

Sam tapped on the open door. "I found some clothes, soap, and a towel." He brought them inside and gestured toward my feet. "Your shoes look quite the worst for wear. One of our number was a cobbler and is skilled at making repairs. Let me take them to him."

"Thank you." I removed them and the men departed, shutting the door behind them.

As soon as I was alone I unwrapped my turban, knelt before one of the buckets, and plunged my head into the cool, clean water. That alone was enough to restore me. I washed my hair and then rolled my mud-caked stockings down, wincing as I pulled them off my blistered feet. My shift and stays were too soiled to put on over my clean skin, so after I finished washing I dressed in the new shirt, waistcoat, and breeches and dunked my feminine garments in the bucket. When they were as clean as I could make them, I hung them on the drying line, and then sank down on some sacks of rice and combed my fingers through my wet hair.

I was working on a particularly large tangle when a knock sounded at the door. Thinking it was one of the men bringing food, I opened it.

This time it was Peter who stood before me. I gasped, and a blazing smile swept over his face. He pulled me into his embrace and we clung to each other until I could feel his heartbeat as though it was my own.

His voice was husky with emotion. "How did you know where to find me?"

"I didn't. I was looking for General Marion, to deliver intelligence from Charles Town."

"I've been with him since March." He gave me a searching look. "I'm sorry for leaving you at such a precarious time. After the siege began I feared you would never forgive me."

"If you'd refused to enter the field in our country's Cause, I would despise you from my soul." I brought his mouth down to mine and as we kissed, the months of separation, hardship, and danger ceased to matter. Instead, my thoughts flitted to our last night together, when we'd come home spattered with mud, kissed, and made promises. I could have stayed in that moment forever, but someone whistled behind us. As we broke apart, I turned to see a grinning group of soldiers.

"We brought you something to eat." James extended a wooden trencher heaped with food.

I thanked him as Peter took the offering and then wrapped his free arm around my waist to pull me close again. "I daresay I'll even kiss you in front of the general if I get the chance, for it was he who realized who you were to me and sent a swift rider to call me back from the other camp."

I followed him into the cabin and he shut the door to prying eyes. Then he moved sacks of rice and spread a blanket on the dirt floor, and soon we had a comfortable couch and a picnic laid before us. He settled beside me and watched me as I ate.

"When were you ill, *mon cher*?" I was not usually self-conscious about my smallpox scars, but as he touched my cheek the concern on his face made me pull away.

"Around the time of the surrender."

He raised my chin with a gentle hand. "I cannot bear to think of all the ways I might have lost you. You can't imagine how helpless I felt, wanting to protect you but not knowing how."

"It tormented me, not knowing whether you were dead or alive. After I recovered my health, I did relief work, and I always hoped to learn something of your fate. I fell in with some extraordinary ladies and helped bring off the escape from the *Pack Horse*."

"I know. When those men brought the first news of you and what you were about, I wrote to you in care of my family. I told myself it was safe because my messages were in an unbreakable code unless one possessed the book needed to transcribe them."

"I received the first message, but Captain Sandford intercepted the second and claimed it as proof I was a spy."

He nodded. "Sandford. The intelligence officer. I knew he was the one who'd given you trouble last fall and I tried to warn you he was in Charles Town. As his name did not appear in the text of the book, I improvised my warning as best I could."

"So that was what you meant. He was assigned to live in your house, which was no coincidence. He missed seeing me by a quarter-hour the day your family refugeed. Later when he knew I'd moved to Polly's, he placed one of his agents in her house. He would have pursued me regardless, but the encoded letters proved to be my undoing. They made me seem more important to the intelligence network than I was."

Peter hung his head. "My selfish choice was your undoing."

After that he listened in silence as I continued my tale. When I reached the part where Sandford attacked me in Balfour's chamber, I broke down in sobs, and he gathered me into his arms, rocking me as though he was comforting a child. "Oh, *mon cher.* I'm so sorry."

I sniffled and shook my head. "No. You mustn't be. I prevailed unharmed and I'm here now. That's all that matters."

"Ah, but you're wrong. There's one more thing I must bring to light." He brushed my tumbled hair back from my face and settled us more comfortably against the sacks of rice. "I went to that Christmas party to receive an assignment from Colonel Skirving. I had no plans to socialize, but Maman insisted I take my sister along.

"You interrupted my solitude in the library. With no warning, you kissed me in front of everyone, and that flamed my desire beyond anything I had ever known. I wanted to pursue you then, but I had committed to intelligence work that would take me into occupied Savannah. Later, when Maman's summons reached me I came in haste, for I was burning to see you again. Then she laid the blame for Mary's troubles on you, insisting you were a heartless coquette. She had known you longer, and I began to doubt my first impression of you."

He took his copy of *The Wealth of Nations* from his haversack and brought out a folded sheet of writing paper addressed to me at the Porcher house in Ansonborough. "This may have been the most important lesson in intelligence I ever had."

I read the single page.

January 1780

My very, very dear Mrs. Wilkinson,
I am pleased to learn that you were not content to stay buried in the country after your triumph at the Christmas party.

In response to your expressed desire to continue your conquests in the 'Ton, I have procured a number of invitations for you and Miss Porcher and look forward to continuing our intimate social intercourse.

Charming coquette, I do love you most abominably.

H McC

I could not hide my indignation. "Where did you get this?"

"It arrived with some party invitations. Maman opened it along with the others before she realized her mistake."

"Mistake? More likely she considered it her duty as my chaperone to read my correspondence."

"That would come as no surprise, but I only know what she told me." He glanced away before meeting my gaze. "When I arrived on your birthday, Maman insisted you were trying to steal Mary's suitor and produced that letter as proof of your character flaws."

"I shall take the greatest pleasure in burning this. Why have you kept it?"

"To remind myself that things are not always what they seem. I made a shamefully poor analysis of the intelligence I was given, and by the time I arrived at the truth and learned you still cared for me, it was too late again. Early the next morning, Colonel Marion sent orders for me to report to his home."

"He recognized you when you came to his aid."

"Yes. When I reported to him, he asked me to serve as a scout and forager, rightly anticipating that the British would soon take the city. While he recuperated from his broken ankle, I and several others spent the final weeks before the siege gathering supplies and weapons and preparing safehouses and camps like this one. After the city fell, we recruited dispossessed soldiers, escaped slaves, natives, and back-country militiamen. Now we act under Marion's orders to disrupt the British communication lines and steal their supplies."

"You are regarded as mythical heroes in Charles Town." I snuggled against him. "When I first saw you in the library, it was plain you didn't want company."

"After the first few minutes with you, I no longer minded." He gave me a gentle kiss. "Whatever comes next, we shall face it together, yes?"

I nodded and when I turned my face up to his again, he chuckled. "Eliza, I never thought of you as a sister, nor as a brother for that matter. But in those clothes, you're even more alluring."

I laughed with him. "It was easier to travel in men's clothes." Then I cast a pointed glance toward my underthings hanging on the drying line. "I daresay you notice a difference when you hold me."

He feigned surprise. "Really? May I explore the situation further?" He pulled at the neckline of my shirt and I giggled as I turned aside to keep him from peeking. He pulled me closer and his fingers raised a pleasant shiver as they trailed down my side. Just as he leaned in to kiss me, someone knocked on the door. "General's ready to address the troops."

"Duty calls again." Peter gave me a quick peck on the lips before he released me, and as we left the cabin I found my clean and mended shoes outside the door. We joined the others who grouped around Marion in the clearing.

"Gentlemen and lady, new intelligence leads me to conclude that I must dismiss you from service until the threat from Tarleton's troops has passed. This fight is not about South Carolina alone. It is about forging one nation, and our Cause is far from lost. Get yourselves to safety and await word from me."

The men dispersed, and soon the camp hummed with activity as they packed up supplies and readied their horses. I returned to the cabin and rolled my damp underthings into a tight bundle, and then followed Peter to the corral, where he saddled his horse.

"How far is it to your place at Black Swamp?"

"Too far, but I have so many cousins in the Santee region that we shall never want for a place to stay." He tightened the girth strap. "Ophir can carry us both if we travel light." He swung into the saddle and extended his hand.

I put my bundle in the saddlebag, used a stump for a mounting block, and wrapped my arms around his waist. As he guided Ophir through the clearing, one of the men gave Marion a hand up into his saddle. The general turned his horse's head and rode off to the north.

Peter squeezed my hand. "I have to remind myself I'm not dreaming. I should prefer it if you never left my side again."

"As would I, but you'll have to return to the fight." I hesitated before I asked, "How can we prevail when commanders like Gates turn cowardly and their men are too discouraged to fight?"

"When King George ordered his troops to America, the Britons expected to encounter no opposition, for they believed their colonists lacked experience in the art of war. Instead they learned that we are able warriors with a true sense of our rights and liberties. We will prevail and drive out tyranny by daring to oppose it." He turned in the saddle. "When that fight is won, I intend to take up an even more important cause."

"What might that be?"

"To restore my home."

"Oh. I see." I'd expected a flirtation or something of a more personal nature, but then a smile broke through his viz.

"Yes, to restore my home and live with you there as your husband and generous companion, if you so desire."

I pretended to consider his proposition. "I'd been planning to search out some smart lad and beg him to take me away, but I daresay you'll do."

Afterword

Eliza Yonge Wilkinson Porcher (1757-1806) was a prolific letter writer. Copies of her correspondence to various friends and dated between 1781-83 survived and report the events of those years, including the British presence in the sea islands in the weeks leading up to the Battle of Stono Ferry in June 1779; a visit to soldiers on board a prison ship during the British occupation; and the surrender of Cornwallis at the Battle of Yorktown.

Her chief correspondent during that period was Mary Porcher, who would later become her sister-in-law.

Little is known about Eliza's later life, but the letters she saved from her youth convey powerful emotion and intellect. I chose to build upon the information in her letters and craft a story that celebrates the brave deeds of women patriots in South Carolina, who, according to an essay of Eliza's

> exhibited an example of more than masculine fortitude. They displayed so ardent, so rare a love of country that scarcely could there be found, in ancient or modern history, an instance more worthy to excite surprise and admiration. Far from being offended by being called rebel ladies, they esteemed it as a title of distinction and glory. Instead of showing themselves

assembled in the seat of joy and brilliant pleasure, they repaired on board ships, descended into dungeons, where their husbands, children, and friends were in confinement; they carried them consolation and encouragement.

The occupation of Charleston lasted from 1780-82, but the narrative in *Patriot of the Lowcountry* ends in August 1780. I took liberties with the timeline in order to include examples of the civilian experience during the city's occupation.

Plantations

Eliza's father, Francis Yonge, Sr. (1730-1780) inherited Toogoodoo Plantation when he was in his early twenties. Throughout his life he bought and sold property in the sea islands, including Toogoodoo, two properties consistently mentioned together as Plainfield and Pawletts, and what would become known as Yonge's Island.

Toogoodoo

Toogoodoo Plantation consisted of two land grants to Abraham Eve, one for 500 acres conveyed in January 1705, the other for 456 acres conveyed in January 1710. It appears it was known as Mount Laurel at this time.

After his death, his widow Hannah inherited the plantation. She married Robert Yonge in 1723, and it was he who called the place Toogoodoo. After his death in 1751, his second wife, Elizabeth, inherited the property, which then passed to Robert and Hannah's son Francis after her death.[1] Newspaper advertisements show that Francis Yonge bought and sold numerous tracts of land in the area.[2]

---

1. *Huguenot Society of South Carolina Transactions No. 8* (1975) 103-104.

2. Newspapers.com, The South-Carolina Gazette, Tuesday, January 1, 1754 https://newspapers.com/image/605123157 and Saturday, August 11, 1759 https://newspapers.com/image/605073856.

Two advertisements in *The South-Carolina Gazette* in early 1765 announced "The valuable plantation called Mount Laurel, belonging to Francis Yonge, upon a branch of Toogadoo-creek" was to be sold at public auction on February 18 of that year. The advertisements specify that the present owner must make a reserve of his family's burying place.[3]

Francis seems to have decided to sell the property after the death of his first wife Sarah Clifford Yonge in 1764, though some sources say he owned Toogoodoo as late as 1769. It appears Edward Wilkinson, an older brother of Eliza's first husband Joseph, acquired the property around this time, though whether he purchased it from Yonge is unknown.

Edward's will inventory and appraisement dated July 23, 1771 lists the contents of the house at Tobodoo Plantation [sic].[4] His will, dated June 8, 1771, directs his executor to "let out occupy, exercise, repair and improve the Premises and every part and parcel thereof, and collect receive and apply, as he or they shall see fit, the Profits of the same, towards defraying the Expense of Suitably Cloathing, Educating, and Maintaining my three Children in such manner as his discretion shall judge."[5]

It stands to reason then, that Edward's younger brother Joseph rented Toogoodoo from Edward's estate until his own death in March 1775. Advertisements placed in the *South Carolina Gazette and Country Journal* on March 6 and 14, 1775, advertise an estate sale to be held

---

3. Newspapers.com, The South-Carolina Gazette, Charleston, South Carolina https://www.newspapers.com/image/605094222 and https://www.newspapers.com/image/605094498.

4. Ancestry.com, South Carolina Probate Records, Files and Loose Papers, 1732-1964. https://www.ancestry.com/imageviewer/collections/61962/images/FS_004754683_00080?usePUB=true&_phsrc=Gam1962&pId=641572.

5. Ancestry.com, South Carolina Wills Wills, Vol 14-16, 1771-1779, https://www.ancestry.com/imageviewer/collections/9080/images/004753752_00076?pId=17159.

"at the Plantation on Togadoo, where the late Mr. Joseph Wilkinson, deceased, lived."[6]

Thus, it seems likely that Eliza lived at Toogoodoo at two different points in her life, as a young child and as a bride.

Plainsfield and Pawletts

Plainsfield and Pawletts plantations were established around 1690 by Joseph Blake, one of Carolina's Lords Proprietors and governor of the colony in 1694 and again from 1696-1700.[7] The property is a private residence, and a historical marker was placed at the site in 2012.

Francis Yonge purchased Plainsfield and Pawletts, totaling 2796 acres, in 1761.[8] Because none of Eliza's letters specify which of her father's properties she managed, I chose to establish her at Plainsfield.

Yonge's Island

Yonge's Island was part of a 640-acre land grant that dates to 1694. Francis Yonge purchased the southern side of the island in 1775, and the remainder at an unknown date.[9] In her letters, Eliza referred to her father's home as Island House.

---

6. Newspapers.com, *South Carolina Gazette and Country Journal,* https://www.newspapers.com/image/605365418 and https://www.newspapers.com/image/605383152.

7. Historical Marker Database, "Plainsfield Plantation," https://www.hmdb.org/m.asp?m=56562

8. St. Paul's Garden Club, *Close to Heaven, The History and Cuisine of St. Paul's Parish,* (2000) p. 19-20.

9. Jennifer H. Gililand, *Images of America: St. Paul's Parish* (Arcadia Publishing, 2012) 24-25.

Family

The information pertaining to Eliza's immediate family on Ancestry.com is sparse and full of discrepancies. Births and deaths recorded in the family Bible are as follows:

Francis Yonge, Sr. (1730-1780) m. 1st Sarah Clifford (1732-1764) in 1752.

Mary (1754-1810)

Francis Jr. (1755-1789)

Eliza (1757-1806/7)

William (1758- bef. 1807)

Mary Peter (1760-?)

Married 2nd. Susannah Peckham Johnson (1747-1819) in 1768.

Susannah Sarah (1773-1773)

Sarah Hope (1776-1783)

Harriet Peckham (1778-1870)[10]

Mackworth (1780-1784)

---

10. Images of pages from family Bible provided by Clayton Rhodes, a descendant of Eliza's half-sister Harriet. Private collection.

ELIZA'S HUSBANDS

I was able to learn very little about Eliza's husbands aside from their birth, marriage, and death dates and will inventories, which left me free to create those characters with only the barest framework of facts.

Joseph Wilkinson

Joseph Wilkinson (1745-1775) was the fourth son of a wealthy planter family. His three elder brothers had received large inheritances from a relative, while Joseph, who was not yet of age, received a cash bequest. There is no evidence of him owning land. He was twenty-nine years old and Eliza seventeen when they wed in 1774. He died of unknown causes before their first anniversary and the birth of their son.

I elected to send the character based on Joseph to the Philadelphia Medical College, where I imagined him coming under the influence of Quaker citizens and some of the medical school faculty and returning to South Carolina with abolitionist ideals.

Though South Carolina's economy relied on slave labor, the private manumission of slaves was not as uncommon as we might assume.[11] As the American colonies moved toward declaring independence from Great Britain, people began to look at the institution of slavery with a new perspective.

Henry Laurens, who served as president of Congress from November 1777 to December 1778, was a partner in the largest slave trading house in North America and one of the richest men in the colony. He wrote to his son John, who was a captain in the Continental Army and an aide-de-camp to Washington:

> You know, my dear son, I abhor slavery. I was born
> in a country where slavery had been established by

---

11. Charleston County Public Library website, "Private Manumission: An Intimate Path to Freedom," https://www.ccpl.org/charleston-time-machine/private-manumission-intimate-path-freedom.

British kings and parliaments, as well as by the laws of that country ages before my existence. I found the Christian religion and slavery growing under the same authority and cultivation. I nevertheless disliked it...I am not the man who enslaved them; they are indebted to English for that favour; nevertheless I am devising means for manumitting many of them, and for cutting off the entail of slavery. Great powers oppose me — the laws and customs of my country, my own and the avarice of my countrymen.[12]

During the American Revolution, John Laurens proposed the idea of arming slaves and granting them freedom in return for their service. He wrote, "We Americans at least in the Southern Colonies, cannot contend with a good Grace, for Liberty, until we shall have enfranchised our Slaves." I chose to have Joseph Wilkinson share Laurens' belief that black and white people shared a similar nature and could aspire to freedom in a republican society.

Though Congress approved the concept of a regiment of slaves in 1779, 1780, and 1782, Laurens met with overwhelming rejection each time he tried to raise troops.[13]

Peter Porcher

Eliza's second husband Peter Porcher (1753-1796) came from a prodigious family of Huguenots. He had more than one cousin by the same name and of similar age. In historical and genealogical records,

---

12. Library of Congress website, *A South Carolina protest against slavery: being a letter from Henry Laurens, second President of the Continental Congress, to his son, Colonel John Laurens; dated Charleston, S. C., August 14th, 1776. Now published from the original.* https://www.loc.gov/resource/gdcmassbookdig.southcarolinapro00laur/?sp=1&st=image.

13. American Battlefield Trust website, "John Laurens," https://www.battlefields.org/learn/biographies/john-laurens.

he is often confused with the cousin who owned the plantations Ophir and Peru in the Santee region.

Eliza's Peter owned property at Black Swamp, near the Savannah River, and served in Colonel Waters' regiment of the South Carolina Militia in 1779.[14]

The character based on Peter has a pensive, brooding nature, which hints at his losses at the hands of the British and his work on behalf of the Cause.

Eliza was twenty-eight when she and Peter married on January 7, 1786. They had four children over the next ten years: Francis Yonge (1789-1862) Sarah Caroline (1791-1833) Eliza Maria (1793-1855) and Harriet Ann Porcher (1796-1853).

Virtually nothing is known of their lives with their young children or the circumstances that led to Peter's death in 1797 at age 44.

A document filed in the Colleton County Court of Common Pleas dated November 13, 1807 pertains to dividing land owned by William Yonge among his nieces and nephew. It lists Peter and Eliza's four children as minors of deceased parents and Peter's younger brother James as the children's guardian.[15]

Though family trees on Ancestry.com and other sources list Eliza's date of death as around 1813, the relatively obscure court record from 1807 definitively proves that she died much sooner, likely in 1806 at the age of 49.

---

14. Ancestry.com. *North America, Family Histories* for Peter Porcher, Daughters of the American Revolution Lineage Book Vol. 159, 1920. https://www.ancestry.com/imageviewer/collections/61157/images/46155_b290461-00047?pId=3717529.

15. South Carolina Historical Society Collection. Porcher–Gift of Miss Anne Porcher. Call# 30-04.

Quotable Eliza

Caroline Howard Gilman, (1794-1888) published *Letters of Eliza Wilkinson: during the invasion and possession of Charleston, S.C., by the British in the Revolutionary War* in 1839. Gilman was not a descendant of Eliza. Her daughter, Abby Louisa, married Francis James Porcher, Eliza's grandson.

The opening chapters of *Patriot of the Lowcountry* are drawn heavily from Eliza's published letters. I used excerpts from her unpublished correspondence to craft the characters and develop a storyline set against the backdrop of the siege of Charleston and the first months of occupation.

The following quotes allow the reader to compare Eliza's words to their applied use in the context of the story. Eliza's idiosyncrasies of punctuation, spelling, and capitalization appear as found in the transcribed letters, which are on file at the University of South Carolina library.

Social
We each got a book and determined that neither shou'd profit, or amuse themselves by one; and so read aloud and confus'd one another,

then Laugh'd aloud at our nonsense; do you think Books were published to create Nonsense and Folly?

I can emerge from Obscurity, and once more have the company of friends to share my gloomy hours, talking of friends, pray have you heard from my brother Hext McCall—how and where he is? I wish you'd let me know, and I wou'd fain write to him, but know not how; shou'd you be sent off before I see you, I charge you to remember my sisterly wishes for his welfare and happiness. I should be glad of a line or two from him when opportunities offer.

Remember me to all my friends and Christmas acquaintances that we had at Pon Pon in 1779. Ah! What a contrast was this last! How was the two most remarkable days spent, to what they were then! In less folly and vanity, I'll grant—but how far from me was mirth and gaiety! How many reflections and comparisons I made, how scattered and how far apart are those who were then assembled at Pon Pon!

Suppose upon entering the room, you address the Ladies with some such lines as these (no matter what the gentlemen think)

> Ye Fair, your charms are such, I cannot come
> Unarm'd within this gay Assembly Room,
> Therefore excuse the armour, o'er my Eyes,
> Or else the lustre of your own disguise.

As these are extempore, and I think not expressive enough; you may compose some more so, for the Occasion.

So I've betrayed a great want of taste! As how pray? Why, because I prefer the peacefull Serenity of a harmless Country life to the noise and bustle of the Town!

So you may laugh at "rural felicity" as much as you please, Sir - but I say - may Heaven Allways give me a mind to relish these Humble and Innocent Amusements, and then I shall enjoy perfect; the unwearied repose; however, I'm glad to find you so completely blest, and happy, amid the noise and Tumults.

The music play'd sweetly, so sweetly that I cou'd not keep my feet still; it Inspired me with such a Strong Inclination for dancing I promis'd myself some agreeable, happy hours—but ah! How precarious and fleeting are all sublunary enjoyments!

I've got so tir'd of dancing that I shall hurry to my peaceful home to regroup, for my Spirits are quite exhausted; I'm very fond of that amusement, and look on it to be very Innocent when it is not carried to an excess. Indeed excesses of ev'ry kind become sinfull, and besides I hate to make a toil of pleasure. I think too much mirth as bad as too much melancholy.

The elder Miss Sarrazin I think perfectly amiable; her countenance and address are expressive of ev'ry virtue, and I shou'd wish to cultivate a further acquaintance with her.

I had a deal to write to you; but as I'm told there are some Persons who make it a point to open my letters, I write nothing but what they may see.

Ah! The poor Doves are sometimes in danger of falling in the Tallons of the Hawk of the Forest, the treacherous Hawk! Who void of pity, makes a prey of defenseless, unprotected Innocence.

How must the poor unhappy woman feel whose character has been so wantonly sported with! The wound which her reputation has receiv'd [is] a wound which is seldom, or never cur'd. People who act ungenerously and those who countenance it don't consider that what is sport to them is the most cruel injustice to another, and death to all their happiness in this world; what satisfaction anyone can feel in ruining the peace of mind of their fellow-mortal I can't think!

O where is my dear Mrs. Brewton?… I have a hundred things to tell you – to ask you – but I can't trust them to paper; the distance of eight hundred miles seems rather precarious & I wou'd not choose my *whole heart* carry'd in people's hands…I ain't received a letter in some time but what has been open'd before it came into my hands.

Before I go any further I must beg Pardon for my Servant's unreasonable intrusion; to wait upon a Town Lady at Seven o'clock in the morning! I confess I shew'd a total want of reflection, and at the same time discover'd her Ignorance of the gay world! She knew not that the Nights were *much longer* in Town than in the Country; pray excuse the rustic. She pleads the necessity she was under by her very short stay in Town, of catching Time by the forelock, to be expeditious in finishing her business; but promises a future conformity to the Customs and fashions of City-Dames; so hopes this one blunder will be forgiven and forgotten.

I have just got the better of the Small Pox! Thanks be to God for the same. My face is finely ornamented, and my nose *honored with thirteen spots*. I must add that I'm pleas'd they won't pit! —for as much as I revere the number, I wou'd not choose to have so conspicuous a mark. I intend in a few days to introduce my spotted face in Chas. Town. I hear there are a number of my friends and acquaintances to be exil'd, and I must see them before they are.

Love and Relationships

I must really go and search out some smart Lad and beg him to take me away.

I can't see why the two Sexes shou'd act as if they were at continued open war with each other; and to commence a friendship with, or behave sociably to a gent shou'd put us under the dread & fear of some sad catastrophe; such notions are a bane to society, they keep us under a constant reserve and constraint, and we fear to open our mouths, lest the *Enemy* should find some advantage over us; as if they had nothing in view but our destruction.

Are not such the Characteristics of a narrow soul, or an uncharitable disposition? I wou'd not insinuate by this, that we are right, or that we can be justifiable in contracting Friendships and Intimacies with ev'ry Fop, Fool or Rake that we come across! No, the two former are not worth our Notice, the latter are (on more accounts than one) dangerous *Animals*.

For my part I choose to receive no letters from gentlemen but what ev'ry body might see.

O how sweet, how comforting, the presence of a friend in such distressing times, especially those we look on as the protectors.

Possible References to Peter

As to a description of Black Swamp, I shall only tell you it's not unlike other places I have seen...I'm desir'd to correct a *terrible error* I made. Mr. Porcher has discover'd a great aversion to the word "Bog," and desires I'll say Rivulet. I won't contradict him, but shall only beg your Opinion or judgement whether a piece of dirty, muddy water, can resemble a purling stream?

I'm not so simple Mary, but what I can see is something more than a call in somebody's visiting his Sister! "He'll probably call on his Sister" - very simply said Indeed! - and you really think it won't be a premeditated "Call" O, Mary! Mary! When I see you we'll have it out; I'll drag the half smother'd secret from its lurking place. But harkee Child, I beg you won't take it upon yourself to make so free with my letters: shewing passages to this one, that one, and the other one! And now to your brother Captain forsooth! You shan't show him. I told you to burn that letter, Miss, and you've dar'd to disobey orders.

At my heart I Love all such little sociable amusements and excursions; and wou'd prefer them to the grandest Parade which pride and Ostentation cou'd suggest—but no such scheme of pleasure cou'd enter the Beau's Noddles while I had it in my power to partake. Wretches! I cou'd abuse them for it—all but the one who wishes to see me—who is he—tell me—may be *I may wish to see him too.*

After having a Comfortable fire made in my little sequester'd apartment, I once more took possession of it, and seemed more easy and satisfy'd alone than I had been in a Crowd; sitting down by my fire, I wish'd for you—or a Certain some-body else, to make my fireside more sociable and cheerful; I won't tell you who it was I wish'd for beside yourself! So you may save yourself the trouble of asking.

Feminism

I won't have it thought that because we are the weaker Sex (as
to bodily strength my dear) we are Capable of nothing more than
minding the Dairy - visiting the Poultry house, and all such domestic concerns; our thoughts can soar aloft, we can form conceptions of
things of Higher Nature; and have as just a sense of honor, glory, and
great actions as these "Lords of Creation" – what contemptible Earth
Worms those Authors make us! They won't even allow us the liberty of
thought! And that is all I want.

To the women of Carolina, it is principally to be imparted, the love
and even the name of liberty were not extinguished in the Southern
provinces. The English hence begun to be sensible that their triumph
was still far from secure. For in every affair of public interest, the general opinion never manifests itself with more energy than when the
women take part in it with all the life of their imaginations.

I'm determined you shan't persuade me that I have any other heart
than my own in my bosom, *I know it mine*, my own, yes, I'm still mistress of it; but I tell you again, cou'd I find the Clever fellow I have
pictur'd in Imagination, and wou'd he give me his, *whole and entire* I
would with joy exchange - yes I wou'd - and resign my freedom to a
generous *Companion* (not a Lord and Master) who wou'd restore it to
me again and *rule* with *love*. But when, or where shall I find him? In
my own brain I fear, for doth such a one now exist?

No sooner are we enter'd our teens but we hear nothing else but
Encomiums on our beauty: Air! Voice! Mien! All cry'd up to extrava-
gance; not a word is said of our mental accomplishments, while Beauty
is spoke of to a degree of enthusiasm: this naturally makes a young
Creature turn her whole thoughts to the study of embellishing and

ornamenting those charms she has been accustom'd to hear praised as Angelic; she neglects the cultivation of her mind as frivolous; little thinking that to be the only *lasting* charm, the Bloom of Age: and wholly studious to make the Charms of her person more pleasing, becomes almost, nay - oftimes as much an Idiot as an Idol.

On seeing a man beat his Wife with his walking stick

Poor wives are made to honor and obey.
Must yield to a husband's lordly sway.
Whether you live in Peace, or horrid strife,
You must stay with him, aye, and that for life.

If he proves kind, then happy you will be,
If otherways—O! dreadful misery!
Kind husbands nowadays you scarcely find
The lover's seldom in the husband's mind.

The imperious Mortal makes his wife his slave,
He will, he won't yet knows not what he'd have.
While she—poor trembling soul! In vain doth try,
To please him, marks the motion of his eye;

He still storms on, while from his eyes flash fire.
She trembles more—is ready to expire.
Wou'd any stander by but hand a glass
He'd start! Amazed! To see his frightful face.

O shameful sight, he cou'd not then dispute.
But that he made himself a very brute.
Guard me good Heaven whene'er I change my state!

That this may never be my wretched fate.

War

I've no husband to fight against them, (tho bye the bye, if I had one who refus'd to enter the field in his Country's Cause, I believe I shou'd despise him from my Soul).

[I] with the utmost compassion beheld their tatter'd raiment, and miserable situation...they will fight from principle alone, for from what I could learn these poor Creatures have nothing to protect and seldom get their pay—and yet with what alacrity will they encounter danger and hardships of ev'ry kind!

He told me he fear'd my dear little heart was among the Rebels. I told him it really was so.

I've often wonder'd since I wasn't packed off too; for I was very saucy and never disguis'd my sentiments.

Don't you think it a little spitefull to laugh at them? I can't help it, I must—I will! And I've ventured out to laugh at some to their very faces out of a little sweet revenge.

A week or two ago I learned that the Britons are accusing their Commandant for losing this state; they say "if the Inhabitants had been treated with mildness & generosity, they wou'd have join'd them, but that their property's [sic] have been taken from them, and they could find no redress, which was the reason that they are so exasperated against them and the British government.

They've lost America past redemption; and may thank their own Avarice Pride and Cruelty for it. They envy'd us our possessions and thought to build themselves on our ruins; but Heaven is just! The Pit they dug for us, they've fell in themselves—and there may they lie groveling!

It was the constant Topic of conversation, some said one thing, some another, and depend upon it never was greater Politicians than the several knots of ladies who met together. All trifling discourse of fashions, and all such low or little Chat were thrown by and we commenc'd perfect statesmen—and I don't know but if we'd taken a little pains, we shou'd have been qualify'd for prime Ministers, so well wou'd we discuss several Important matters at hand.

Tho our troubles were great, in the midst of them my Brothers, with the Willtown hunters arriv'd from Chas. Town, judge our joy upon that account—which was augmented from their assuring us that they had heard from Genl. Lincoln, that he was hurrying on to our assistance and would soon be with us. We us'd to see parties of our friends—mostly the Willtown hunters, pass the avenue toward Stono Ferry, where they rode daily in search of adventures.

We cou'd neither eat—drink—nor sleep in peace, for as we lay in our cloaths & stays every Night, we cou'd not enjoy the little sleep we got, the least noise alarm'd us, up we'd jump, expecting ev'ry moment to hear them demand admittance. In short, our nights were wearisome and painful; our days spent in anxiety and melancholy.

When they embarked for America, they were sure of success, for they expected no Opposition from a people so little skill'd in Arms, and who had no experience in the Arts of War, but to their cost they found that those who have a true sense of their rights and Libertys will conquer difficulties by daring to oppose them.

A brave and generous people can never be overcome but by acts of generosity; had you endeavored to conquer that way, we should ever thus have been united in Bonds of Friendship and happiness, but by repeated and manifold Injuries, the spirit of resentment and opposition will subsist.

O day of Sorrow, must America indeed fall, after resisting so long, too, after so many of her Sons have nobly dar'd to die in her defense—must they die in vain?

South Carolina groans beneath the British yoke, her Sons and Daughters are exil'd, driven from their native land, and their pleasant habitations seized by the *Insulting Victors*.

Depression and Suffering

Hang dull life 'tis full of folly
Why shou'd we be Melancholy?

Aye, why shou'd we–does it answer one good purpose? No–very well then I'll 'een banish it and make the best of what I can't prevent. To indulge melancholy is to inflict ourselves.

Your account of suffering Old Age has brought to mind my dear late and venerable Parent, his sorrows and misfortunes came afresh in view, and I cou'd not but congratulate his escape from them, the grave seems a refuge in these distressing times. "He and his sorrows now are safely laid within its cold and hospitable bosom." How many at this awful alarming period envy the dead! How many retches do this fatal Cause make to groan under a weight of woes!

Both of my brothers are allmost destitute, and to whom else can I apply? Indeed ev'ry body our way Labor under the same difficulty, a want of horses is the general cry, so what's to be done! say—what shall I do? O dear! O dear! That ever we shou'd be subjected to so many disappointments.

Lately an Indifferency—an Insensibility has crept on, which make me regardless how the world goes; I can't account for it, unless it is that frequent and repeated misfortunes have render'd me so even my belov'd Pen is become more a trouble than an Amusement.

To indulge melancholy is to afflict ourselves, and make the edge of Calamity more keen and cutting, so I'll endeavor to maintain a calm, let what will, happen. I'll summon Philosophy, Fortitude, Patience and resignation to my Aid; and sweet hope which never forsakes us, will be my chief support.

No sooner do we enter this World but we are Immediate heirs to all its misfortunes and heart-rending sorrows, and oftimes what a large share, a double portion do we inherit! But I'm glad to find you have those aids, Religion and Philosophy, so necessary to uphold and strengthen weak desponding mortals.

The great Creator knowing our weak desponding natures, seems to've endow'd us with [hope] to smooth, soften and heal the Wounds of keen distress and anguish, and to make us bear with Fortitude the many misfortunes which attend mortality. Without this gentle, heal-ing Passion, dreadful despair would take possession of us.

For Additional Reading

Aigniel, Lucien. *The Late Affair Has Almost Broke My Heart: The American Revolution in the South, 1780-1781*. Riverside, CT: Chatham Press, Inc., 1972.

Bell, Karen Cook. *Running from Bondage: Enslaved Women and Their Remarkable Fight for Freedom in Revolutionary America*. Cambridge: University Printing House, 2021.

Borick, Carl P. *A Gallant Defense: The Siege of Charleston, 1780*. Columbia, SC: University of South Carolina Press, 2003.

— *Relieve Us of This Burthen: American Prisoners of War in the Revolutionary South, 1780-1782*. Columbia, SC: University of South Carolina Press, 2012.

Bostick, Douglas W. *Sunken Plantations: The Santee Cooper Project*. Charleston, SC: The History Press, 2008.

Buchanan, John. *The Road to Charleston: Nathanael Greene and the American Revolution*. Charlottesville, VA: University of Virginia Press, 2019.

Butler, Nicholas Michael. *Votaries of Apollo: The St. Cecilia Society and the Patronage of Concert Music in Charleston, South Carolina 1766-1820*. Columbia, SC: University of South Carolina Press, 2007.

Clinton, Catherine. *The Plantation Mistress: Woman's World in the Old South*. New York, NY: Pantheon Books, 1982.

Daigler, Kenneth A. *Spies, Patriots, and Traitors: American Intelligence in the Revolutionary War*. Washington, DC: Georgetown University Press, 2014.

Ellet, Elizabeth F. *The Women of the American Revolution, Volumes One and Two*. New York, NY: Baker and Scribner, 1849.

Eastman, Margaret Middleton Rivers, with Edward Fitzsimmons Good. *Hidden History of Old Charleston*. Charleston, SC: The History Press, 2010.

Fraser, Walter J., Jr. *Patriots, Pistols and Petticoats: "Poor Sinful Charles-Town" during the American Revolution*. Columbia, SC: University of South Carolina Press, 1993.

Kennedy, Cynthia M. *Braided Relations, Entwined Lives: The Women of Charleston's Urban Slave Society*. Bloomington, IN: Indiana University Press, 2005.

Maloy, Mark, with Foreword by Richard W. Hatcher III. *To the Last Extremity: The Battles for Charleston, 1776-1782*. Published by the author, 2023.

Moultrie, William. *Memoirs of the American Revolution Volume 2*. New York, NY: Printed by David Longworth, for the author, 1802.

Nagy, John A. *Invisible Ink: Spycraft of the American Revolution*. Yardley, PA: Westhome Publishing, LLC, 2010.

Ramsay, David, MD. *The History of the American Revolution in Two Volumes*. Lexington, KY: Printed and Published by Downing and Phillips, 1845.

Smith, Adam LL. D. and F. R. S. *An Inquiry into the Nature and Causes of the Wealth of Nations in Two Volumes*. London: Printed for W. Strahan and T. Cadeli, The Strand, 1776.

Taylor, Dale. *The Writer's Guide to Everyday Life in Colonial America From 1607-1783*. Cincinnati, OH: Writer's Digest Books, 1999.

Acknowledgements

Many thanks to:

Fallon Chiasson of chiassoneditorialservices.com for tackling the first edit on this book.

Jenny Q of Historical Editorial for helping put the puzzle pieces of the story in the right order.

Carl Borick, Director of The Charleston Museum, for information about women and spycraft in occupied Charleston.

Marshall T. Willis, Assistant Director City of Charleston Department of Budget, Finance and Revenue Collections for providing details about the Old Exchange.

Clayton Rhodes, descendant of Eliza's younger sister Harriet Yonge Haygood, for sending copies of letters, documents, and the birth and death entries in the Yonge family Bible.

Kim Stone, beta reader who gave thoughtful feedback and helped shape and refine the book.

The Rebecca Motte Chapter National Society Daughters of the American Revolution, particularly Katie Hyman and Elizabeth Gay, for their support, encouragement, and assistance with research.

Kathy Meis, Shilah LaCoe, and the team at Bublish.com for their expert formatting and production.